MW00873727

USA TODAY BESTSELLING AUTHOR

GIN JONES

MY OLD KENTUCKY HOMICIDE

··· THE ···
BOURBON B&B
MYSTERIES #1

MY OLD KENTUCKY HOMICIDE
Copyright © 2024 by Gin Jones
Cover design by Janet Holmes

Published by Gemma Halliday Publishing Inc
All Rights Reserved. Except for use in any review, the reproduction or
utilization of this work in whole or in part in any form by any electronic,
mechanical, or other means, now known or hereafter invented, including
xerography, photocopying and recording, or in any information storage and
retrieval system is forbidden without the written permission of the publisher,
Gemma Halliday.

This is a work of fiction. Names, characters, places, and incidents are either the
product of the author's imagination or are used fictitiously, and any resemblance
to actual persons, living or dead, business establishments, or events or locales is
entirely coincidental.

MY OLD KENTUCKY HOMICIDE

BOOKS BY GIN JONES

Bourbon B&B Mysteries:
My Old Kentucky Homicide
Bluegrass Homicide
Old-Fashioned Holiday Homicide

Danger Cove Mysteries:
Patchwork of Death
A Christmas Quilt to Die For
Clues in Calico
A Death in the Flower Garden
A Slaying in the Orchard
A Secret in the Pumpkin Patch
Deadly Thanksgiving Sampler
Two Sleuths Are Better Than One

CHAPTER ONE

I wanted to strangle my baby sister.

I'd forgotten how often I'd felt that way when we were kids. Ten years since our last real reunion when CJ graduated from high school, and apparently all it took was thirty seconds together to remind me of how infuriating she could be.

She and our middle sister, Em, had been waiting for me on the broad front porch of their B&B on the bourbon trail. They were in a pair of rocking chairs with a small table between them, and they'd pulled up a third for me. Em had also offered me a glass of sweet tea, but I'd already realized something was up and wasn't ready to be mollified.

It was dark out, with little more than the light from a baby monitor's display screen on a side table to illuminate the area, but even from the bottom of the porch steps, I recognized the guilty looks on their faces. They were both hiding something, and they expected me to fix whatever the problem was. I didn't mind helping out. That was what big sisters did. But I hated not having all the information I would need.

CJ was trying to look innocent, but she wasn't as good an actor as Em. I switched my attention to my middle sister, but she wasn't giving away any clues. I was tempted to strangle her too for her role as an enabler. She was usually the more levelheaded of the two, but Em had frequently been a co-conspirator when they were kids, claiming she'd hoped to be a moderating influence.

I leaned against the railing across from my sisters and took a deep, calming breath of the fresh spring air. It wasn't really their fault that I was so annoyed. I was the one who'd let nostalgia create unreasonable expectations for our reunion.

I'd just driven nine hours from Washington, D.C. to Cooperton, Kentucky, leaving behind the city's pollution, along with the stress of my work as a probate lawyer. It wasn't until the last section of the trip though, winding through the forests of eastern Kentucky, that I'd really felt refreshed. It was impossible not to notice how beautiful my home state was. As soon as I'd crossed the border, everything had seemed magically cleaner, brighter, and greener. I'd forgotten so much about the place, having left when I was eighteen and never spending any real time here in eighteen years, just a few quick overnight trips, including one for a wedding and then for the groom's funeral. The drive had reminded me of how I'd taken the stunning landscape for granted as a child, making it easier to forget it once I left.

I should have come back sooner, but I'd been busy with school and then my career, and I'd lost track of time passing. But I was here now, and I'd built up this fantasy of how we'd all happily celebrate my only nephew's third birthday, and make the most of this chance to get to know each other again, now that we were all that was left of the family. That was, after all, the plan that Em had laid out two weeks ago when she'd finally convinced me to take a long weekend off to visit their newly acquired B&B in a town near where we'd been born and raised, deep in rural farmland.

I took another deep breath of the invigoratingly fresh air. I'd never make it through the long weekend if I couldn't get past the knee-jerk responses triggered by our childhood conflicts. Unfortunately, it looked like that gulf between us wasn't ever going to shrink. They were still united in some battle against me, and I was frustrated by my inability to understand what they wanted from me.

They were both supposedly mature adults, in their late twenties, and I was no longer tasked with watching over them. I was just here for a pleasant vacation, a relaxing weekend surrounded by rolling hills, bluegrass, and horses. And distilleries, of course, the reason for much of the tourism in the area. I was here to do tourist things, not to be the fixer of family problems.

I finally dropped into the rocking chair, setting it in motion. "What are you two up to?" It came out as more of an accusation than the simple curiosity I'd aimed for. Apparently, they weren't the only ones who needed to grow up.

"Nothing," the aforementioned baby sister, CJ, said with

a note of petulance.

That wasn't like her at all. Em had always been the one to invoke her right against self-incrimination while CJ had gleefully confessed her misdeeds, babbling along about how great everything had been going until she'd tumbled off the sled/bicycle/skateboard and accumulated a head-to-toe collection of cuts and bruises. For weeks after, she'd excitedly tell anyone who asked about her scars, just how much fun she'd had, and how much she'd wanted to do it again, except her mean parents and even meaner big sister wouldn't let her.

Worry was starting to replace my irritation. "What about the black eye and the cast on your arm?"

"Oh, that just happened yesterday," CJ said lightly, sounding more like herself. She'd never been fazed by physical injuries. "I was working on the stable renovations and fell off a ladder. No big deal." Her tone turned petulant again. "You'd know I've been through much worse in recent years if you ever visited."

"I'd have visited if you'd ever invited me before now," I snapped before I could stop myself. I hadn't meant to rehash old arguments.

Em, always the peacemaker, intervened. "The thing is, as long as you're here, Jess, we could use some help. CJ can't exactly cook for our guests at the moment." She glanced at CJ who raised her cast-wrapped arm and waved it, as if I might have missed it otherwise. "You know I'm a disaster in the kitchen, and we've got a full house this weekend. All five rooms are booked for two nights, starting tomorrow."

Em had sent me pictures of the B&B shortly after they'd bought it the previous November. At the moment, the porch was too dark to see anything clearly—oddly, there weren't even indoor lights visible in the windows—but I knew it was a rambling two-story white farmhouse with ells added to each side over time. Inside, there was a lobby, kitchen/dining area, and six guest rooms. Presumably we'd be sharing the last room since the other five were booked.

"How are we going to have Noah's birthday party with all those guests around?"

"They'll be gone by then," Em said. "It's on Sunday afternoon. And we arranged for the food and everything to be delivered, so there won't be any cooking for you to do. All you have to do is be there."

"I'm looking forward to it." They still hadn't told me everything. I was sure of it. But they weren't ready to talk, so I'd just have to deal with things I could control. First up was getting some sleep. "I don't mind working for my dinner. But can we go inside the B&B now? I'm too tired to do much tonight."

"Um," Em said. "The rooms are all set up for the guests. You can't sleep in there."

"Aren't we sharing the sixth room? You said there were only five booked."

"The last one isn't finished yet," Em said.

"But I thought I was supposed to be staying here this weekend."

"You are." CJ jumped to her feet and grabbed the baby monitor. "You'll be bunking with us out in the stable. It'll be fun, like when we went camping as kids. You loved camping."

I'd hated camping. Every minute of it.

Glamor camping—glamping—in what amounted to luxury hotel suites on wheels hadn't been invented back then. What we'd done in the forests of eastern Kentucky was old-fashioned roughing it, with canvas tents, sleeping bags on the ground, and no running hot water. Worse than the discomfort was the way that I'd always ended up spending the whole time babysitting.

It was too late to find a hotel room now, so at least for one night, I'd have to experience camping again. I'd be fine, as long as it didn't involve babysitting my adult sisters.

* * *

Beyond the farmhouse was a stable that, from what CJ told me, had once housed sixteen horses. For several generations, both the house and the stable had been part of the Rackhouse Saddlebreds horse-breeding farm next door, but during an expansion of their business twenty or thirty years ago, they'd sold this corner of the property to help finance a larger, more modern commercial stable, along with a new home for the owners.

Given that history, I was expecting a decrepit outbuilding that was falling down and every bit as rustic as our childhood camping sites had been. I was pleasantly surprised to find that, at least from the outside, it looked much more like a luxury-magazine spread on converting a barn into a residence. The exterior had a new roof, new siding shingles that hadn't had time to darken with age, and large new windows above, where the sliding barn doors had been replaced with a solid wall. A smaller entrance had been installed just off-center, and skylights had been added to the roof. Maybe my sisters had just been pranking me with the suggestion that we'd be roughing it.

CJ opened the door and gestured for me to go inside first, with Em at my back.

They hadn't been pranking me.

The interior had been gutted, exposing the original posts and beams. A new subfloor had been installed over the original slab, but like the walls, it was unfinished, and there was no kitchen. I was a little afraid to check out what was apparently a bathroom in the dry-walled but unpainted bump-out in the right back corner.

The sparse furnishings consisted of two sets of bunk beds lined up end to end along the back side wall across from the bathroom, plus three wood chests that apparently served as both storage and seating. The chests were perhaps twice the size of my wheeled rollaboard, which held just enough for a long weekend. I couldn't imagine how my sisters, who'd once thrown tantrums over the prospect of parting with even a single stained and holey t-shirt, could possibly have reduced their belongings so they fit in such a small space.

"Isn't it great?" CJ asked with seemingly genuine enthusiasm. "There's a lot left to do, but it's going to be perfect when it's finished. Two bedrooms, a tiny galley just for snacks and beverages since we can use the kitchen in the B&B for serious cooking, and a tiny office so Em can do all the paperwork."

"It definitely has potential." The place wasn't to my taste, especially as rustic as it was now, but it obviously made CJ happy, and that was all that mattered. She'd been through a lot in recent years, losing her husband to an ATV accident not long after they'd married, and then raising their son as a single mother. If the stable renovations helped her move forward, then I was glad for her.

"You can have whichever bunk you want," CJ said. "Except for Noah's of course."

I headed over to toss my suitcase on the nearest bed, and then turned to glance at the other bottom one, which had side rails to prevent its occupant from falling out. At the far end was a blanket-covered lump that I assumed was my three-year-old nephew, Noah. Seated next to the pillow was a black-and-white tuxedo cat whose one eye glared at me suspiciously. I liked cats—I had two at home—but this one didn't seem to like me.

I took an involuntary step back.

CJ apparently noticed my concern. "That's Pappy." She went over to kneel down and pat him briefly on the head. He wasn't having it. His glare remained focused on me. "He was a barn cat until he was injured. After we took care of his eye, we didn't think it would be safe for him to live outside again. He's still not very social, so don't try to pat him until he gets to know you. The only human he really likes is my son, and they're inseparable."

Em added, "Best not to touch Noah just yet either. Not until they both know you better. Pappy doesn't like strangers getting near his human."

That seemed to sum up everything about this reunion. I was a stranger to my own family.

I glanced at Pappy again and noticed a little hand that was the only part of Noah sticking out of the covers. It was snuggled up against his guardian cat's haunch, as if the contact helped him feel secure enough to sleep.

My sisters and I had once been like that, I thought.

They might not need me to watch out for them any longer, but their determination to get me to visit this weekend suggested that they might crave, at least subconsciously, that old feeling of the three of us being a united force against the dangers of the world. I hadn't realized until now how much I'd missed it myself.

It might take more than this weekend to recapture that feeling, but I was going to do my best to make it happen.

CHAPTER TWO

The bunk bed turned out to be surprisingly comfortable, and the sheets, part of the B&B's supply, were softer than anything I'd ever slept on before, so I was well-rested the next morning when I heard CJ get up at dawn. She threw on some clothes and herded her son outside, presumably heading for the house and breakfast. She'd always been an early bird to Em's night owl.

I got up and dressed quietly so as not to wake Em, who had her covers over her head like Noah had the night before. Pappy watched me from his new perch on the top bunk that CJ had just vacated. I kept my distance and successfully escaped to go greet my nephew inside the B&B.

The kitchen was massive. About a third of the space, at the far end from the back door, featured a dream setup for cooking, laid out in an L shape, complete with what looked like commercial appliances and infinite counter space. The remainder of the room held a trestle table large enough to seat a dozen people comfortably, more if they were a little squished together. From there, guests could look out the oversized windows of the back wall and appreciate the bucolic beauty of the horse farm next door.

Noah was seated at the foot of the table. He looked tall for his age, which was hardly surprising, since both of his parents were above average in height. Other than that, I thought he took after his father more than his mother, with a serious expression, round face, and tousled hair that was such a light brown it verged on blond. In front of him was a clear plastic cup, a quarter full of orange juice, an almost empty bowl of yogurt, and a plate that, judging by the little spots left on the white surface, had originally held a dozen blueberries lined up in three neat little rows. CJ sat beside him, sipping at her own glass of orange juice in between encouraging him to eat. He didn't seem interested in the food at all, focused as he was on a picture book beside his plate. He was pretending to read it, his fingers tracing the lines of words while ignoring his mother. Not unlike how CJ had been uninterested in breakfast when she was little.

As far as I knew, CJ didn't drink coffee, but there was a fresh pot in the commercial coffeemaker on the counter, along with a collection of brightly colored, mismatched mugs that advertised a variety of local businesses. I filled one and took a cautious sip. It was surprisingly good. Sometimes when people who didn't drink the stuff tried to make it, the results were terrible. Either CJ had acquired a taste for coffee, or Em had chosen the beans and then tutored her sister in best brewing practices.

I carried the steaming mug over to the opposite end of the table from Noah so as not to distract him from his breakfast. "Good morning," I whispered.

I needn't have worried about interfering with CJ's attempts to get Noah to eat. He ignored me and continued to pretend-read his book.

CJ sighed and leaned back in her chair to finish her orange juice. She set the empty glass down. "You always said I'd regret it if I didn't eat breakfast. I just never thought this was how karma would hit me, having a kid just like me."

"He looks healthy enough."

She started to say something and then stopped. "Thanks."

"You're welcome."

An awkward silence followed. I'd planned to spend this weekend fixing our relationship, but I wasn't sure where to start. If complimenting a mother on the health of her child evoked a response that had to be self-censored, I didn't know what other topic might be safe.

After another few seconds of silence, I decided CJ couldn't possibly object to me asking for more information about my role as cook. "If I'm going to be making breakfast for the next few days, I might as well start now. What would you like to eat?"

"I'm fine," CJ said. "I'll grab a muffin later. First, I need to get Noah settled into his morning routine. He's got a little fort with all his books out in the lobby, where I can keep an eye on him while still working at the front desk."

"Do you need any help getting him settled?"

"No, I've got it down to a science." She stood and encouraged Noah to get up from the table.

I got the unspoken message. She didn't want my help with Noah despite the cast that had to make it difficult to corral a rambunctious toddler. I doubted she even wanted my help in the kitchen. This might have been one of the rare occasions when she'd let Em talk her into something.

"Before you go," I asked, "could you give me an idea of what I'm supposed to be cooking tomorrow morning?"

She looked up from awkwardly using her left hand to dab at Noah's blue-stained lips with a paper napkin while he closed his eyes and accepted it with impatient resignation. "I emailed the menu and recipes to you last night. Nothing complicated. Traditional breakfast foods with just a bit of a Kentucky flavor. Custom omelets, plus ham, of course. For sides, there's hash browns, grits, a variety of made-from-scratch muffins, fruit salad, and locally made yogurt. We do biscuits and gravy too, but only on Sundays."

"That sounds easy enough."

"It is." CJ tossed the napkin on the table. "Especially since I grated and froze a ton of potatoes for the hash browns right before I broke my arm. There's a supply of muffins in the freezer too, and you can make the grits in the slow cooker tonight so they'll be ready in the morning. That mostly just leaves the omelets and the fruit salad to make for the guests at the last minute."

"And you do this every day now?"

CJ shrugged. "Pretty much, although it depends on how many guests are staying, and we're still building our reputation as the new owners, so we aren't usually fully booked, like we will be this weekend."

"I won't have much to do after I familiarize myself with the kitchen and the recipes," I said. "Do you want me to keep an eye on Noah for you when the guests start to arrive?"

"No, he doesn't know you well enough, and it would upset him to be alone with you." She picked Noah up awkwardly with her uninjured left arm and hugged him against her hip, taking care not to dislodge the book he clutched in one hand.

It was a little odd, the way he hadn't seemed interested in a stranger at the table with him. Some kids were just naturally shy, but why was his mother so reluctant to let me spend any time with him, not encouraging him to get to know me? Meeting Noah had supposedly been the reason for inviting me to visit for the weekend. But CJ hadn't even introduced us this morning. How were we supposed to stop being strangers, so Noah would acknowledge my existence, and maybe Pappy would even stop glaring at me as if I were a serial killer?

CJ was definitely hiding something, and pushing her would only make her defend the secret more fiercely.

I was the patient one, though, so I could wait for her to confide in me, laying out the problem she needed me to fix. I just hoped she didn't wait until it was too late.

* * *

I cleared the few dishes from the table and then ran back to the owners' quarters to grab my phone and check on Em. She was still sleeping, and I didn't see any reason to wake her yet.

Once back at the massive kitchen table, I opened the file of recipes CJ had sent me and confirmed that they were as simple to make as she'd said they were. All I really had to do today would happen in the evening—start the grits around ten, and take the potatoes out of the freezer to defrost overnight. No problem.

Then I looked at the menu. Down at the very bottom, in large, bold lettering, were the words, "Don't forget to try our specialty: bourbon bacon jam."

I was equal parts fascinated and repulsed by the idea of eating sweetened, alcohol-soaked bacon first thing in the morning. But apparently the jam was an important part of breakfast at the Three Sisters B&B. And, okay, maybe I felt more fascination than repulsion as I got used to the idea.

Em shuffled in just then, wearing flannel pajamas that looked like the ones she'd gotten for her twelfth birthday, right after she'd become obsessed with horses. Like that set, the one had stylized galloping horses printed in black on a pale blue background.

"Coffee." Em dropped into the seat beside me and slumped over the table, her head resting on her forearms. "I need coffee."

Some things hadn't changed at all.

I went over to the counter to fill a mug for her, grabbed a spoon and some sugar packets, and hurried back. I held on to my leverage though, keeping the coffee just out of reach. "You can have it after you tell me about bourbon bacon jam."

"Ugh." She reached blindly in my direction for the mug. Defeated, she dropped her hand and slipped it back under her head. "It's too early to talk about food."

"Is the jam that bad?"

Her laugh was muffled. "No, it's great as long as you've first had coffee. Everyone loves it. In fact, you need to make some more because yesterday's guests bought the last six jars CJ made before she broke her arm."

I didn't remember seeing the recipe in the file. Maybe CJ considered it her secret and wasn't any more willing to share the recipe than she was to share time with her son. Or maybe I was just reading too much into CJ's standoffishness this morning. She might have thought there was plenty of jam in the pantry, so I wouldn't need the recipe.

Either way, I didn't have time to worry about CJ's secrets. "Perhaps we can skip the jam this weekend."

Em's head popped up, her eyes finally alert and her expression aghast. "We can't do that. Especially not with these guests."

"Why not?"

Em made a gimme motion in the direction of the coffee mug. "I need a drink first. I can't do this without caffeine."

I lowered the mug to the table in front of her, along with the spoon and sugar packets.

Em dumped three packets into the cup, stirred briskly, and then drank half of it before stopping to breathe. Her posture assumed its usual perfection, shoulders back and spine straight. "Ah. I needed that."

"Now talk." I dropped into my seat. "Why do you really need me to be here this weekend? Because I don't think it was just so I could help celebrate Noah's birthday. Or even to cook breakfast."

Em took another long drink and then said, "You're right. The thing is, this weekend's bookings aren't just any guests." She stood and headed back to the coffeemaker for a refill. "Just a second. I need more caffeine if I'm going to explain the rest properly."

I waited patiently until she returned, stirred more sugar into the mug, and then sat again.

She rolled her pajama sleeves up as if preparing for a physical battle. "Okay. So it all started when we applied to become a member of a local group of businesses connected to tourism. Other B&B's, plus restaurants, distilleries, stables, and assorted tourist destinations around here. They've got a website to promote all the members, and then they help each other out, sort of like one big happy family. If someone contacted us for a room and we were full, we'd recommend one of the other B&Bs in the association. And we'd also recommend that our guests frequent the other members' restaurants and the like. Except we're fairly new, so we'd be getting more referrals in the beginning than we'd be giving out."

"That sounds like a great business opportunity." I'd already known that both she and CJ had done their homework about B&Bs, and I trusted that they had a plan for success, even if they hadn't shared it with me.

"It's even better than it sounds," Em said. "The tourism co-op is the brainchild of a local travel agent, Suzi Buford. And she's the queen of marketing. I mean, she's managed to thrive in a business that was mostly destroyed when DIY travel arrangements came to the internet. She couldn't have done that without top-notch marketing skills. We'd be fools not to piggyback on her success."

"I understand that much," I said. "But what's the tourism co-op got to do with this weekend and me being here?"

"We really need to get admitted into this group." She glanced toward the lobby where we could hear CJ and Noah settling in. Em leaned toward me and whispered, "We've been struggling a bit financially. CJ's life insurance money and my savings ran out pretty quickly, between the down payment, the mortgage, and then the renovations, both here and in the owners' quarters. Plus, we reopened at a slow time of year, so bookings haven't come through as consistently as we'd hoped."

"You've got a full house this weekend."

"That's sort of the problem." She took a fortifying glug of the coffee. "The people who are coming this afternoon aren't regular guests. They're here to inspect the B&B for the co-op's decision about whether to admit us to the group. We aren't supposed to know that's why they're here, of course, but the place next door, where I board my horse, is already a member. I happened to overhear someone mention that undercover inspectors were coming to the B&B this weekend. And now that we know, we've got to do everything possible to convince them we're amazing."

"You didn't need to drag me out here to do that. From what I've seen, you two are doing a great job with the B&B."

"Thanks," she said with what I thought sounded like relief.

"Tell me something." I still thought there was more to the story. "When did you find out about the inspection? Before or after you invited me out here?"

"Before," Em said with a sigh.

"But why? You didn't know then that you'd need a substitute cook. What did you think you'd need me for?"

"Everything needs to be perfect."

"You always say that."

"But it's true this time," Em said earnestly. "We knew it was a risk when we chose the name Three Sisters B&B. Our whole image is based on the cozy notion of three sisters running the place, but it seemed like just the thing to set us apart. And then, too late, we realized that the inspectors will wonder where the third one is if they only see two. Regular guests might not notice, but that's exactly the sort of nitpicky thing a representative of the co-op would pounce on, to say we don't live up to our image."

So they hadn't actually wanted to spend time with me, just use me like a grown-up version of show and tell. Not unlike when I'd first gotten my driver's license, and they'd suddenly wanted to do things with me, not because they liked spending time with me, but because I could provide transportation.

It was disappointing to know they hadn't really wanted to have a reunion, but they did need me now, more than they'd originally planned. There was still a chance that we'd grow closer together this weekend, for real, not just for show, and I wouldn't jeopardize that possibility by wallowing in my hurt feelings.

Instead of lecturing my sister about using me, I simply said, "I'd wondered about the name. Why not take all the credit for your hard work?"

"Because everything's better in threes. Mom used to say

that all the time. *Omne trium perfectum.* She claimed that was why she'd been so happy to have three daughters. She'd known we'd be perfect together. Remember?"

I did. And it had always made me wonder how Mom had explained the seven years before Em was born, when I'd been an only child. Maybe she'd had some old Latin saying about independence or sufficiency that was linked to the number one, but I'd been too young to remember it.

Em didn't wait for my answer. "CJ and I can do all the hard work this weekend, I promise." She paused before adding, "Well, except for the cooking as it turns out. Mostly we just need you to be here for authenticity. You're part of the appeal of our B&B, having three sisters working together. Family is a big deal around here."

I raised my eyebrows. "Like we were ever good at the family thing."

"We've gotten better," Em said. "Me and CJ, at least. I think you could figure out how to do it too, considering how smart you are."

"No more than you are." I might not have spent much time with my sisters since leaving home, but I'd kept current on the biggest pieces of their lives. "You're a vice-president at your bank, while I'm just a boring estate lawyer."

She ducked her head, letting her shoulders slump, and mumbled something.

More secrets. "What?" I asked.

"I'm not a bank vice-president anymore." Em straightened and raised her head to look at me defiantly. "I quit last year when I got passed over for promotion yet again. It seemed like a good time to try something different, and I didn't find anything that really appealed to me, so when this place came on the market, I threw in with CJ to buy it."

"Why didn't you tell me about quitting?"

"CJ thought you'd try to talk me out of it. And we both wanted to show you we could do this on our own before we told you all the details."

"You still haven't told me all the details," I said. "What are you holding back?"

Em hid behind her coffee mug for a long moment, and then said, "I've told you everything I can. The rest isn't for me to share."

After that, Em refused to say another word. She quickly finished the last few sips of her coffee, grabbed a muffin from the oversized wooden breadbox on the counter near the coffeemaker, and raced out into the backyard. The slam of a distant door suggested she'd gone back to the owners' quarters, presumably to get dressed.

Somehow, I'd managed to chase away both of my sisters instead of bringing us closer together.

CHAPTER THREE

———

I puttered around the kitchen, familiarizing myself with the contents of the many cabinets before venturing into the butler's pantry, where I almost tripped over a large orange cat. He rubbed against my ankles until I stooped to pat him, and then, apparently satisfied that I wasn't a security risk, he ambled over to a big round bed in the corner to take a nap.

The pantry was large enough to hold a dozen more cat beds, the shelves overflowing with baking supplies, kitchen linens, and duplicate small appliances. When I was done in there, I texted CJ for the bourbon bacon jam recipe. She sent it just a moment later, so maybe I really had been reading something unintended into its absence from the original file.

On my way out of the pantry, I grabbed one of the blue floral cobbler-style aprons to protect my clothes from bacon spatters. It had the B&B's logo printed on a patch pocket, so wearing it would make me an official part of the sisterhood, at least on the surface.

It was almost noon by the time I had a dozen jam-filled jars cooling on the counter. The kitchen smelled of bourbon and bacon, while my fingertips reeked of onions and garlic no matter how many times I washed them or dunked them in lemon juice. When I took off my apron, intending to drop it into a laundry basket in the pantry, it clanked, and I realized I'd managed to fill the pockets with assorted equipment, like spare canning lids, a candy thermometer, and a set of metal measuring spoons.

I'd just emptied out all the pockets when I heard the commotion of guests arriving out in the lobby, so I went to help get the guests settled in their rooms. I might not know anything about the hospitality business, but I could at least carry luggage or do other physical chores that someone with a broken arm shouldn't do.

A short man in a casual jacket and chinos stood in front of the registration desk. A pair of women with a strong family resemblance—sisters perhaps, given their matching outfits consisting of floral dresses, white sandals, and coordinating headbands that pulled back their blonde hair—had settled on a sofa and were almost hidden behind a mound of luggage. Just inside the front door was a middle-aged Black woman in a wheelchair, accompanied by a White man about the same age, who fussed over her, more like a romantic partner than a nurse.

As I approached the front desk, CJ said, "Here she is," to the man at the front of the line, waving her cast in my direction as if she were introducing a product on a display pedestal. "Jess is the oldest of the three sisters. You already met Em, the middle sister, out in the driveway." She turned to me. "Jess, this is Mark Pleasant. He'll be staying here until Sunday."

The man stared at me thoughtfully. When I'd first seen him from a distance, he'd looked to be in his forties, but up close, I could see the wrinkles in his darkly tanned face, and the lifelessness in his thick dark hair, which screamed bad dye job. He had to be at least mid-sixties, possibly early seventies.

Having finished his inspection of me, Mark said, "Are you sure you're not an actress, here to play a part? You don't look anything like your so-called sisters."

At least superficially, he was right. If you lined us up from youngest to oldest, we looked like a set of nesting dolls. I was a good six inches shorter than CJ, and Em split the difference between us. We all had the same facial structure though—inherited from our mother—which lent itself best to the basic pixie haircut that we all wore. No one really paid any attention to my average brown hair, and that was how I liked it since I preferred to keep my clients focused on their cases and not on me. Em's darker hair was more memorable, projecting an image of a strong woman who would keep your financial assets safe, although what she liked most about the style was that it didn't interfere with wearing a riding helmet. On CJ, whose blonde hair had only darkened a little since childhood, the cut created a fragile appearance completely at odds with her daredevil personality.

I considered thanking the man for reminding me that CJ was the pretty one of the sisters, and Em was the striking one while I was emphatically plain in comparison. But it probably wasn't wise to antagonize the guests, even when they deserved it.

"We're sisters, not clones," I said mildly. "We're very different people, so it's only right that we look different."

"I suppose." Mark signed the paperwork CJ had put in front of him. He looked up and asked me, "Are you joining us on the barrel company tour today?"

"No," I said. "I've got work to do here."

"All work and no play makes Jess a dull girl," he said. "Besides, if you really cared about your guests, you'd come with us to make sure we have the best possible experience. This tour is included in the package we... I signed up for, so you should come along to make sure it's up to your standards."

"I'm sorry, but we'll just have to trust the tour guides today. I can't leave CJ all alone here with her broken arm."

CJ spoke up. "Sure you can. Paperwork doesn't require two hands, and Em can help with anything heavy."

"Excuse us for a moment," I told the man as I took CJ's unbroken arm by the wrist. "We need to have a sisterly conversation in private. We'll be right back."

CJ dug in her heels. "I can't leave Noah out here alone."

I glanced at the blanket fort behind the far end of the registration desk. I could see just far enough inside to tell that Noah wasn't paying the adults any attention. He was sitting next to a bin that was almost as big as he was, filled with plastic building bricks. In front of him was a collection of the little pieces, which he was sorting by color, preparatory to building something, the tip of his tongue stuck out in concentration. I doubted he would even notice if we stepped away. He looked like a miniature construction foreman, far too serious for his age. But what did I know about kids? I hadn't been around them for more than a few minutes at a time since I left home almost twenty years ago.

I tugged on CJ's arm again. "We don't need to go far, and we can keep him in sight."

CJ seemed to recognize my determined tone of voice. She nodded at Mark, said "Sorry. This will just take a minute," and let me pull her the twenty feet or so to the hallway between the lobby and the kitchen.

Once there, she demanded, "What?"

I kept my back to the guests and lowered my voice to a

whisper. "You really don't want me to go with them. I only agreed to be the short-order cook, not the traveling concierge."

"Please," CJ said. "We need this to go smoothly, and Mark doesn't like to be told no."

"It's not so much that I don't want to do it," I said. "I'm being realistic. I'm terrible at networking. I almost didn't make partner because I'm so bad at socializing. I'm more likely to insult or annoy the guests than I am to convince them the B&B is perfect."

CJ kept her voice low, but determined. "You don't understand. Mark is a retired tour operator, and we'll be rejected for sure if he reports back that we're not sufficiently supportive of our guests' requests. We have to satisfy his every whim. And that means going on the tour with him apparently. Someone's got to do it, and you're better than no one."

"Gee, thanks."

"I didn't mean it that way," CJ said, waving her casted arm as if to erase her words. "It's just that Noah needs me to keep an eye on him. In other circumstances, Em could watch him, but she'd have to miss a critical session with a busy trainer at the horse farm next door, and it's not fair to ask her to do that. And you can't watch Noah because you're still a stranger to him."

I desperately wanted to remind her that it was her own fault that Noah didn't know who I was, but now wasn't the right time. We had guests to deal with." All right. But once we get the guests settled into their rooms tonight, then I expect you to tell me what you've been hiding from me. I can't help fix whatever's wrong if I don't know what the problem is."

"I don't need your help."

"Yes, you do," I said softly. "Big sisters always know. So promise me we'll have that talk, or I'm not going on the tour with Mark."

"All right, all right," CJ said. "I promise. Now go be nice to the guy."

I wrinkled my nose in exaggerated disgust. "If you insist."

"I do."

I returned to the lobby desk and gave Mark a smile as false as his hair color. "I'd be delighted to join the tour with you."

* * *

I returned from hefting Mark Pleasant's oversized and wheel-less suitcase to his room—the last one on the left—in time to help the two women, who turned out to be a mother and daughter, not sisters, get their mound of luggage to their room. And by "help," I meant carrying all of it myself, with multiple trips up and down the stairs and the two women supervising from the upper hallway and asking me questions about local attractions and amenities, which I couldn't even begin to answer. The B&B was located in Cooperton, the town closest to the extremely rural area we'd grown up in, but it was still some distance from our childhood home, too far to walk or bike. I hadn't spent much time exploring it back then, and I had no idea what had changed in the intervening years.

Admitting my ignorance instead of trying to fake it was the right thing to do, but it left me annoyed with my sisters for putting me in this situation without a chance to prepare. I hadn't felt this incompetent since the days when I'd been a brand-new associate and had frequently been sent to cover depositions at the last minute, without any time to even read the case files. I'd worked hard to make sure I never again ended up in situations where I was unprepared, but here I was.

When I returned from delivering the women's luggage, the lobby was empty. The couple in the ADA room must have decided not to wait for me and taken care of their own bags. A moment later, two men who appeared to be a father and son arrived to check in. They looked to be a father and son with matching buzz-cut brown hair, similar facial features, and the same stocky build. Unlike the mother-daughter pair, the two men traveled light, with nothing more than a small duffle bag for the father and a backpack for the son. I offered to carry the bags for them anyway, but they declined. CJ gave them their room key and told them their room was the last one on the right at the end of the second-floor hallway.

I wasn't needed again until about half an hour before the shuttle bus was scheduled to take everyone to the barrel company. That was when the last pair of guests arrived. They were twin brothers who, with their button-down shirts, slightly shaggy dark brown hair, and traditional bow ties, looked like professors or scientists attending a conference. At least they spared me questions about local businesses while I led them to the last remaining room, pulling the rollaboard for the one who spent the entire time shouting to some unlucky assistant on his phone. The other one took care of his matching bag and studied the B&B's brochure taken from the front desk.

The shuttle bus arrived about fifteen minutes before its scheduled departure time of two o'clock. Em had changed into her casual riding clothes, but she took over at the front desk while CJ went outside to talk to the bus driver. I hurried back to the owners' quarters to freshen up after carrying all the luggage. When I returned, most of the guests had assembled out in the driveway near the bus. The women in matching dresses were at the front of the line, and in the better light, I could see that there was far too much age difference between them to be sisters. Mother and daughter then, with the younger woman's blonde hair a lighter and more natural shade. Behind them were the twin brothers, and at the back of the bus, next to the ADA door, was the woman in the wheelchair and her partner.

We were just missing the father-son pair and the annoying Mark Pleasant. Personally, I wouldn't mind if he decided not to join us.

CJ emerged and called out, "All aboard."

The bus looked like the sort used for shuttling people to and from airport parking lots. It was white, with *Bourbon, Bridles, and Bluegrass* printed where a company name would normally go. Double doors toward the rear opened, and a wheelchair lift started to lower. The woman in a wheelchair and the man with her waited for it to be ready while the rest of the guests climbed the front steps.

I went over to ask CJ if I should go knock on the doors of the missing guests.

She shook her head. "Not quite yet. Mark said he had a migraine and needed to take his meds, so you may luck out and not have to go with him if he doesn't feel well enough for the tour." She looked toward the B&B's front porch. "There are the other two guests now."

The father and son came trotting up to the bus.

"Sorry we're late," the older man said to CJ. "We lost track of time."

"Not a problem," CJ said, gesturing for him to board.

He turned to hold out an encouraging arm for his son to go first and froze briefly in what appeared to be surprise. I followed his gaze to see Mark Pleasant coming toward us from the front porch. So he was joining us after all. Assuming he ever made it to the bus. He walked slowly, like a man with a hangover, taking care not to do anything to trigger the pain, seemingly oblivious to how he was holding up the bus's departure.

The father and son hurried up the steps and into the bus and were seated before Mark finally reached the doors where I waited for him.

"Why aren't you inside?" he asked me, his voice surprisingly loud for someone nursing a migraine. "You're not going to back out on your promise now, are you?"

"Of course not."

His expression made it clear he wouldn't board until after I did, so I started up the steps with him following too close behind me. As I reached the top, I heard him stumble, so I turned to make sure he was okay.

"I'm fine," he insisted, a little pink in the face. "Just miscalculated the height of the first step."

He'd landed on one knee on the bottom-most step. His hands were still tightly gripping the side rails, which had at least saved him from a face-plant. He seemed more embarrassed than injured. He probably hadn't appreciated the reminder that he was both weak and old, not the impressive, spry lady-killer he tried to portray himself as.

I continued down the aisle, and he followed me all the way to the empty seats in the back of the bus. I slipped into a window seat so I could admire the scenery that I'd once treated with the contempt of familiarity, but now couldn't seem to get enough of.

Mark dropped down beside me instead of claiming one of the other unoccupied pairs of upholstered seats.

I took out my phone and pretended to be absorbed in it. Tilting it for privacy, I texted CJ. *You owe me.*

He pushed my arm off the center rest and smirked at me. Another text: *Big time.*

Not content with having claimed the center rest, Mark leaned over into my space and peered at my screen. "What's so important on that thing that you can't talk to me?"

I should have known he wouldn't observe the etiquette

rule against talking to someone who was intent on her phone. I couldn't even chide him for his rudeness without undermining my assignment to charm the guests during the trip.

I put away my phone and let Mark tell me all about himself. If I hadn't known better, I would have thought he was being completely transparent. As it was, I noticed when he glossed over the type of company he'd once owned and forced myself to pretend to believe the elaborate nonsense he invented for why he was staying at the B&B for the weekend.

Being nice to Mark could well be the key to getting Em and CJ an invitation to join the tourism co-op, so I could grin and bear it for a few hours. Maybe then my sisters would trust me with their other secrets.

CHAPTER FOUR

The bus parked outside a complex of buildings, most of which looked like standard warehouses. The one exception was an oversized, weathered barn with as many odd little additions built out from the sides and the back as a traditional farmhouse that had grown to accommodate several generations of a family. A hand-carved wooden sign identified it as the headquarters of Hills' Barrels, established in 1873. The barnlike building was on top of a hill that sloped gently down to a river about five hundred feet to its left. Half a dozen picnic tables had been set up a safe distance from the edge of the water, so workers on break as well as tourists could gather there to appreciate the view.

The bus driver, a man who appeared to be in his midtwenties, with dark, closely-cropped, curly hair on both his head and his chin, wearing jeans and a sports shirt embroidered with the same tagline as the bus, opened the front door and engaged the lift in the back. He got up from his seat and turned toward the passengers to say, "Enjoy your time at Hills' Barrels, everyone. I'll be waiting here for your ride back to Three Sisters promptly at four."

The passengers rose and started to file out, causing a bit of a backup. Mark stood and bumped into the back of one of the twins. While their friends might be able to tell them apart, I couldn't.

The bumped man turned around abruptly, and the snarl on his face made me think he was going to yell at Mark. Fortunately, the man flicked a glance at me, realized he was being observed, and decided not to cause a scene. He looked past Mark to focus on me. "I didn't realize you were still on the bus." His anger, while not completely dissipated, was at least under control, and his tone was mild. "I suppose you've been to Hills' Barrels a million times before, so you're staying behind."

I needed a break from Mark, so I nodded my head in mock disappointment. "I wouldn't usually turn down a chance to take the tour with you, no matter how many times I've been inside, but I just received some critical emails that need an immediate response. I'm confident the guide will take good care of you."

Mark turned to say, "You have to come with us. Otherwise, I'm not going. I can't stand the thought of a sweet young thing like you locked away in a boring old bus while everyone else is having fun."

I was normally quite even-tempered, but it felt like ever since I'd come home, people were intent on making me want to strangle them. And I couldn't even roll my eyes without my rudeness possibly costing my sisters their B&B.

"How about if I walk out of the bus with you?" I said, getting up and into the aisle, and then taking a step back to provide us both with personal space. I'd have moved farther away, but the guest in the wheelchair was blocking the last few feet of the aisle, waiting for the lift to finish locking into place. "Then I'll head on over to the picnic tables to answer my emails while you go on the tour. It's beautiful over by the river, so I won't be stuck in the bus at all."

Mark grumbled, but by then the aisle in front of him had cleared, so he headed for the door and then down the steep steps. I was worried he'd fall down them and wished he'd use the lift, which would have been safer. Fortunately, he held on to the rails tightly enough that he managed to get down without another stumble.

Once outside, I encouraged him to join the rest of the guests, who were listening to a teen-aged girl enthusiastically reciting the history of Hills' Barrels. A step behind her and slightly to one side, a man stood with his arms crossed over his chest, as if offering backup without trying to overshadow her. He looked to be about my age and had a compact build—average height but muscular—wearing khakis and a sports shirt with the Hills' Barrels logo and the words "Master Cooper" on the left side of his chest. His red hair was short, dotted with some bits of white that could either be evidence of aging or just shavings from making the staves that would later be assembled into barrels.

He left the tour guide and came over to ask, "Is there a

problem?"

"No, I'm fine. I'm not going on the tour."

"Why not?"

He looked perplexed, which was understandable. After all, I'd arrived on a shuttle bus with just one destination, Hills' Barrels. Most people didn't ride a shuttle bus just for the fun of it.

"It's complicated," I said, keeping my voice low enough not to be overheard by the guests. "I'm Jess Walker, of the Three Sisters B&B, not part of the tour group."

He reached out to pinch me lightly on the forearm.

"Hey!" I pulled my arm back. "What was that for?"

"Just making sure you're not a ghost," he said with a grin. "I always thought CJ and Em made you up, like they had an imaginary sister instead of an imaginary friend."

"I'm real. Just haven't been back here in a while."

He nodded toward the tour guide, who seemed to have been waiting for permission to leave, and she promptly herded the group toward the entrance. Mark glanced back at me mournfully, and I pretended not to notice.

"I'm Reed Hill."

"Like the equestrian apparel company?" I'd sent Em gift certificates from there for assorted birthdays.

"Nah, my family's only ever been coopers. And that company's only been around for about forty years. There are records of Reed Hills going back almost two hundred years. I'm just the latest to own the family business. Although you probably know that from your sisters."

"I'm afraid the three of us haven't talked much in the last few years. And when we did, it was mostly about family matters, not the B&B or the other businesses it's connected to."

"I'll have to catch you up on all the latest gossip then." Reed turned to point at the picnic tables overlooking the river. "Let's go on over there and talk. That way, the bus driver can get some studying done without us distracting him."

The driver was indeed intent on an ebook reader propped on the steering wheel. He looked up, waved at us, and said, "See you back here at four."

I did have some emails from my paralegal that needed responses, but they weren't as time-sensitive as I'd claimed to get Mark to detach himself from my side. Maybe I could find out from Reed what Em and CJ were hiding since he'd spent more time with them than I had in recent years. Besides, I was supposed to be on vacation, and there were few things more fun than a vacation fling with a good-looking man.

As we headed for the picnic tables, I asked, "Have you known my sisters for long?"

"I knew CJ before she bought the B&B. Her husband was a friend of my youngest brother. I used to join them on some hikes, although I was never as adventurous as the two of them were. My brother still is, although he's trying to be more careful, setting a good example for Noah and providing him with a good male role model."

"Is he seeing CJ?" Was that another secret she'd been keeping? It was too innocuous to be the main one, I thought, but the last I'd heard, CJ had still been mourning her husband and adjusting to single motherhood, vehemently resisting any suggestion that she should go out and date again.

"No, they're just friends," Reed said. "It's more about honoring his friendship with her husband than anything else."

"That's kind of him," I said. "What about Em?"

"He's not dating her either."

"No, I meant, when did you meet her?"

"I'm disappointed," he said with a grin. "I thought you were leading up to asking if I was dating Em. Or CJ."

He would be totally wrong for them, I thought. Not that I could warn him if he was dating one of them. For the most part, my sisters and I had always been careful never to offer each other advice about boyfriends. I'd practically had to wear a gag to keep from telling CJ what I thought of the irresponsible man she'd eventually married, and then when he'd died, I'd wondered if I could have saved her some heartbreak by speaking up earlier in their relationship. Probably not, but it still bothered me sometimes that I might have had an opportunity to protect her, and I hadn't taken it.

"Well?" I asked. "Are you dating one of them?"

"Nope. CJ's way too young and wild for me. And Em's too obsessed with her riding to even notice men most of the time. Besides, she's still too bitter about the end of her banking career. She needs to work that out before she can be in a stable relationship." Reed waited for me to sit on the side of the picnic table facing the river before he settled across from me. "So, how come I know more about your sisters than you do?"

"You'd have to ask Em and CJ," I said lightly. That wasn't the entire truth though, and while I had no compunctions about telling social lies to the annoying Mark Pleasant, I didn't want to lie to this man, not even to be flirty. And I didn't want him to just humor me in return.

I held up a hand to forestall his response. "No, you don't have to say it. I know it's my fault too. It's hard to be a family long-distance."

"But you're here now," Reed said. "It's a start."

That was what I kept telling myself, but I hadn't really understood just how difficult it would be to find some privacy for serious family conversations in a setting where guests took priority, and one of them might interrupt at any moment. Probably Mark Pleasant with some new and unreasonable demand.

* * *

Flirting with Reed had been so much fun that, an hour and a half later, I was surprised to see the guests emerge from the factory's front doors and wander over to the bus.

"Sorry," I said. "I've really enjoyed meeting you, but I've got to go take care of our guests."

Reed rose to his feet. "I understand. Work has to come first for both of us. I hope you'll stop by sometime when I can give you a personal tour of the place."

"I'd like that." Unfortunately, I doubted I'd have time to return this weekend since I was needed at the B&B, and I wasn't sure when I'd be back to Cooperton. I wasn't even sure my sisters would ever want me to visit again once they had their coveted invitation to join the tourism co-op.

Reed went inside, and I joined the guests waiting to board the bus. Mark Pleasant was last in line again, and he had one hand pressed against his forehead. When the person in front of him took a step closer to the bus, Mark followed, wobbling so much I was afraid he'd fall over. If he couldn't walk on flat ground, he definitely wasn't going to be able to scale the steps into the bus.

I moved to his side to ask, "Are you okay?"

His face looked strained, and he was paler than he'd been earlier.

"I'm fine," he said, letting his hand drop to his side. "Just a migraine."

"Do you need to see a doctor?"

"No, no," Mark insisted with a forced smile. "I get them all the time, nothing to worry about. I might lie down for a bit once we get back to the B&B, though."

He must feel really terrible if he was willing to admit to the need for a nap. I glanced toward the back of the bus. The driver had already lowered the handicapped lift, and the wheelchair was on its way up.

"Why don't you take the lift?" His pride might make him resist the sensible approach, so I added, "There's no line there, so it'll be faster, and then you can sit down and close your eyes to get some relief more quickly."

"Will you come and sit next to me if I do?"

It was only about a twenty-minute drive back to the B&B, and Mark looked like he didn't have the energy to insist on being entertained on the return trip. It wouldn't kill me to do as he asked. Besides, saying no was too risky. If he ignored his limitations, tried to scale the steep front steps, and instead fell and hurt himself, that wouldn't be good for anyone.

"Of course I'll sit with you." I herded him toward the back of the bus.

Mark used the lift without any further difficulty and slid into the nearest seat, scooting over to the window. He patted the space beside him, and I dropped into it. That seemed to satisfy him. He leaned his head against the glass and closed his eyes.

Twenty minutes later, the bus parked in front of the B&B. Mark slept through the announcement that we'd arrived at our destination. The driver opened the doors and engaged the back lift, and still, Mark slept. I waited until the wheelchair behind me had exited the bus, and in the other direction, most of the other passengers had made it outside. Then I twisted in my seat to face Mark and gently tapped his upper arm. "We're at the B&B. It's time to go inside."

No response.

I tried again, and he remained unresponsive.

Not good.

I glanced toward the front of the bus, where the last two guests, the twin brothers, were chatting with the driver. I couldn't get his attention without advertising to all the guests that we had a problem, and the last thing I wanted to do was cause a panic.

I took out my phone, fumbled it in shaking hands, and it dropped on the seat beside me. Somehow, I managed to pick it up again and dial 911.

"Police, fire, or ambulance?"

"Ambulance." I kept my voice low so the last, reluctant-to-disembark guests couldn't hear me. "There's an unconscious man at Three Sisters B&B." The dispatcher said she knew where it was, and she'd send help immediately.

I hung up and stared at Mark, wondering if I should do something while I waited. Recline the seat? Cover him with a blanket in case he was in shock?

It was only then that I realized he was unnaturally still. As far as I could tell, he wasn't even breathing.

I picked up his hand and searched frantically for the pulse at his wrist, but there wasn't one.

I leaned back in shock and dismay. My sisters were counting on me to help their B&B succeed, and instead, I'd just let a guest die on my watch.

CHAPTER FIVE

———

While I waited for the first responders, I sent a group text to my sisters to warn them that things were going to get crazy in a few minutes.

I think Mark Pleasant is dead. Police/ambulance on the way.

Em and CJ responded almost simultaneously with the exact same question: *What happened?*

Explain later

CJ: *What do we tell guests?*

Dunno

Em: *You always know what to do*

I usually did, but I'd never had anyone die practically in my arms. It wasn't something I could have prepared for. And there was no time to make a plan now, let alone carry it out. I could already hear sirens in the distance. I thought Mark was beyond my help, but I still couldn't abandon him to go inside the B&B and help with the other guests. What if I was wrong, and he was still alive? Either way, someone had to stay near the bus to direct the EMTs and explain the situation to the police. CJ and Em were going to have to handle the situation indoors on their own. They knew more about the hospitality industry than I did, anyway. They'd even taken enough online courses to get certificates from an accredited school.

I texted: *Is there a standard procedure to keep everyone calm when there's been a death on the premises?*

CJ: *Not that I know of, but we'll deal with guests if you deal with cops.*

Will do

The sirens grew louder, so I moved away from Mark just enough to lean out the handicapped ramp doors so I could signal the first responders. A moment later, an ambulance was sliding to a stop on the gravel driveway, with a police cruiser a few yards behind it. The sirens cut off abruptly, but the flashing lights remained on.

Two EMTs raced over to the bus, pushing a gurney topped with a bulging, extra-large, red and white duffle bag. The apparent leader, a middle-aged man, asked from near the front of the bus, "Where's the victim?"

Fortunately, by then, the bus driver had realized something was wrong and had evacuated along with the two guests he'd been talking to.

"In here," I called out.

The EMTs left the gurney outside and raced up the steps with the younger one in the lead. I stayed out of their way near the wheelchair lift while they hurried over to Mark. They hunkered down in the aisle, and I couldn't see what they were doing, but as they worked, the older one asked me questions.

"What was he doing before you noticed he was unconscious?"

"Sleeping. At least, I thought that was what he was doing. He drifted off right after he sat down, about twenty minutes ago."

More activity that I couldn't see, then, "Did he complain of not feeling well?"

"He had a headache," I said. "He had one earlier too. Told me he suffered from migraines. I think he took something for it before we left for the barrel factory tour, and he seemed okay, but it must have returned later."

Again, a pause while they did whatever they did. "We found his wallet, and it says he's on blood thinners. Do you know anything about that?"

I knew that blood thinners were for preventing strokes and heart attacks, but that wasn't what the EMT was asking. "I'm sorry. I don't know anything about his medical history. I only met him a few hours ago."

The EMT grunted in acknowledgment, and they went back to work. A few minutes later, the older one sat back and shook his head. The younger one rose and hurried out the front of the bus. I heard the gurney being rolled toward me, presumably so they could use the wheelchair lift to move Mark out of the bus.

I took the opportunity to go outside and wait until they'd brought him out and settled him on the gurney. They had an oxygen mask on him, but I didn't think that was necessarily an indication that he was still alive. They probably had to continue treating him until a doctor pronounced him dead at the hospital.

"He's gone, isn't he?" I asked.

The older EMT asked, "Unofficially?"

"Of course."

"Yeah," he said. "I'm sorry. There isn't really anything more we can do but go through the motions. It might help our report though if you can think of anything else that happened before he fell asleep."

"Nothing." I was completely stymied. "I wasn't with him on the tour itself, but when he came out, he seemed tired and insisted he just needed a nap, and he'd be fine."

The EMT handed me a business card. "Well, if you think of anything else, let me know."

"Actually," I said. "There's one other thing. He seemed unsteady on his feet, almost like he was drunk, but he couldn't be, so I thought it was just fatigue."

The two EMTs exchanged a glance, and the younger one muttered, "Talk and die."

The older one nodded and asked, "Could he have hit his head sometime in the last few hours?"

"Not that I saw." He could have fallen during the tour, I supposed, or even in his room at the B&B before getting on the bus, but I didn't want to suggest it without knowing the facts. Rumors based on mere supposition could spread quickly and ruin a business. "He didn't say anything about a fall when he came out of the factory after the tour, and from what little I'd seen of him, he seemed like the sort who would definitely take advantage of an opportunity to complain if something had gone wrong."

"Well, if you think of anything else, you've got my info." He gestured for his partner to resume pushing the gurney, and they headed for the ambulance.

The police officer—he was with the county sheriff's department, according to the markings on the cruiser—talked to them briefly, getting Mark's driver's license from them and making a few notes on an official-looking, pocket-sized notepad before handing the ID back and heading in my direction.

I'd dealt with quite a few cops in my legal career, although never in a particularly hostile setting. Generally, it had just been a matter of getting police reports from fatal accidents to deal with insurance claims for the estate. I always offered to take care of matters like that for my clients, aware that it would be emotional and stressful for them. I could be objective about it since I had no personal connection to the decedent or the accident.

It was different now that I was personally involved in the incident. Not that I'd known Mark that well or had any emotional attachment to him. It was just that I didn't have any experience talking to cops on my own behalf. Maybe I should have asked CJ to talk to the officer. She was the one who had dozens of run-ins with the law. Nothing serious, just fallout from her daredevil activities that had frequently involved trespassing, and she'd always managed to talk them into letting her go with nothing but a warning.

Too late to switch places now. I was going to have to convince the deputy that there was nothing to see here, just an elderly man in poor health succumbing to his pre-existing medical conditions.

It had nothing to do with me. Nothing to do with the other guests. And most especially, nothing to do with the B&B.

* * *

As the officer approached, some of my apprehension faded. He looked about twelve years old, too young to have a driver's license, let alone a badge. How intimidating could he get?

The thought brought me up short. When had I become old enough to start thinking that adults were just kids?

He did have a baby face, so maybe I hadn't entirely gone over the line into old-geezer territory. He truly did look like a teen, if not a pre-teen, all gawky and soft, with drab brown hair and no hint that he was capable of growing a beard, not even incipient stubble. I had to wonder how much teasing his youthful appearance had generated while he was qualifying to become an officer.

"I'm Evan Shurette," he said. "Deputy sheriff. I understand that you were the last person to see the deceased alive."

"Yes. I'm Jess Walker." I nodded toward the front of the B&B where its sign was clearly visible from where we stood.

"One of the three sisters."

"Right." He wrote something, presumably my name and address, in his little notepad.

I probably should have mentioned that I didn't live here permanently, but one of the first things drilled into practicing lawyers, even the ones like me who didn't handle criminal cases, was never to volunteer extra information to the police. The standard advice, applicable to both lawyers and their clients, was to answer honestly but to listen to the question carefully and only address what was specifically asked, not what you thought they might be interested in. I didn't have anything to hide, but it was an ingrained habit, and you never knew what might lead down a wrong path.

He didn't seem to notice my reticence when he asked, "And your relationship with the victim?"

The deputy would find that out soon enough, so it would seem suspicious if I didn't mention it. "He was a guest at the B&B."

"Did you witness anything that might have caused his death?"

"So he is dead? I wasn't entirely sure."

Deputy Shurette looked embarrassed but apparently concluded it was too late to deny it, so he nodded. "It's unofficial, but yeah, he was gone before the EMTs arrived. So did you see anything I should know?"

"I'm sorry. No."

"Who else might have witnessed anything relevant to the situation?"

"No one, as far as I know," I said. "There were nine other people on the bus, but I was sitting closest to Mr. Pleasant in the back, and the other people had left the bus before I realized he was unconscious."

Shurette flipped the pad closed. "I'll still need to talk to them. I should get their names and contact information, just in case the medical examiner has any questions."

Yeah, that would give the guests a warm, fuzzy feeling about their stay at the Three Sisters B&B.

My expression must have given away my moment of panic because Shurette added, "It's just a formality. I'm sure the death will turn out to be from natural causes. The deceased looked pretty ancient."

"I hope you're right." Although as we headed toward the B&B's front door, I couldn't help thinking that Mark hadn't seemed ancient to me. Perhaps because I was about fifteen years older than Shurette, and I'd done plenty of estate planning for men who were in their late eighties, a few even in their late nineties and fully competent to get their affairs in order. Mark, at somewhere between sixty and seventy, had another ten to twenty years left in the average male lifespan, and he had appeared to be in reasonably good health as far as I could see, other than his migraine and unsteadiness.

Inside, the guests were distributed throughout the lobby, each pair keeping to themselves, not mingling with the others. The woman in the wheelchair was parked near the hallway to the ground floor ADA room, with her partner leaning over her solicitously. The father and son were near the front door, inspecting the shelves along the wall to its right, which served as a gift shop, displaying CJ's jams and an assortment of other Three-Sisters-branded keepsakes for purchase. The women in matching outfits had settled in a pair of chairs that had a good view of the front yard, although the younger one seemed more interested in the long-haired gray cat in her lap than anything else, indoors or out. And finally, the twins were standing at the front desk, one of them yelling at Em. Despite his loud voice, his words made little sense, other than that he felt he was being treated like a child, which of course would only have been fitting since he was acting more infantile than Noah. His brother stood beside him, unwilling to interfere, despite appearing mildly embarrassed by the scene.

Fortunately, Noah wasn't being subjected to the shouting or the anxiety that hung in the air. His little fort behind the front desk was unoccupied, and I assumed CJ had taken him with her to go get some beverages and snacks, judging by the sounds emanating from the kitchen.

Em finally succeeded in calming the belligerent twin, or perhaps it was the sound of the door shutting behind us and the presence of a uniformed officer that did the trick. Everyone turned their attention on me and the deputy, except for the young woman who remained focused on the gray cat in her lap.

I expected Shurette would introduce himself and explain the situation, but he appeared to have developed a sudden case of stage fright and was struggling to get his notepad back out of his inner jacket pocket, as if it would tell him exactly what to say.

Em gave me a look that I remembered from our childhood when she'd expected me to argue her case with our parents, either to get permission to do something, usually horse-related, or to prevent her and CJ from being grounded for whatever latest bit of trouble CJ had gotten them into.

I'd never minded being her mouthpiece and had long since learned that there were advantages to being the one who controlled the narrative. It had worked with our parents, it worked at the office with my clients, and it would likely work with the deputy.

I cleared my throat and stepped forward so the deputy was slightly behind me, still struggling with his notepad. "I'm sorry to have to tell you that Mark Pleasant has been taken to the hospital, and his condition is critical." It was worse than that, but it was better to ease into bad news. I turned to indicate the officer, who'd finally gotten his notepad ready. "This is Deputy Sheriff Evan Shurette, and he'd like to collect your contact information, just in case he has any questions later."

The mother-daughter pair exchanged anxious glances while the twins took the news in stride, responding the same way they had to everything so far, with complaints and anger by one and resigned embarrassment by the other. On the other side of the lobby, the man beside the wheelchair had his head bowed and his hands clasped together, whispering what sounded like a prayer. The father and son looked at each other, and the younger man said, "Who?" His father leaned down, presumably to explain, but in a tone too quiet for me to make out the words. Then they both shrugged and returned to inspecting the different varieties of jams for sale.

Under cover of the sudden resumption of the guests' chatter, Deputy Shurette leaned closer to me to say in a tone just above a whisper, "I think I need to take brief statements too. Is there a space where I can talk to everyone privately? They'll need to be separated in the meantime so they can't influence each other's memories."

I gestured for Em to join us. "My sister can arrange that. She's good with logistics." And I didn't have a clue where we could sequester all eight guests and the driver. Which reminded me: where was the driver?

I explained the situation to Em, and she said, "CJ is in the kitchen with the bus driver, and they'll be out with drinks and snacks in another minute or two. Then the kitchen can be used for the interviews. The guests who aren't being questioned can stay in here or hang out on the front porch since the weather is still mild."

"I'll talk to the driver in the kitchen while you two get everyone else settled," the deputy said.

So for the next hour, while CJ kept an eye on everyone to make sure they weren't coordinating their stories, Em and I escorted the guests to and from the kitchen. When all but the last interview—with the quieter of the twins—was completed and the guests were free to return to their rooms or wander the B&B's grounds, everyone chose instead to remain in the lobby and compare notes. The shared brush with possible death gave them a sense of intimacy with each other that random guests wouldn't have. Of course, they weren't truly random guests and had probably known each other somewhat before coming to the B&B, through their connections with the tourism co-op, but I wondered if they knew they were revealing that fact by the way they skipped over more usual small talk about their backgrounds.

I went out to the front porch to take a break, leaving the front door open so I could hear when the deputy emerged from the kitchen. The bus driver was slouched in one of the wicker chairs. He'd been the first to be questioned but had been asked to stick around until all of the interviews were completed, in case the deputy thought of anything else to ask. The young man exhibited far more patience than I would ever have under the circumstances, reading what he referred to as homework on his phone until a few minutes after I joined him.

Finally, he ran out of patience, got to his feet to pace, stuffing the phone into his jeans pocket. He came over to where I leaned against the railing. "We never got formally introduced," he said. "I'm Lucas Verano."

"Jess Walker."

He nodded. "CJ's told me all about her big sister."

"And you're still willing to talk to me?" I asked. "She likes to tell people how mean and bossy I am."

"Well, she did mention a tendency to tell people what to do," he said, "but I guess that's better than telling them where to go."

"I've been known to do that too."

"Wish I could do that without losing my job," he said with a glance at the bus. "Any idea how much longer I'll be stuck here?"

"It shouldn't be too long." The last guest had already been in the kitchen with the deputy for longer than anyone else, I thought.

"I really need to get back to the campus," Lucas said. "I've got an exam next week, and my study group meets tonight."

"I'm sorry you got caught up in this."

Just then, I heard voices in the lobby and glanced through the door. The deputy and the twin he'd been interviewing were walking down the hallway from the kitchen to the lobby. Judging by their equally irritated expressions, I might have been mistaken about which twin had been the last of the guests to be interviewed. Perhaps it had indeed been the more aggressive one, but he'd managed to exert enough control over his temper not to yell at someone who had the authority to arrest him.

Deputy Shurette seemed to have gotten over his fear of public speaking, and said, "Thank you, everyone, for your cooperation. I've heard from the sheriff, and he would appreciate it if you'd stay here in town overnight, in case we need to talk to you again after we know more about Mr. Pleasant's condition."

The guests all looked at each other, as if waiting for someone else to be the first to speak, either to argue or agree.

Lucas moved over to the doorway so the deputy could see him. "That's fine for the guests, but I don't have a place to stay within the town's technical limit. I live about half an hour away, and you can always find me either at the graduate school or at my apartment if that's okay with you."

"That's fine," Shurette said. "But I'll need the keys to the bus. Just until we know for sure that it's not a crime scene."

Lucas hesitated, and I shared his reluctance to leave the bus where it was parked, right in front of the B&B, where it would serve as a billboard announcing that something bad had happened here. Not just for the guests, who'd lost a colleague, but to everyone in town, once they'd heard about why the bus was parked out front.

I couldn't think of a good reason to move the bus though, and apparently, neither could the driver because, after a long moment, Lucas dug the keys out of his pocket and handed them over.

Now I had one more problem to fix this weekend, along with healing the rifts with my sisters: Make sure no one started thinking of the Three Sisters B&B as the one where a guest had died.

CHAPTER SIX

CJ volunteered to give the stranded bus driver a ride home, leaving Noah with Em. I tried not to dwell on the fact that she hadn't even considered handing my nephew over to me. It was probably just habit. And I had plenty to worry about without getting offended by what was probably an unintentional slight.

The guests finally withdrew to their rooms since apparently none of them had noticed anything amiss while on the bus or at the barrel factory. Em said she could handle both Noah and the front desk alone if I wanted to take a break. I went out to the owners' quarters to quickly answer the emails from my paralegal, which Reed Hill had distracted me from earlier. Then I used my laptop to do some research on what the EMTs had suggested was Mark's cause of death, in case I needed to head off any speculation that it had been the B&B's fault.

I was still reviewing information about epidural hematomas—the official term for what the EMT had called "walk and die" syndrome—when Em texted to let me know CJ had returned and wanted to talk. Perhaps now I'd finally get to hear what they'd been hiding from me.

I found my sisters in the B&B's kitchen, with Noah nibbling on a grilled cheese sandwich and reading a different book than the one he'd had at breakfast. He was at the foot of the oversized table, like he'd been for breakfast, but with CJ and Em on either side of him this time. Em stared gloomily into the half-full mug of coffee in front of her while CJ absently rubbed at the skin along the bottom edge of her cast. She stared at it so intensely that I wondered if she was considering removing it against the doctor's orders. It wouldn't be the first time she'd done something like that.

Over on the counter were two fresh pots of coffee. The decaf was all I could handle at this hour, so I poured myself a cup and carried it over to join my sisters. I chose a seat about halfway down the table so as not to be close enough to Noah to risk upsetting him, although I wasn't sure he'd even noticed I was in the room. There was definitely something different about him in the way he was oblivious to me, but CJ would only get defensive if I asked her about it. I'd steeled myself to wait until she brought it up herself, and I was determined not to give her any more reasons to be annoyed with me.

"So," Em said, "what really happened to Mark?"

"I'm not sure. The EMTs mentioned something that I think refers to an epidural hematoma, basically swelling in the brain that can lead to death if not treated immediately. They called it 'talk and die syndrome' because the patient seems to be fine initially, able to walk and talk, completely unaware of how seriously they're injured, so they don't see a doctor. And then it's too late."

"Like an aneurysm?" Em asked.

"Sort of," I said. "But an aneurysm can happen without any external cause, while a hematoma is the result of a blow to the side of the head. Sometimes you see them in sports when an athlete is hit by a ball or puck. Or it can be caused by a fall."

"So where did Mark get injured? It wasn't here, was it?" Em asked anxiously.

"It's hard to say," I said. "The amount of time a patient can seem okay can be up to about four hours."

"So it could have happened here." Em was always good at math.

I nodded. "Or during the tour or even in the hour or so before he checked in here. All I know for sure is that it didn't happen on the bus. I was right next to him the whole time, both directions, and he didn't fall or bump his head."

CJ finally looked up from her cast. "A fatal injury happening here will ruin the B&B. The tourism co-op won't want anything to do with us, and word will get around that the place is unsafe."

"We might have been able to weather some negativity if we'd been around for years and this was the first incident, but we've only been open under the new name for a few weeks," Em explained. "If something happened here toward the end of when the prior owners had been running it, with their thirty-year track record, it wouldn't have been a big deal. One death in all that time wouldn't have been surprising. Almost makes it worse that the place was perfectly safe for all that time, and then the minute we took over, someone died."

CJ added, "Our only chance of surviving this mess is to prove that we had nothing to do with Mark's death before the rumor even gets started. All anyone will remember is the gossip, not that we were absolved of any involvement."

CJ was too young to be that cynical without having been to law school. She'd had her own kind of legal education, though, since there were some who blamed her husband for the accident that had killed him and injured two other people. His estate had been sued and eventually settled by the insurance company for a pittance. The small payment was a clear sign—to anyone with a legal degree, at least, if not to the general public—that the insurance company did not believe CJ's husband was responsible for the accident, but it made business sense to pay off the plaintiffs with an amount less than it would cost to continue to fight the claims in court like CJ had wanted to do. As a result, while most locals fully sympathized with CJ, speculation over her husband's role in the accident would never completely go away.

"We'll just have to prove the injury happened elsewhere, and it was nothing more than a fluke that Mark happened to die here," Em said firmly. "Jess will know how to do it."

They looked at me expectantly, just like they had when, as kids, they'd relied on me to plan outings to the movie theater or the summer fair. At the time, I'd considered some of our activities to be fairly complicated logistically, but they were nothing compared to the current situation.

Still, I had to try. But I also needed to set reasonable expectations. Despite our recent separations and some simmering resentment that I didn't fully understand, my sisters seemed to believe that I could fix their adult problems as easily as I'd fixed their childhood ones.

"I'll do what I can," I said. "But I'll need some more information before I can make a plan. Like a definitive cause of death and how the sheriff's investigation is proceeding. For all we know, he could have the whole thing resolved this evening, with a culprit in custody or a determination that it was a sad accident, nothing to do with us."

CJ snorted, and Noah copied her, repeating the sound

several times. She tapped his plate, drawing his attention back to the barely touched sandwich, encouraging him to have another bite before saying, "No chance this sheriff will resolve the case quickly. He's probably still panicking over having a suspicious death in his county, something that will actually require an investigation rather than just catching someone in the act. It's probably the first suspicious death around here since he took office some twenty years ago."

"The deputy seemed okay," I said. "A bit inexperienced, but he must have colleagues who can guide him."

"You'd think so," CJ said, "but he's probably the best of the bunch. Did you know that Kentucky doesn't require sheriffs to have law enforcement training? Ours certainly doesn't. He's a political hack who takes credit for the low crime rate in his jurisdiction, which is only low because he manipulates the statistics and doesn't report everything that actually happens. He's not going to know what to do with a death that doesn't fit neatly into one of the three usual categories around here: accident, natural causes, or a brawl that got out of hand."

"He can call in the state police for help," I said.

"In theory he could," CJ agreed. "But he won't, for political reasons. He'd have to admit to needing help, and that wouldn't look good when he runs for re-election. Plus, as long as he controls the investigation, he can guide it to a conclusion that benefits him, regardless of what it does to the truth. Or to us. If he can't pretend it was a heart attack or something like that, he'll say it was just a tragic accident, a slip and fall, which will give the gossips free rein to blame us. I'm telling you, the sheriff's a hack, and all he cares about is keeping his job, not getting to the truth."

Em explained, "CJ has some personal experience with him. He was already sheriff when we were teens. There was one incident in particular when you were in college, and CJ joined a parkour group that refused to acknowledge *No Trespassing* signs."

"I remember the parkour phase." Em had told me about it at the time, and I'd known it would spell trouble. A sport that involved running through public spaces, vaulting onto or over barriers, and occasionally leaping from one elevated location to another was just the sort of thing that would appeal to CJ. Her fearlessness, along with her competitiveness, would lead her into taking even more risks than usual

"I don't think I told you about the trouble she ran into. Apparently all the best places for parkour were owned by rich cronies of the sheriff, so he and CJ had some... encounters at his friends' properties. It's probably a good thing she'd been dating someone whose parents were both lawyers, and the boyfriend was with CJ every time she ran into trouble, or she'd have a more extensive juvenile record."

"I'm not the only one who had bad experiences with the sheriff, back then or more recently," CJ said. "I've heard about a few from Lucas Verano, the bus driver, who gets the scoop from his cousins in law enforcement."

"How bad is it?"

"Let's just say that the whole way home today, Lucas kept fretting about how he'd be blamed for Mark's death if the sheriff was in charge of the investigation. Lucas thought the sheriff would make up something about how young men always drive recklessly, and that was what must have caused the hematoma, so the bus driver should be fired, and his boss wouldn't have any choice but to do it. Even if Lucas isn't blamed, he could still be suspended, without pay, until the investigation concludes, and if it drags out for a few months, it would be really bad for him. He needs his job, or he'll have to drop out of graduate school, and that would be terrible for everyone. He's brilliant, studying to become an engineer."

Em said, "If anyone's going to get solid answers about Mark's death, it's not going to be the sheriff. We need you to figure it out, Jess. You're good with that sort of thing. I can follow the money if that becomes an issue, but you're the one who can untangle a puzzle."

"And I'll chase the perp down and handcuff him," CJ said cheerfully before looking down at her cast. "Well, I can chase him down and sit on him, but you two will have to cuff him."

Em laughed. "We always did make a good team. Remember when you decided we needed a vegetable garden, Jess, and you drew up the plans while I helped with the planting, and CJ built a fence around it to keep out the rabbits?"

"All I remember is that Mom and Dad wouldn't let me use the rented tiller," CJ said.

"You were seven," I said. "And weighed about half of what the tiller did."

CJ shrugged. "I'd have managed."

"We grew the best pumpkins in the county that year," Em said.

"True," I said, "but catching a killer isn't the same as gardening."

"I know," Em said. "But no one thought we'd get anywhere with the garden, and look at what we did. All it took was working as a team."

"And the prospect of getting a ribbon at the fair," CJ added. "We've got even more motivation to succeed in catching a killer. I mean, the ribbon was nice, and I still have it somewhere, but this is a matter of life and death. For Em and me and the B&B."

I shook my head. "It's not that bad. No one's going to kill you."

"They might as well," CJ said glumly. "Our lives are over if the B&B fails."

"It won't come to that," I said. "But even if it does, you'll both recover."

Em sighed. "Maybe not. Buying this place took everything CJ got from her husband's life insurance, as well as all of my savings, other than what I spent on buying a horse right after I quit my job. But we still needed to take out a mortgage and even some unsecured financing to cover the renovations. If we had to sell the B&B now, especially if it's discounted due to bad press from Mark's death, we'd be broke. And homeless."

"I'd never let you be homeless."

CJ laughed. "Do you really think we'd all fit in your townhouse?"

"It would definitely be better for everyone if it didn't come to that."

CJ grew serious and looked at Noah. "Especially for my son. He needs stability."

I might not be able to help much with raising Noah, as long as CJ maintained her overly protective wall around him, but I could at least do everything possible to make sure he'd grow up safe and secure, without any worries about losing the roof over his head.

"Then we'll just have to save the B&B by figuring out who killed Mark Pleasant."

CHAPTER SEVEN

My sisters looked at me expectantly.

"Give me a minute to think." It was one thing to agree to investigate a murder, but quite another to figure out how to actually do it.

The B&B's guests were the most likely suspects since I refused to even consider that either of my sisters might be a killer. They'd undoubtedly changed in the years since I'd left our childhood home, but I just couldn't believe that the young girls I'd once known better than I'd known myself could have become murderous adults. No one changed that much.

So. Any investigation had to start with the guests. If the cause of death did indeed turn out to be a blow to the head, and there wasn't a murder weapon that could identify the killer, then it would come down to motive and opportunity. It would take some digging to see if the guests had known Mark before this weekend, which might have given rise to a motive for murder. But it was immediately obvious that the guests, more than anyone else, had had plenty of opportunities to have assaulted Mark, both at the B&B and on the tour at Hills' Barrels.

The bus driver and everyone at the barrel company, other than Reed Hill whom I could alibi, had to be on the list of suspects too, but only if I couldn't find any motives among the B&B guests. It seemed more likely that someone who'd known Mark before this weekend—due to their connections to the tourism co-op—would have a sufficient reason to want him dead, compared to someone who'd just met him during the tour. Mark had gotten on my nerves from the moment I'd met him, but surely anyone who dealt with the public, like the bus driver and the factory guides, had dealt with troublemakers before without actually killing any of them.

It definitely made sense to start the investigation by

learning more about the B&B guests and their connections, if any, to Mark. The trick would be to ask them in a way that wouldn't make it seem too much like we were accusing them of murder.

While I was considering how best to approach the guests, the phone on the table in front of CJ pinged. She looked at it, muttered "uh-oh," and handed it to Em to look at the screen, who pointed to something and then at herself. CJ nodded and raced out of the kitchen toward the lobby.

Em stayed just long enough to explain, "The guests are getting restless. We forward calls from the front desk's number to one of us when we're not in the lobby, so guests can contact us. Usually one of us can handle all the calls without help, but nothing's normal this weekend. CJ's taking the upstairs guests, while I'm responding to the ADA room."

A moment later, Noah and I were alone together for the first time.

Noah darted a glance at me, three feet to his right, looked down at his book briefly, and then up again in another peek at me. I smiled encouragingly, but he just bent his head back to his book.

I understood the clear message everyone had given me, from Noah himself to his mother and even his guardian cat, Pappy: stay away. At this rate, I was going to run out of time to get to know my nephew before it was time to go home to DC.

Noah and I remained in our separate little worlds, close enough to see each other but with an invisible barrier between us, for another fifteen minutes until CJ came back to scoop up her son. "The guests are mutinying, threatening to go home now instead of finishing out the weekend, despite what the deputy said about staying here until the sheriff says otherwise."

"We have to discourage that," I said. "Not just so they don't get into trouble with the sheriff's department. We need them to stick around so we can question them about their interactions with Mark."

"I know," CJ said. "Plus, the stupid sheriff would probably blame us if the guests left. He loves throwing people under the bus to hide his own incompetence. If it came out that he didn't do a thorough job, he'd claim he couldn't do anything more because we obstructed his investigation. Em and I gathered everyone in the lobby so we can convince them to stick around. We'll probably need to bribe them."

"Right." I cleared the table of my mug and the ones my sisters had abandoned when they'd gone to respond to the guests' calls. "Do you want me to do the talking?"

"It depends on what you intend to say," CJ said. "We're hoping this will all be resolved quickly, and the guests will still be able to file their inspection reports to the association, so we can't admit that we know why they're here."

"Are you sure?" I asked. "It might be better to get it all out in the open and ask for a do-over later on when the experience won't be tainted by a death."

"We considered it, but there's too much risk that by waiting we'll just let rumors about the B&B get out of hand, and the co-op will reject our application without even bothering with a full inspection."

It was CJ's and Em's livelihood at stake, not mine, and therefore ultimately their decision. "All right. Let's go."

CJ set Noah down to toddle after her, and they both followed me into the lobby.

Each pair of guests had established their own little territory, maintaining a bit of distance from the others. The mother and daughter were in the same adjoining chairs as earlier, facing the front yard, where the view, including the bus-slash-potential-crime-scene, was fading into shadows as the sun set. The woman in the wheelchair and her partner were on the opposite side of the lobby, near the hallway to their room. The father and son leaned against the front desk. The twins paced irritably near the front door, one of them occasionally feinting as if he intended to make a run for their car, only to stop short and look back at me with a smug grin.

I forced myself not to react to the irritating twin. I was one of the B&B's three sisters, after all, even if just temporarily, so I had to act like a gracious hostess.

"Thank you all for joining us in here," I said. "You probably already know, but I'm Jess, the oldest sister. We understand that this weekend hasn't turned out as you'd hoped, and we're anxious to do whatever we can to make you comfortable until we hear back from the deputy about their investigation into Mr. Pleasant's accident. Is there anything we can do to help you pass the time?"

"We're starved," the louder twin said. "Can you make us some dinner, or are we supposed to die of hunger while the sheriff decides what to do with us?"

I knew what food we had on hand, and there was plenty to make a simple dinner for everyone. I could throw together some grilled ham and cheese sandwiches with a side salad topped with bacon. Not gourmet, but filling.

I was about to see if that would satisfy the guests, when Em elbowed me into silence and took over. "By law, we're not allowed to serve any meals except breakfast, but fortunately, there are some excellent restaurants in town that deliver pretty quickly. We've got all their menus so you can choose what you want."

"I'd rather eat at the restaurant," the older man of the father-son pair said. "No offense, but eating take-out in our rooms kind of ruins the dining experience."

"You don't have to eat in your rooms," Em said. "You're welcome to use the kitchen and its dishes and utensils. And the coffeemaker."

"You can't keep us locked up here," the loud twin complained with a longing glance at the front door. "The cop only said we can't leave town. So we can go to the local restaurants ourselves."

The problem, of course, was that once the guests got into their cars, there was a very real chance that they wouldn't come back. Especially the twins. I wouldn't trust them even if they left their luggage behind as a guarantee of their return.

"You're not prisoners," I said. "We're just trying to make things simpler for you."

"And," Em said, "if the food is delivered here, we'll be able to pick up the expense as an apology for the inconvenience."

The mother-daughter pair looked at each other and squealed happily. The mother spoke for them. "We never turn down a free lunch. Or dinner, in this case. We'd be quite happy to eat here. The kitchen really is lovely, and I'm sure that, as locals, you know more than we could possibly know about the best places to eat in town."

"Staying here is fine with us too," the woman in the wheelchair said. Her partner nodded, saying, "Blessed are those who hunger, for they shall be satisfied."

"Whatever," the loud twin said. "Just hurry up."

"In that case," the father said, "would it be all right if I chose the restaurant? It's just that I'm a chef, and my son is in training to become one. Trying food from the local restaurants is a big part of why we're here for the weekend."

"Of course," I said and looked at Em, who turned to go fetch the promised menus.

"Just get on with it," the loud twin grumbled. "This has to be the worst vacation of my life. First, one of us ends up in the hospital, and now the rest of us are going to slowly starve to death."

* * *

Em reappeared with multiple copies of several menus, from which the father narrowed the options to just one restaurant, and then copies were distributed to everyone. CJ and Em mingled, in case anyone had questions for us, until the problem twin complained that we were trying to influence their choices in order to keep the bill low. To placate him, my sisters and I adjourned to the kitchen, leaving the guests alone to write out their orders without any input from us.

Once safely out of hearing, Em said in a low voice, "Jerk. The Hammett twin, I mean. He was trying to trick you into breaking the law by serving dinner. Now he's probably maxing out the cost of their take-out just to see if we'll refuse to pay for all of it. Men think everything is about money."

"Better to pick up a large tab than risk getting bad marks from him on the inspection report," CJ said calmly. "We can't expect perfect scores on everything from all of the guests, and the rest seemed to be perfectly fine with eating here. We'll be fine if it's only the Hammetts giving us a bad review."

"Are you sure they're even going to complete the inspection? There's an even number of judges now, no one to break any ties."

CJ shrugged. "I don't see what else we can do except hope for the best. It's not like we can ask what their plans are for the inspection since we're not supposed to know that's why we're here."

Em nodded. "We're probably doomed anyway. The women in the group are outnumbered by men, and the best features of our B&B are more likely to appeal to women, starting with the emphasis on family and sisterhood. I guess we're lucky the inspection team isn't all men since the governing board of the co-op is predominantly male."

"The partner of the woman in a wheelchair seems reasonable," I said. "And the father and son."

"Men can seem reasonable even when they're not," Em said. "And the reasonable ones tend to knuckle under when bullied by people like the twins. We need to find a way to get the Hammetts on our side, and I'm not sure how to do it. Or if it's even possible. They're players. I've seen enough of them in my finance career to recognize them from a mile away. They don't care about anything except winning."

"Then the key to getting their cooperation," I said, "is to define the game so that supporting us counts as winning."

Em frowned. "How do we do that?"

"I don't know yet. I'll work on it once I've figured out all the details of a plan to investigate Mark's death."

"Do you at least have a general idea for the investigation?"

"I do." It was rough, but I could trust my sisters to improvise once they had a basic assignment. And it helped that I knew their fundamental strengths and weaknesses.

"Well?" Em asked impatiently.

"You're good at acting, so that's what you're going to do." She'd had lead roles in several high school theater productions, and as an adult, she'd done some amateur theater in the summer, all to good reviews. But more important than that, she'd always been something of a chameleon even when not on the stage, able to be whatever other people needed or expected her to be. It had enabled her to succeed in a male-dominated industry, but apparently, constantly being someone she wasn't still hadn't been enough to get her through the glass ceilings she'd encountered. "I want you to become the best friend of each guest. Don't ask them about Mark or anything they'd have to lie about to maintain their cover, not yet. Just cozy up to them, get them talking about their lives in general, so when it's time for you to question them about possible motives for murder, they'll be inclined to answer without wondering why you're asking."

"What about me?" CJ asked.

"You've always had a knack for making friends, so I'm betting you started getting to know everyone in town the minute you bought the B&B." It was something of an understatement to say that she had a knack for making friends. Everyone she met— except for the sheriff apparently—was drawn to her enthusiasm for life. They were instantly eager to become her BFF, and she generally and genuinely reciprocated the feeling. She'd lost some of her sparkle with her husband's death, but she still had enough to enchant most people. "Some of your local contacts must know the guests since the judges have to be a little familiar with the local tourism industry, but not connected enough that we'd recognize them as an inspection team. See if you can find out the guests' real backgrounds, and anything that might indicate they had a history with Mark that would give them a motive for assault or murder."

"I can do that," CJ said. "I'll get Noah settled for the evening first, and then I'll make some calls from the owners' quarters. What will you be doing?"

"I'm going to focus on opportunity instead of motive. I'll go ahead and interrogate everyone about whether they were ever alone with Mark to see if anyone claims an alibi. I'll try to be subtle, but if they figure out I suspect them of murder so they hate me, it doesn't matter as much as if they came to hate the two of you. I'll be gone soon, and you two can explain that I've always been the mean sister, and you bought me out or something."

"See?" Em told CJ. "I told you Jess would be a big help this weekend. She always has a plan for everything."

To my surprise, CJ nodded without any hint of resentment. "I'm not sure what we'd have done without you this weekend, Jess."

They might not be quite so grateful if they knew my plan involved more than just asking questions. Until we had the initial answers, it was probably better if my sisters didn't know I was planning to violate the laws of hospitality—but technically not the Fourth Amendment since I wasn't a cop or someone working for law enforcement—by snooping around the guests' rooms without permission.

CHAPTER EIGHT

———

Dinner had been ordered, and all the guests were settled in the kitchen to wait for the delivery. Em joined them, diligently becoming everyone's best friend. CJ was in the owners' quarters with Noah, making calls to anyone she thought might have useful information about our suspects. Time for me to snoop.

I still had a master key from earlier in the day when I'd been helping the guests with their luggage, so I headed out to the lobby. I planned to start with the ADA room since it was on the ground floor, and if I propped the door open, I'd be able to hear if anyone left the kitchen.

I was halfway across the lobby when the front door opened, and Reed Hill came inside. I stuffed the master key into my pocket and said, "What are you doing here?"

He laughed. "Nice to see you too."

Okay, so I hadn't exactly sounded like a gracious host, but he already knew I wasn't really involved in the running of the Three Sisters B&B.

"I'm sorry," I said. "You startled me. We weren't expecting any visitors this evening, and it's been a long day."

"I heard." Reed closed the door behind him. "That's why I'm here. To get the real story of what happened. And to offer any assistance you and your sisters might need."

All I could think about right now was getting the guests' rooms searched before they finished their dinner, but I couldn't ask a virtual stranger to help me do it.

"I assume you're talking about the unexpected hospitalization of one of our guests." I wasn't as good an actor as Em, but I tried to project nonchalance as I crossed the lobby to the pair of comfortable chairs with a view of the front yard, which now was fully dark. I dropped into one, gesturing for Reed to take the other. "What have you heard so far?"

"Just enough to be concerned." His words were calm, but he didn't try to hide his anxiety over the situation. He leaned forward in the chair as if expecting to have to jump to his feet on a moment's notice. "All I know is that one of your guests died on the ride back from Hills' Barrels, and it wasn't immediately clear whether it was from natural causes. That can't be good."

"I only know a little more than that," I said. "Mark Pleasant fell asleep on the way back here and then never woke up. The EMTs thought it might be an epidural hematoma. If so, he had to have sustained some sort of injury to his head in the four hours or so before he died."

Reed paused long enough to do the math. "That puts both the B&B and Hills' Barrels under suspicion."

"I'm afraid so."

"The sheriff's going to love painting a bullseye on me." He leaned back in the seat, but his posture remained tense.

"CJ thought the same about us."

"You mean because of her juvenile escapades?" At my nod, Reed shook his head. "I think you're okay there. He probably doesn't even remember CJ. He only cares about his big donors who keep him in office. Everyone else is disposable. He might help his smaller donors, anyone who supported his campaigns, but only if their interests don't conflict with the big-money people. And he saves his real hate for business owners like me, who not only decline to donate to his campaign but who have gone on the record as being willing to support anyone who has the guts to run against him. Except no one ever does."

"Maybe he'll do the right thing and turn the matter over to the state police. I assume they have more resources than a small town does."

"I suppose it's possible he'd consider the investigation too much work for too little benefit to himself personally," Reed said. "But just in case, we both need to be prepared to protect ourselves against his botched investigation. I understand you're a lawyer."

"Not the right kind for criminal defense."

"You aren't going to just wait for the sheriff to railroad your sisters, are you?" Reed asked. "From what Em and CJ have said about you, I wouldn't expect you to be that cold."

Much as I liked Reed, I didn't really know him, and he could well be responsible for Mark's death. Not intentionally, I thought, or directly, but factories—even low-tech ones for hand-building barrels the same way they'd been made two hundred years ago—had to be dangerous places where a visitor might be injured. Until I was sure Mark hadn't hit his head at Reed's factory, I wasn't letting him in on my plan to investigate the death myself.

"There isn't much I can do," I said.

He gave me a long appraising look and then stood. "Okay, if that's your story, I understand. But if you change your mind and can use my help, just give me a call. Your sisters know how to reach me. And I'll let you know if I find out anything useful."

"Thanks." He had to be tied into the local grapevine far better than I was, even better than CJ and Em since they hadn't lived in Cooperton as long as he had, and they certainly didn't provide jobs for dozens of employees like he did. His insights could be really useful, but first I had to check with my sisters to be sure he was trustworthy.

If something similar had happened in DC, at least I'd have known who, besides my sisters, I could turn to for help. Here, I was stumbling around in the dark. Which would merely have been annoying and stressful, not catastrophic, if the stakes weren't so high. My sisters could lose everything if I trusted the wrong person. I couldn't risk that, no matter how appealing and seemingly transparent Reed Hill was.

* * *

After Reed left, I confirmed that all of the guests were still eating and socializing in the kitchen. Then I grabbed some towels from the hallway closet, to have an excuse if I got caught, and headed for the ground floor ADA room. I paused just inside the doorway to take a picture of the interior. I knew the couple had been inside it, both before the barrel factory tour and after, but it looked unoccupied. The bed was still perfectly made, and there weren't any clothes laid out or any luggage visible. I'd seen the man carrying a paper bag from Hills' Barrels' gift shop, but it wasn't in the trash or on the desk or dresser top.

I ventured deeper into the room, and still, the only personal belonging I could see was a well-worn Bible placed on the nightstand next to the far side of the bed. It had *Property of*

David A. Miller embossed on the cover.

I found the couple's suitcases inside the wardrobe, and a quick peek in the dresser drawers confirmed that they were full of clothes. A large collection of pill bottles was laid out neatly on the bathroom counter, most in the name of Tanya Miller, but a few prescribed to David Miller. I was working on the assumption that Mark had died from a blow to the head, but it was always possible he'd been poisoned, or he'd been drugged, causing him to be lightheaded, which in turn caused him to fall and hit his head. There was indeed a heavy-duty painkiller among the collection, along with routine anti-cholesterol medications and several I didn't recognize, but everything was legitimately labeled, and nothing stood out as particularly suspicious. Just to be thorough, so I wouldn't have to risk being caught searching a second time, I took pictures of all the labels.

Aware that I only had a limited amount of time before the guests were likely to return to their rooms, and with nothing to suggest a deeper search of the Millers' room would reveal anything useful, I decided to move on.

I slipped out and headed to the lobby. Before crossing it, I peeked down the hallway to the kitchen, where the guests were chatting amiably with no signs of becoming restless. Even the twins were relaxed enough to laugh in what sounded like genuine amusement at something another guest had said instead of sniping at everyone.

Reassured that none of them was on the verge of abandoning the kitchen, I crept upstairs to check the three other assigned rooms. The first door to the right opened into a housekeeping closet, filled with linens and other supplies. The first to the left hadn't been assigned since its renovations weren't complete. The one next to it belonged to the mother and daughter, as I recalled from helping them with their voluminous luggage. It was much more obviously occupied than the ADA room. Matching nightgowns had been laid out on the pillows, and toiletries were scattered across the six-foot-long countertop in the bathroom. I quickly photographed the room, looked for any obvious anomalies, and left, having found nothing suspicious. The last room on that side of the hall belonged to Mark Pleasant, so I skipped that for now since there was no reason whatsoever that would satisfactorily explain my presence in there if I were caught. I'd have to save that for a time when there was less risk of being seen.

I crossed the hall to the last room on the right, assigned to the father and son. They hadn't bothered to unpack anything into the dresser or closet, but their duffle bag and backpack were open, one on each bed, with some of the contents dumped out onto the duvet. A pair of unremarkable and barely distinguishable nylon dopp kits had been tossed on the counter near the sink. I checked quickly to see if there were any prescription bottles but found none.

As I left the second upstairs room, I heard the front door open, and a moment later, I heard Em greeting the delivery driver and guiding him toward the kitchen. The guests should be busy eating for the next half hour at least, giving me time to search the one I dreaded most, the twins' room, since they were the most likely to make a huge fuss if they caught me.

I slipped inside, and the first thing I saw was the twins' rollaboards lined up just inside the door, where it would be easy for them to grab and go. The beds looked like they hadn't been touched, not even to support their suitcases briefly. A quick peek inside the dresser drawers and bathroom confirmed that nothing had been taken out of the luggage, not even toothbrushes or toiletries to set on the bathroom counter.

This room looked like it belonged to people who were prepared to run on a moment's notice.

I was debating what to do next when something brushed against my ankles. I looked down to see a tortoiseshell cat wearing a rainbow-striped collar. She must have slipped inside when I opened the door, and I just hadn't noticed, probably distracted by taking a picture of the room.

I couldn't leave her here, or the twins would know someone had been in their room, and they would be sure to complain loudly. I could leave the extra towels I was still carrying, and claim that was why I'd been there. Normally, it would have been a credible excuse, but today hadn't been a normal day, so everyone was likely to be suspicious of every little thing, especially the twins who seemed inclined to complain about every little thing. And their unpacked luggage suggested it wouldn't take much to trigger them into flight.

I started to bend down to pick up the cat and carry her out with me, but she took that as an indication that I wanted to play hide and seek. She ducked under the nearest bed, and I dropped down to crouch on the carpet to see where she'd gone. Unfortunately, she seemed to be able to calculate exactly how far I could reach from that position, and she hunkered down a foot beyond my grasp with a distinctly gloating expression.

I wiggled my fingers at her and said, "Come here, pretty kitty," in the high sweet tone that my own cats tended to respond to. At least when they felt like it.

The tortie inched closer, as if daring me to try to catch her, and then danced away.

Argh. I didn't have time for this. And I hadn't thought to come prepared with cat treats.

Then I remembered the brochure one of the twins had taken from the front desk. He'd left it on the dresser, where it was the only thing out of place in the room. I got up to grab it, tore a lengthwise strip off one end to serve as a lure for the cat, and dangled it in front of her.

To my relief, she chased it all the way to the edge of the bed, where I was able to catch her. I got to my feet, hugging her to my chest in a tight grip. Fortunately, she seemed to accept that I'd won the game and didn't struggle. I stuffed the two pieces of the brochure into a pocket and then carried the cat out to the hallway, where I made sure the door was securely closed behind me before releasing her.

Just in time, too, because I could hear people leaving the kitchen and congregating in the lobby. Any moment now, someone would likely come up the stairs and wonder what I was doing up there.

The cat remained sitting at my feet, apparently intent on washing my germs off her.

That gave me an idea.

I scooped her up again, checked the name on the tag hanging from her collar, and headed down the stairs. When I reached the bottom, I said, "I hope no one's allergic to cats. Taylor here thinks she's in charge of greeting guests and checking on their rooms. I just saw her sneaking upstairs again, and she's a pro at slipping into rooms without anyone noticing."

I tensed, waiting to see if the guests believed my excuse for having been upstairs.

CHAPTER NINE

Em gave me a suspicious look and plucked the cat from my arms. The mother and daughter pair, apparently incapable of doing anything alone, came over to coo at the cat and insist that they'd be thrilled if Taylor chose their room to visit.

The loud twin, on the other hand, complained, which I was starting to think he would do even if we announced he'd won a prize of some sort.

"Ugh," he said. "Keep it out of our room."

"Are you allergic?" I asked.

"Nah." He shook his head. "Just don't like animals indoors. They're fine outside, but it's just unsanitary to have cats and dogs in the house. Even worse when it's a place of business."

I was somewhat surprised he hadn't made a fuss earlier when the long-haired gray cat in the lobby had been fawned over by the mother-daughter pair. Perhaps the twin hadn't noticed since he'd been so busy yelling at Em about some other minor irritation. Odds were good he'd be similarly distracted if the orange cat ever decided to emerge from the pantry while the guests were in the kitchen.

"Some of our guests do enjoy the cats." I nodded toward where Em had settled the tortie on the lap of the younger of the mother-daughter pair. "But we do try to keep them out of the bedrooms. You should be safe enough in there."

He grunted, and then instead of hurrying up to the privacy of his room, he nodded for his brother to join him at a small table where a jigsaw puzzle had been started. The image on the box was a vintage-looking map of Kentucky that highlighted recommended locations to visit along the bourbon trail.

No one else seemed inclined to retire to their own rooms. Perhaps they were all on edge after the murder and didn't want to be alone with their thoughts. The father and son were inspecting the display of jams and other gifts again, although they'd had plenty of time earlier to have memorized the offerings. David Miller pushed his wife's wheelchair over so they could enjoy the fireplace. Em had apparently started a fire while I was upstairs, perfect for a chilly June evening, with the added benefit of soothing anxious guests.

The various pairs were maintaining their distance from each other, but that might change if Em and I left the room. Without us nearby, they might decide to compare notes for their inspection reports, and I thought it would be better if they waited to render judgment until after the shock of Mark's death had worn off.

Em was continuing to befriend the guests, as she'd been assigned to do, chatting with the mother-daughter pair, but I caught a questioning look from her, presumably asking if she could continue. I nodded and then went over to the fireplace to introduce myself to the Millers, who hadn't needed my assistance with their luggage earlier. "I'm Jess, the oldest sister."

"I'm Tanya Miller." The woman in the wheelchair indicated the man who was still standing behind her, his hands on the handles. "And this is my husband, David."

He nodded a greeting. "Peace to you and your house."

It was a little too late for that, but I thanked him and then asked, "So how are you two doing this evening? Do you have everything you need in your room?"

"We do," Tanya said solemnly. "The setup here is quite well done for accessibility."

"It must be challenging to travel with a wheelchair," I said.

"It is." Dave added with a fond smile down at his wife, "It's taken me a while to adjust to driving a van, after getting one with a chair lift for Tanya. But I'm happy to be her chauffeur so she can continue to go wherever she wants. We are not frightened or dismayed, for the Lord God is with us wherever we go."

"And now that we know how accessible this place is, we'll be back," Tanya said. "I'm from Cooperton originally, and I still have business here a few times a year."

Assuming that was true, not just a cover story for the inspection, it might be useful to know more about what brought the couple to town. "What kind of work do you do?"

She hesitated a moment, as if trying to decide whether she'd be jeopardizing her cover by answering honestly. "I'm a juvenile court judge, but that's not the work that brings me here. That's due to my being part of the family that owns Rackhouse Saddlebreds next door. We have quarterly meetings to go over the earnings and make plans for the future. There's no meeting this weekend, but sometimes I miss being around the horses. I practically lived in the stables when I was a kid. I've gotten used to not being able to walk, but I'll never get used to not being able to ride."

"I'm sorry." I glanced at where Em was still chatting with the mother and daughter. "My middle sister would feel the same way in your circumstances. She competes in dressage and boards her horse at Rackhouse."

"I never did dressage. I was in it for the speed and the jumps." Tanya smiled ruefully. "And I paid the price."

"But you're not afraid of horses?"

"Oh, no," she said. "I don't blame the horse for my injury. She got spooked, which horses do, sometimes for no apparent reason, and it was my responsibility to be prepared for that sort of thing. Unfortunately, I wasn't paying as much attention as I should have been, so I lost my balance, and then on top of everything else, I fell wrong. My fault entirely."

I couldn't quite imagine being that accepting of the situation, but I couldn't see any indication she was putting on a good face rather than telling the truth about how she felt. "I hope you'll still be able to enjoy visiting the horses tomorrow despite the damper that Mr. Pleasant's accident is putting on everyone."

"Not your fault," Tanya said easily, "any more than my fall was my horse's fault. Sometimes things just happen, and you have to make the best of what's left."

"Still," I said. "I can't help thinking that I was distracted, like you were before your fall, and maybe if I'd been paying more attention, I'd have noticed something wrong with Mr. Pleasant earlier and could have intervened somehow."

"You can't think that way or you'll go crazy," she said. "The what-ifs can consume you. I learned early on that it's best to just accept a situation and move forward instead of dwelling on things you can't change."

My need to fix things had always fought against accepting that some things couldn't be changed. "I know you're right, but it will take time for me to accept it. Until then, I can't help going over everything that happened. I think what's keeping me in that loop is that I can't figure out how Mr. Pleasant could have been injured without anyone noticing."

Tanya glanced over her shoulder to catch the eye of her husband, and they exchanged a look before she turned back to me. "We didn't see anything out of the ordinary. We saw the man in the lobby while we waited to check in, of course, but I'm afraid we weren't paying any attention to anything other than getting settled. Car rides tire me, and all I could think of was getting to my room to lie down for a bit. And then, of course, we were in the back of the bus where the lift is, all by ourselves, rather than mingling with everyone else."

"I'm sure nothing happened on the bus," I said. "I was next to Mr. Pleasant the whole time. I'm mostly wondering if something happened during the tour. Maybe if I'd gone inside with everyone ..."

"No," Tanya said firmly. "You can't think that way. Your being with the tour wouldn't have changed anything. As far as I can recall, nothing happened out of the ordinary while we were inside the factory. Isn't that right, dear?" She glanced up at her husband again.

"That's my recollection too," he said immediately. "The tour took about an hour, and then they gathered a few workers from different areas to answer questions for about ten minutes, and finally, we were introduced to the gift shop. We were all together the whole time, except for maybe fifteen minutes when Tanya and I had to take the long way around to use an elevator while everyone else took the stairs. I suppose something could have happened then, but we wouldn't have known about it."

"What about in the gift shop?" I asked. "Could there have been some sort of situation there but hidden from you behind a display?"

"I suppose." David tapped the handles of the wheelchair. "This old thing is a bit awkward in confined spaces, and I didn't want to risk knocking anything over. We've redone our townhouse to have an open floor plan, so I haven't had to learn to maneuver the chair through tight spaces. I stuck to the main aisle, and Tanya isn't much of a shopper, so we didn't stay very long before going back to wait in the lobby to be escorted out to the bus."

I was going to ask if everyone else had remained in the gift shop the whole time, but just then I got a text from Em, who had left the lobby without my noticing.

I was needed in the kitchen.

* * *

It was tempting to ignore the summons since I preferred not to leave the guests alone in the lobby, but a moment later, I got a second text with the same message but this time from CJ.

I gave my excuses to the Millers, intending to head for the kitchen, then I noticed the two men inspecting the jams on display had sidled over to the front door, clearly intending to go outside. I knew their luggage was still in their room, so they couldn't be leaving for good unless they were prepared to abandon their bags, which seemed unlikely. But where could they be going?

Small towns like Cooperton didn't have the round-the-clock sightseeing and cultural events that I'd grown accustomed to in DC. Unless things had changed significantly since I was a kid, pretty much everything here closed by seven even on a Friday. For anything later than that, they'd have to go to Lexington, about an hour away. Too far to come back before the deputy sheriff noticed if he stopped by with more questions for the guests. And then my sisters and I would get the blame for potentially letting a killer get away.

I detoured over to the door to ask, in what I hoped was a casual, light tone, "You two aren't leaving us already, are you? We were hoping your vacation wouldn't end prematurely."

"No," the older man said. "Just stretching our legs. We're not used to sitting around so much."

"Would you like a tour of the yard? I understand you're both chefs, and there's a culinary garden out back that you might find interesting."

"It's dark out," the younger man said.

"Don't mind my son, who apparently isn't aware of the existence of artificial lighting." He glared at the younger man before turning his attention back to me. "You're right. We are chefs. Or at least I am. The name's Jack Dell. Jonny is still in training, but he's going to be even better than his father before long. That's why we're here this weekend, in fact. Exposing him to other places' menus. Me too, actually. I like to try different things, and the customers seem to appreciate a little variety. But for right now, we could use a few minutes alone to clear our heads. Can't do that with a stranger joining us. No offense intended."

"I understand." I really did. I would have liked to take a few minutes all alone to clear my head too. The men probably weren't planning to run, not without their luggage, but if they had killed Mark, they could be planning to sabotage the bus if there was any incriminating evidence on it. The deputy had surrounded it with police tape, but that was more of a moral warning to people with good intentions than a physical deterrence against people with bad intentions. For Mark's killer, the risk of being prosecuted for interfering with an investigation probably wasn't very compelling if they thought there was something incriminating on the bus, and they could destroy it. I might not be able to stop them, but perhaps I could discourage them by letting them know we'd be popping in and out of the B&B to check on them.

"There are chairs on the front porch for after you've stretched your legs, and we can bring you some coffee if you'd like."

"We just want to be left alone," Jonny said irritably.

"The porch sounds like a good option, though," Jack said. "For after our walk."

"Let me just check that the chairs are ready for you." I opened the door to lead them outside.

Jack closed the door behind them and started for the front steps. He paused at the top and then turned to say, "I'd forgotten about the bus still being here. Maybe it's not such a good idea to go for a walk by ourselves. Wouldn't want the cops thinking we'd tampered with the crime scene."

"Much better to stay up here on the porch," I agreed. "We've got surveillance cameras watching over the yard. As long as you stay up here, they'll show that you weren't anywhere near the bus." I didn't know if there were in fact any cameras, but it didn't matter as long as they believed me.

"Good to know," Jack said. "In that case, I think we will stay right here and accept your offer of coffee. We can come get it if you'd like."

"I don't mind delivering it," I said. "And I think you made the right choice to stay up here. Not that there's any reason for them to suspect you of being involved in Mark's injury. I mean, you only met today, after all."

Jonny snorted. "I'm pretty sure everyone who meets him is tempted to punch him within the first sixty seconds." He stomped over to the nearest chair and threw himself into it. "I take my coffee black."

"Me too," Jack said. "And Jonny's right about how irritating that Pleasant guy was. He sure doesn't live up to his name. If I were a cop, I'd suspect anyone who met him, however briefly, unless they had a rock-solid alibi."

"What about you? Do you have an alibi?"

Jack shrugged. "Depends on whether you'd believe a family member. It's kind of a miracle, but my son and I were together all day without getting on each other's nerves. The only time we were out of each other's sight was when we stopped by the restaurant first thing this morning so I could check on the early shift's prep work. But once we hit the road, we were pretty much glued at the hip."

"Even during the factory tour and the time in the gift shop?" I glanced at Jonny. "Your son doesn't seem like the sort who'd be interested in knickknacks."

Jack chuckled. "You might be surprised. He inherited his love of clutter from his mother. And her need for everyone to *ooh* and *aah* over her finds. I've long since accepted my lot in life as the prime admirer of stuff he's found. I wouldn't dare try to get out of it even for a moment."

A grunt came from where Jonny sat hunched in the chair, studying his phone. "Where's the coffee?"

"Sorry," I said. "I'll go get it now."

CHAPTER TEN

—————

I hurried into the kitchen to get the coffee and find out if there really were security cameras watching over the guests.

Em was waiting for me just out of sight in the kitchen. She herded me toward the far end of the room. I made her stop at the coffeemaker so I could set it up for a fresh pot.

We ended up in the pantry, not out back on the veranda as I'd expected originally. Fortunately, there was more than enough room in there for me and both of my sisters. Five more people could have joined us, if they didn't mind a little invasion of personal space.

CJ was kneeling next to the bed occupied by the orange cat, with Noah on his stomach on the floor beside her, reading his book. CJ looked up to say, "Have you met Beam? He came with the house. His official name is Sunbeam, and maybe it fit his personality as a kitten, but now he's more like bourbon—smooth, well aged, and a little reserved. He's friendly with us but prefers to stay out of sight when there are guests around."

"We met this morning when I needed supplies."

CJ rose. "Good. Now you've met all of the friendlies, Pappy, Beam, Russell—that's the gray longhair in the lobby this afternoon—and Taylor, the tortie. There are also a few semi-ferals who live in the backyard, but you won't be here long enough to get to know them."

"I appreciate the introductions, but that's not why you dragged me in here, I assume."

"No." CJ said, "We got some information on Mark Pleasant that we thought you should know."

Em said, "I'll let CJ tell you while I keep a lookout for guests."

"Could you keep an eye on the coffee too? I promised to send some out to the Dells on the front porch. They take it black."

"Sure."

Em slipped out of the pantry, and I asked CJ, "Before you tell me your news, is there any way to keep an eye on guests when they're outside? The Dells wanted to go for a walk alone, and I told them there are security cameras everywhere, so they wouldn't go near the bus. It would be nice to know if it's true."

"Not everywhere," CJ said, getting out her phone. "But we do have a couple cameras trained on the driveway and parking lot, in case someone tries to blame us for damage to their vehicles. One of them should have the bus in its line of sight. I'll pull up the feed on my phone while we talk."

Before I could thank her, CJ asked, "Do you really think the Dells intended to sabotage the bus?"

"I don't suspect anyone in particular," I said, "but if one of the guests killed Mark, then we have to be prepared for them to try to either destroy incriminating evidence or go on the run. I was more concerned with keeping the Dells away from the bus at the moment since it doesn't look like they're planning to leave. They don't have their luggage with them."

"They could have put it in their truck earlier."

"No," I said. "It's still in their room."

I braced myself, anticipating that CJ would ask how I could possibly know what was currently in the guests' room, but Em returned just in time to say dryly, "I'm pretty sure we don't want to know how you know that."

"Which is why I wasn't going to tell you," I said. "You've got your secrets, and I've got mine."

"Okay," Em said. "I just wanted to let you know the coffee's ready, and I'm heading out front. Keep an ear out for other guests who might wander nearby."

She left again, and this time, CJ held the swinging door ajar with her foot, so she could see the hallway between the kitchen and the lobby. Satisfied that she'd have some warning before anyone came close enough to hear us, she said in a tone just above a whisper, "I think someone may have tried to kill Mark before today."

"You think? But you're not sure?"

"Well, in retrospect, it seems pretty certain, but I can also understand why no one put it all together before now. About two weeks ago, he filed a police report saying someone tried to run him off the road, which sounded pretty crazy at the time."

"What did the investigation turn up?"

"There wasn't one." CJ huffed in frustration. "You've got to remember we don't have big-city law enforcement departments here. And the sheriff doesn't set a good example by keeping up with best practices or providing educational resources for the cops who, unlike him, are at least trying to do good work."

"It doesn't take a lot of training to go out and look over the car and the crime scene to confirm the incident happened. Even without forensic skills, they could have taken pictures of skid marks and broken glass and the like."

"Oh, they went through the motions. The problem is that they went into it already convinced that Mark was lying. They thought he'd just had an accident that was his own fault, and he was making up a story so his insurance company wouldn't blame him. Or so he could keep his driver's license. Apparently, he had some driving-under-the-influence charges five or ten years ago, and he claimed to have cleaned up his act since then, but maybe he just got better at not getting caught. Plus, there's a rumor that he'd had several strokes in the last year or two and probably shouldn't be driving."

"Still, a reported attempt on someone's life is too serious an allegation to simply go through the motions of investigating."

"That's all they usually do," CJ said. "All that's necessary for most road incidents, according to what one of the officers who'd looked into Mark's story told my source. That around here, if you're going to kill someone, you face them like a man, and take the consequences. You don't run them off the road."

"Seriously, he said 'face them like a man'?"

"Yep. Women never get violent. Didn't you know that? We're paragons of virtue and all sweet and kind and upbeat, like our guests, the Readings."

At my quizzical look, she explained, "The mother and daughter in the matching outfits. Gotta admit it's hard to picture them getting violent, face-to-face. But I can totally see them running someone off the road, especially if one of them felt the other was being abused by Mark."

I agreed.

"What about the Millers? Do you think they could have run Mark off the road?"

"The wife doesn't drive any longer," CJ said as Em

returned to the pantry. "But she's strong-willed enough to plan a murder and get her husband to carry it out. But I doubt they'd have risked damage to their expensive and highly identifiable wheelchair-lift van as the murder weapon."

Em nodded. "I think you can rule out the Hammett twins for the road incident too. No way they'd risk a brand new, top-of-the-line Tesla that way."

My eyebrows rose. "What kind of work do they do to be able to afford a car like that?"

Em interrupted. "Not just one, but two identical ones. They keep one here in Kentucky, and the other is in New York, where they live most of the time."

"So how can they afford two expensive cars? Are they trust fund babies or something?"

Em disappeared briefly, apparently having heard something in the kitchen, but reappeared in the door opening again almost immediately. "I don't know. They're new to town, arriving after I left banking, so I missed out on all the best gossip. All I know is that they work in finance and are starting up their own brand of bourbon, with the headquarters here in Cooperton, presumably so they can put Kentucky on the label. But I know a lot more about the Tesla out in the parking lot. It's worth more than the estimates we've gotten to finish all our renovations here, even if we did all of our dream projects, like a pool. And they treat it like it's worth even more. I offered to help retrieve their luggage from the trunk, but they wouldn't let me get near the car, like I might damage it just by breathing on it."

"So definitely not going to use it to push another car off the road," I said.

Noah yawned loudly, and CJ announced, "Time for someone to go to bed."

"And I need to go next door to visit my horse for a few minutes, or I'm not going to have the patience to deal with human beings tonight," Em said.

I sighed. "I guess that leaves me to keep an eye on the guests until they're finally ready to retire."

"Thanks." Em keyed something into her phone. "I just transferred the B&B's incoming line to your number, in case the deputy sheriff calls."

"Maybe it will turn out that Mark's death was from an

aneurysm, not a head injury," CJ said as she encouraged Noah to get to his feet. "Then we can all get a good night's sleep tomorrow. But as long as I'll be awake tonight anyway, I'll monitor the surveillance cameras and let you know if any of the guests does anything suspicious. With luck, we'll just have the one restless night."

I doubted we'd be sleeping soundly any time soon, but I didn't say anything to burst her bubble. When we were kids, my sisters had complained constantly about my being the very epitome of a Debbie Downer. I still was, but I'd changed in one way—I kept my worst-case scenarios to myself.

I could see any number of worst-case scenarios arising from Mark's death, and no good ones. But my sisters didn't need to worry about them yet. I would worry for all of us. Just like when we were kids, except that the stakes were a lot higher now.

* * *

The Millers had retired to their room before I returned to the lobby, and the Dells were apparently still out on the front porch. The remaining guests had rearranged the furniture, so that a large square end table was surrounded somewhat awkwardly with upholstered seating. The older Reading woman was on the sofa, her daughter was in a wingback chair across from her, and the Hammett twins were in the two remaining seats, facing each other.

As I approached, the younger woman was in the process of setting her cards down in front of her, face up.

Her mother glanced at the cards before greeting me. "You're Jess, right? The oldest sister? I'm not sure you caught our names earlier. I'm Shelly Reading and my daughter is Candy."

"Thanks for the reminder. I'm terrible with names." I remembered belatedly that I was supposed to be the part-owner of a B&B. "Pretty sad for someone in the hospitality business."

"Names aren't as important as your attitude, and you've all been lovely in very trying circumstances," she said, closing the fanned-out cards in her hand. "We used to own a B&B, you know. I hope you don't mind that we moved things around in the lobby, but we couldn't pass up the chance to play some bridge. It turns out that we're all dedicated players, and I never go anywhere without a pack of cards."

"We're always happy to accommodate our guests if we can, so moving furniture is perfectly fine," I said. "Is there anything else you need?"

"Least you could do is break out a bottle of bourbon," the twin to Shelly's right said, his voice both loud and demanding.

His brother laughed and said, "He's just kidding. Even if you have a liquor license, you wouldn't have anything worth drinking. B&Bs never do. It's why we hardly ever stay in them."

"No offense intended," his brother said in the less than convincing, sing-song manner of someone who'd said the words too many times for them to have any meaning.

If they weren't fans of B&Bs, then why had they been chosen to do the evaluation for the tourism co-op? I couldn't ask though, so I ignored him.

"It's legal to drink in a B&B if you bring your own," Shelly said, catching and holding the eye of the more sociable twin to her left. "I don't suppose you brought some samples of your own bourbon that you'd be willing to share?"

"We won't have anything worth drinking for another five years or so," he said.

The louder brother added, "We don't make the rotgut you're probably used to."

I was impressed by how unaffected Shelly seemed by the insult. She just smiled and said, "You might be surprised. I'm used to the best in life. In both bourbon and card games. I'm a life master, you know."

"We were life masters in college," the loud twin said scornfully. "But sure, show us what you've got."

Candy pushed back her chair and stood. "That's my cue to leave. I don't do trash talk, and you don't need me for the rest of this hand. Perhaps Jess will be kind enough to show me where I can get some ginger ale."

"Of course." I led her back to the kitchen and opened the beverage refrigerator. "Help yourself."

"Ooh, you have Ale-8." Candy chose a can and a glass from the adjoining counter and eagerly carried them over to the kitchen table. "I wasn't really all that thirsty, but this is such a treat. I mostly just wanted a break from the game. Mother is obsessed with bridge. Just a warning, but if you play even a little, and she finds out, she'll regale you with summaries of all of her best plays."

"I played a bit in college," I said, "but not since then. I wouldn't mind listening to her."

Candy laughed. "You may regret it, so don't say I didn't warn you. She can go on for days."

"Is that why you don't have the B&B any longer?" I asked. "Did she scare off the guests with her bridge talk?"

"No, we actually had quite a loyal following among serious bridge players, and they were happy to exchange stories about the tournaments they'd been in. We were closer to Lexington than you are, and the city has an active bridge club. Whenever they held big events, we'd get booked by players from all over the state. And word got around—everyone knows everyone in the bridge community—so players would stay with us whenever they were in the area for other reasons too."

"Sounds like you had an excellent marketing plan," I said. "We're still refining ours. It doesn't help that we may end up with a reputation for danger, based on what happened to Mr. Pleasant. I don't suppose you or your mother noticed anything earlier today that could explain his condition."

"I wish we had," Candy said. "I wouldn't want to be in your position, dealing with a critically injured guest. But Mother and I did our best to stay as far away from—what was his name, again? Mark?—as we could. When we owned the B&B, we learned to spot the jerks at fifty paces. We had to deal with them then, but I, for one, didn't miss that part of the business when the place had to be sold as part of Mother's divorce. Now that we're not getting paid to be nice to people, we do our best to avoid the annoying ones."

"Both of you?" I asked. "Your mother seems to like everyone."

"She's good at hiding her annoyance. I mean, she does like most people, and she's always telling me I'm too judgmental. But she noticed that Mark was going to be a problem before I did. Warned me to stay near her the whole time because he was the sort who would try to divide and conquer." Candy shuddered. "Mother and I have our differences sometimes, but I trust her judgment of people. I don't think we've been more than six feet apart since we arrived here today. Until now, of course."

"What about Mr. Pleasant? Did he stick with the group during the whole tour? Could he have gotten into some trouble without your knowing it? Perhaps when you were using the restroom or something?"

"I tried not to pay much attention to him," Candy said. "I stuck close to Mother, and she made sure we both stayed away from him the whole time. I couldn't say for sure if Mark left at any point. I'm pretty sure he was with the group for the official part of the tour, and I know he was there during the Q&A session because he did a few of those long-winded 'more of a comment than a question' things that are so annoying, like he knew more about barrel making than the employees did. But after that, when we were in the gift shop, I can't be sure where he was. You may have noticed the pile of bags I brought back with me. I tend to go into a bit of a fog whenever I'm shopping, and I don't notice anything around me. Mother's that way too, so he could have been dancing on a table or getting his head bashed in right next to us, and we wouldn't have noticed, not once shopping fever kicked in."

"What about before the tour, while you were still getting settled here at the B&B?" I asked. "You were in the room next to his. Did you hear anything unusual? Could he have fallen and hurt himself while he was in there?"

"That's the big fear for a B&B owner, isn't it?" Candy said sympathetically. "But you don't need to worry about that. This place looks to be about the same age as ours was, so I bet the walls are thin enough that I would definitely have heard if someone in the next room had fallen and hit his head hard enough to be a serious injury. Mother took a brief nap, but I was awake and checking social media the whole time. It was quiet as the grave the whole time. I'd actually been meaning to compliment you on how serene everything was, and then, well, things got a little crazy, and it seemed a bit insensitive."

I could confirm that the walls were far from soundproofed. I'd been able to hear activity in adjoining rooms when I'd been delivering luggage, so if Mark had fallen or been assaulted in his room, Candy would definitely have heard it. Unless he hadn't actually been there. "Maybe Mr. Pleasant wasn't in his room. Could he have slipped out without you noticing?"

She sipped her pop while she considered the question and finally shook her head. "It's possible, although I didn't hear him leave. I remember noticing how rude he was and being glad I didn't have to handle a front desk any longer. But when you took his bags upstairs, that was the last I saw of him, other than distant glimpses of him during the tour. He wasn't in the hallway when we went to our room or later when we left. That nice chef and his son came out of their room to board the bus at the same time we did, but they were the only people I saw upstairs before the tour."

That matched my recollection with the Dells, the Millers, and the Readings already at the bus when Mark finally showed up.

Candy seemed to be open and honest, but it was hard to trust her entirely since I knew she was lying about her reason for being at the B&B. Plus, she'd stumbled over Mark's name, pretending not to be sure about it, when I was reasonably sure that the guests would have known each other before today. At least, I assumed they would have been told about who else was on the inspection team. The odds were good that someone who operated a B&B would have had some business dealings with local tour operators like Mark.

Before I could come up with a new line of questions, Candy suddenly squealed in delight. "You have another cat!"

I turned to follow her gaze to where the orange tabby was poking his nose out of the pantry. "That's Beam. You already met Russell and Taylor."

She laughed. "Bourbon-flavored cats. I love it. Will he let me pat him?"

"He's a bit skittish," I said, "but you can try."

Candy patiently wooed Beam, crouching on the floor near but not too near him. He was a little standoffish at first, but eventually succumbed to her patient approach and let her pat him.

It was hard to believe that someone who was so kind to animals might have killed a man. But it was also hard to believe that someone who seemed so naive and transparent was a liar, and yet I knew her very presence at the B&B was a lie. All of the guests were, in essence, conspiring together on behalf of the tourism co-op. What if they had all been working toward another joint goal from the very beginning—getting rid of Mark—and now that, as far as they'd been told, they'd successfully landed him in the hospital, they were continuing to collaborate to cover for whoever had done the actual deed? How were we supposed to identify Mark's killer if there was a whole team of killers?

My increasingly pessimistic thoughts were disrupted by

the sounds of shouting coming from the lobby, followed by a loud crash.

CHAPTER ELEVEN

I found Shelly crouched on the lobby floor beside the overturned table, picking up cards that had been strewn all over the room. The Hammett twins remained in their seats, glaring at her.

Candy went over to help her mother while I asked the twins, "Is there a problem?"

The loud one nodded at Shelly. "She cheats."

Shelly said calmly, "I don't have to cheat. I'm just a better player than you are, Beck. No need to get nasty."

He snorted. "No way an old biddy like you is better than us. Benn and I haven't played much since college—our time is much too valuable to waste on games that don't turn a profit—but there's no way we lost all of our skills. The only explanation is that you cheated."

"There's an element of luck in any card game," I said, wishing Em were here since she was a much better peacemaker than I was. "It could just have been a fluke."

"In that case, we demand another game," Beck said. "We deserve a chance to show what we can do. The first hands were just a warm-up."

Shelly stood with a cheerful smile. "That sounds lovely. But not tonight. It's getting late, we need our beauty sleep, and you'll play better when you're fully rested too. So let's say tomorrow morning after breakfast."

"You're on," Beck said.

Candy picked up the last tossed card, which had made it all the way to the front door, and handed it to her mother as they headed for the stairs.

I thought the twins might decide to retire too, and I wanted to be sure they weren't too close behind the women. "You two don't look like you're ready to sleep," I told them. "You're welcome to stay here in the lobby for as long as you'd like."

"What we'd like to do is go home," the loud one, Beck, said. "We had important things to do this weekend, but now that we're under house arrest, we won't be able to do them. And there's nothing to do here."

"Say, that reminds me," Benn said. "Where are the other guests, the ones who are cooks? They've been gone a long time. If they've decided to ignore the orders to stick around, then we might as well too."

"They didn't leave." I would have heard from CJ if they had. "They're out on the front porch getting some fresh air. There are enough chairs out there for you two as well if you'd like to join them."

"Whatever for?" Beck said. "We get all the fresh air we need from our oxygen bar back home, and they can't be very interesting to talk to. They're just glorified short-order cooks, not true artists like those of us developing new and improved bourbons."

Benn got up from his chair and threw himself into a reclining position on the sofa. "We should have brought a bottle from our collection. Then you'd understand about refined tastes."

"No one prepares for being under house arrest," Beck said with less than his usual level of spite. "But we'll be home by dinner tomorrow and can pour something special then."

"At least we got the factory tour in before things went to hell," Benn said. "That's one thing off our to-do list. We can place our barrel order now."

Finally, we were on a safer topic. "Don't you already have barrels at your distillery?"

"Sure," Benn said. "We're thinking of changing suppliers though, and we wanted to get a look at Hills' Barrels without letting them know we were potential customers."

"Did you like what you saw?"

Beck shrugged. "A barrel's a barrel. We need some customization though, which is easier to do when the maker isn't overly automated. Hills' does a lot of the work the old-fashioned way, so they can accommodate special requests like ours."

"I'd love to hear about your distillery. Despite growing up here, I don't know much about bourbon or its production."

Beck smirked. "Ironic, isn't it, that a couple guys from

New York City are more passionate about bourbon than the locals?"

Benn added, "We've dreamed of making our own bourbon since our college days. Now we're on the verge of remaking the industry. Took us twenty years on Wall Street to get what we needed, but we're about to quit our first career and finally start our second one."

"We've been juggling both for a few years now." Beck sat up and leaned forward. The snarl that had seemed a permanent part of his expression disappeared as he talked about what was obviously his passion. "Took two weeks off from our day jobs to come deal with issues here, and we made good progress before today. In another ten years, the Hammett brand is going to rival the top names of today."

I tried to imagine the kind of cat that my sisters would name Hammett. It would have to be particularly surly and even more arrogant than the average feline.

Benn said, "Our first batch made to our specs will reach the two-year aging mark in a few months, so we'll be able to taste it for proof of concept, but most of the barrels will need to age another two years before we start marketing. By then, we'll be fully retired from Wall Street and focused on the bourbon. Of course, the best stuff will need to age much longer, but we'll be establishing a reputation before then."

"And within ten years, we'll be able to sit back and watch the money roll in," Beck said.

He made it sound like a guaranteed thing, but I had my doubts. Plenty of clients had come to my law office with plans for their estates, and often they involved expectations of hitting the lottery or something equally unlikely in order to provide for their heirs. And if developing an elite brand of anything were as simple as just sitting back and waiting for it to age, Pappy Van Winkle— the bourbon, not Noah's cat—would have a lot more competition.

"I hope it all works out as planned," I said. "With luck, you'll be able to get back to your to-do list for this weekend first thing tomorrow when the sheriff lifts the request to stay here. I don't suppose you noticed anything that might be useful for the investigation. Perhaps something you didn't think of earlier?"

"We didn't see any reason to pay the old guy any attention," Beck said. "I remember him being late for the bus, and he bumped into me when we were disembarking for the tour, but nothing else he did made any real impression on me."

I didn't entirely believe him. He'd looked furious when Mark had bumped into him, as if he thought it had been intentional and much more serious than the light impact of a stumbling old man. Considering how badly Beck had reacted to losing a friendly game of cards, I doubted he would have been willing to overlook what he considered to be a physical assault. He might not have wanted to hit an obviously smaller and weaker opponent when there were witnesses, but he could well have plotted his revenge, waiting for the right moment to intentionally bump into Mark. And not just with an equal force. Beck would have thought the payback impact had to be greater than the original one to show who was the dominant male. He might not have intended anything more than to inflict a bruise or two, but the impact could have caused Mark to fall and hit his head.

"What about you?" I asked the other twin. "Did you notice anything unusual about Mr. Pleasant today?"

"I didn't even notice the assault on Beck," Benn said. "Except, come to think of it, the dead guy did disappear for a while when the rest of us were in the gift shop. We went in just to get a copy of the Hills' book on barrel making, so we were in and out in just two minutes. Everyone was supposed to meet the tour guide in the lobby when we were done, and we were the first ones there. Everyone else joined us on time, but the old guy was late, so the tour guide had to send someone to go find him. Eventually they dragged him out from the direction of the factory floor, not the gift shop."

Beck shoved himself to his feet. "I don't know why we're sitting around here talking about something that's got nothing to do with us. I'm going for a walk."

Benn gave me an apologetic smile and followed his brother, leaving me with no one to interrogate and nothing else useful to do. Despite what my sisters seemed to think, I'd never had all the answers when we were kids, and considering how little I'd been able to learn from either the guests or their rooms, I didn't even seem to have the right questions now.

* * *

That night I slept restlessly, unable to stop thinking about

Mark's death. I even had a series of dreams about it, with different B&B guests starring as the killer each time. None of those scenarios were my worst fear though. Even my subconscious self had been unwilling to play out the possibility that the B&B would be blamed for a guest's death, and my sisters would lose all of their money and, worse, their hopes for Noah's future.

I was almost relieved to leave the dreams behind when my phone beeped to tell me it was time to get up and make the doughnuts. Or, more accurately, make the muffins and eggs and bacon.

I wasn't as much of a night owl as Em, but I couldn't imagine getting up at this early hour day in, day out, like CJ had been doing for the last few months. Even she wasn't naturally this much of a morning person, I noted, since she and Noah slept through my getting dressed and slipping out of the owners' quarters.

By the time the first guests, Shelly and Candy, arrived in the kitchen, some strong coffee had allowed me to be functional, if not exactly perky. The Millers arrived next, parking the wheelchair at the head of the table and exclaiming delightedly about everything they sampled, especially the bourbon-spiked peach jam. The four guests lingered at the table well after finishing their breakfasts, chatting amiably.

CJ ran in just long enough to grab some food for herself and Noah before taking it all back to the owners' quarters. More time passed without the twins or the Dells appearing. A sleepy-looking Em—in jeans and a B&B logo t-shirt instead of horse-print pajamas—arrived for her morning caffeine infusion, and the remaining guests still hadn't shown up.

I was starting to wonder if the Becketts and Dells were even on the premises. Could they have slipped away during the night?

I waited until Em had finished her first mug of coffee before asking her to join me in the pantry, where I could ask her to check the recorded surveillance video to make sure no one had sneaked away while everyone else was sleeping. She agreed and refilled her coffee to take it with her back to the owners' quarters for some privacy.

A few minutes later, as I was about to shut down the omelet-preparation area, the Dells finally trotted into the kitchen.

"Sorry," Jack said. "We usually work late and aren't used

to early mornings. But we didn't want to miss your signature bacon jam."

Jonny silently helped himself to coffee, his eyes looking more hungover than simply tired.

Jack ordered omelets for both of them and sat beside his son, who was hunched over his coffee. While I cooked the eggs, Jack helped himself to toast and bacon jam and tried to engage his son in a discussion of how the jam could be used at their restaurant in sandwiches or possibly a marinade.

The one-sided conversation had dwindled to silence by the time I delivered their plates.

"Do you mind if I sit with you," I asked Jack. "I'm not usually the morning cook, so I'm not used to being on my feet like this. I could really use a break."

"Sure," he said while his son turned his single-minded focus from his coffee to the eggs on his plate. "I don't even notice how long I'm on my feet any more, but I vaguely recall how it felt in the beginning."

"Did you sleep okay?" I asked. "Considering the circumstances?"

"Like babies." Jack gave his son a look that encouraged him to join the conversation, which was ignored.

"I wish I'd slept that well." I'd read once that, contrary to expectation, innocent suspects tended to be anxious and hyper with righteous indignation during interrogations, while the guilty ones tended to fall asleep. Was that why Jack had slept so well? Because he was guilty and thought he'd gotten away with assault? And if so, would he be just as relaxed when he found out that he'd actually killed Mark? "Every time I started to fall asleep, I thought about Mr. Pleasant and how he could have been injured without realizing it before he was unconscious. I kept trying to do the math for when the trauma could have happened. I believe there can be about a four-hour window between a head injury and passing out."

"All I know is that neither of us touched him," Jack said. "The first time he tried to sell us on some get-rich-quick scheme, I made sure we both stayed as far away from him as possible."

This was the first I'd heard of any get-rich-quick scheme, but it certainly fit with Mark's personality.

The son swallowed and finally spoke up, "He was boring

and had nothing to teach me about food. I'm not interested in getting rich. Just want to prove I'm a better chef than Dad before he retires."

Jack laughed. "You're almost there already, and it's going to happen sooner than I'd like to admit."

"Did Mr. Pleasant try to sell his scheme to the other guests? Maybe someone who was more gullible?"

Jack shrugged. "We really weren't paying attention to who he was with, just where he was in relation to us, so we could avoid him."

Jonny set his fork down on his empty plate. "I did notice he kept trying to hang out with the twins. They kept bragging about their distillery, and it takes a whole lot of money to start one. More than opening a restaurant even, and that's bad enough. So the old man probably figured they had deep enough pockets to make a good target for his scam."

"Were the Hammetts interested?"

Jonny shrugged. "No idea. All I know is he kept sidling up to them. He didn't bother with the two women. Musta' figured out they were broke. I heard they had to sell their B&B when they still owed more on the mortgage than the place was worth. I'm not taking that kind of risk when I open my own restaurant. Dad might be happy working for someone else his whole life, but I'm not."

Jack looked like he'd had this sort of conversation about finances before. "You may feel differently down the road," he said calmly. "There's a lot to be said for not having all that responsibility and uncertainty. I've never had to worry about any business debt, and I get paid well enough to send my kid to a top culinary school. Are you sure you'll be able to say the same if you open your own restaurant?"

"That won't be a problem," Jonny said. "I'm not planning to have any kids. I'm more into YOLO than you are, Dad. You taught me to cook, and Mom taught me to live like there's no tomorrow."

Jack shook his head. "Not sure 'you only live once' is the message she meant to convey."

"Back to Mr. Pleasant," I said. "I heard he was late to the rendezvous point at the end of the tour. Do you know where he was then?"

"No idea," Jack said.

"Last I saw him," Jonny said, "he was harassing a gift shop employee, but that was about ten minutes before the tour guide sent someone to look for him."

"What about earlier yesterday when you were checking in at the B&B?" I asked. "I was busy delivering luggage and didn't see where everyone was as they settled in. Did you see Mr. Pleasant with any of the other guests then? I hate to think he was injured here, but it could have happened after he checked in or, really, even as early as an hour or so before he arrived at the B&B."

The two men exchanged a questioning glance and then shook their heads in unison. Jack spoke first. "We didn't see him in the corridor, not on the way in or the way out."

Jonny frowned. "Hey, are you accusing one of us of assaulting the old man? Because that's ridiculous. He was annoying, but we've dealt with worse at the restaurant without getting physical with them. Banning them from ever coming back, or even just the threat of banning them is usually enough to get them to settle down."

"I would never accuse anyone of assault." I still remembered the basics of defamation law from when I was in school, and I wasn't protected by qualified immunity like the sheriff's department was. "I was just hoping you might have seen something that we could share with the police. The sooner they can zero in on a solid suspect, the sooner they'll let everyone go home."

Jack gave his son a calming pat on the shoulder. "We understand. You have to protect the B&B. We'd love to be helpful, but we just don't know anything. Don't worry about us being stuck here. We're not in any rush to get home. If we can't research the local restaurants in person at lunchtime today, we can still order take-out. I'm hoping you'll let us choose which restaurant to order from again, so we can get a good bit of variety. Sometimes people like to stick to a tried and true place, and dinner was excellent last night, but professional curiosity makes me want to see what else is out there."

"Of course." That was the simplest request I'd had so far this weekend. "I'll collect the menus we have for lunch, so you can study them. With luck, though, the deputy will have good news for us soon, and everything can return to normal."

Yeah, I knew there was no chance of that, but I was reluctant to tell any of the guests that Mark had died. Despite how much death was at the core of my legal specialty, my job involved either preparing in advance of the death, or carrying out the final wishes some time after the death, usually after the funeral. I'd never had to deal with witnesses to the death in its immediate aftermath. I had to hope, although it was far from a certainty, that the deputy had been trained on how best to tell people they had been witnesses, not just to a medical emergency but to a death. One that had occurred under suspicious circumstances.

CHAPTER TWELVE

After the Dells headed out to the front porch to study the menus, CJ came into the kitchen from the owners' quarters. "Well?" she asked as she retrieved a large, transparent plastic container filled with kibble from just inside the pantry. "How'd it go, your first morning as a professional cook?"

"I'm just glad it's only temporary. I don't know how you do it every single day."

CJ struggled with the lid of the container, unable to stabilize the base well enough with her broken arm to be able to disengage the lid with her one working hand, but she wouldn't appreciate my helping her unless she asked. "You've always underestimated me."

I hadn't expected the snippy response. I knew she resented being sidelined by her injury—she'd always been restless whenever her escapades had left her in a cast—but she'd never taken her frustrations out on other people.

"I didn't mean to be critical of you," I said. "I meant it sincerely, that it's obvious you're really committed to making the B&B a success."

"Why wouldn't I be?" CJ demanded. "Sometimes it feels like I'll never be able to break free of the reputations we had as kids. You were the smart one, Em was the hard-working one, and I was the cute and adventurous but not-too-bright one."

"I never thought that."

"Then you're the only one. Everyone else thought that just because I liked sports instead of math, I had to be stupid."

"You're definitely not stupid. And I never heard anyone suggest that you were." If I had, I'd have made sure they reconsidered their position.

"You didn't hear it because you weren't here," CJ said. "You abandoned us, and Em was so busy studying for her straight

A's that she didn't have time to help me get even straight Cs. I was all on my own. No perfection of three for me."

"I'm sorry." I'd been so excited to leave for college that I hadn't stopped to think about what it had meant for my younger sisters. I'd come home for summers and major holidays, but I'd had jobs then, so I wasn't around much even when I was back from school. "Is that why you won't let me get to know Noah? You're afraid I'll abandon him too?"

"Why shouldn't I think that? You didn't even want me to marry Nick, so why would you care about his son?"

I hadn't realized she'd known I disliked her husband. Or more accurately, that I'd disliked the prospect of CJ getting hurt by his irresponsibility. It didn't help that my worst fears had been realized, and he'd died so young, leaving CJ pregnant and heartbroken.

"Noah is your son too, and I care about you, so of course I care about him."

"Well, you wouldn't know it from how long it's been since you've spent any time with us. Quick hit and run visits for my wedding and then for Nick's funeral don't count."

"I was trying to give you space," I said. "I didn't think you wanted me here. You've always treasured your independence. I figured you'd ask if you needed anything."

"I needed my big sister," she said plaintively, shoving the kibble container, which had continued to frustrate her, in my direction. "But not if I had to force you to act like a sister."

I accepted the kibble container with a sigh. "You didn't have to force me. Just let me know. And I'm here now. What do you want from me? Besides an extra pair of hands?" I opened the lid and gave the container back to her.

"I don't know." CJ fidgeted with the lid. "You don't have to tell me I'm being irrational. I know it. It's just that the last few years have been stressful, and Em is great, but I always feel like something is missing. I hate that Noah doesn't have a solid family like we had. Nick's parents blame me for his accident, like I should have told him to quit doing the things he loved. Like I could have changed him, even if I'd wanted to."

"His death wasn't your fault."

"I know. At least, I do now. But I had my doubts for a while, and that was hard. Nick would have hated me if I'd tried to get him to stop taking risks. And he didn't know he was about to have a kid to support. I hadn't even known I was pregnant at the time, and I certainly hadn't known—" She stopped abruptly and shook her head before turning away to get a bowl from a nearby base cabinet filled with pet dishes.

"Hadn't known what?"

She kept her gaze on the bowl she was filling with kibble instead of looking at me when she answered. "It's not easy being a single parent."

"You're doing a great job from what I've seen."

She slammed the lid back on the container and glared at me. "Yeah, like you'd know. You've only spent like ten minutes with Noah in his whole life."

I didn't want to argue with her, so I didn't remind her that she'd been the one keeping me from spending time with Noah.

"I know you're a good mother because I know you," I said. "I also know you don't really want me to help with parenting. You used to say that I stifled your independence and never let you have any adventures, and I can't think of a bigger adventure than raising a child."

"Don't try your devil's advocate stuff on me," CJ said. "There's nothing you can say to convince me you didn't just give up on me and Noah. It took me a long time to understand why. You never gave up on Em and me when we were kids, and I thought it was because you cared, but now I figure it was because you didn't really have a choice, like you do with Noah. You were stuck with us. And you played along. You hounded me for hours if I didn't put on my knee pads or whatever."

"I did, didn't I?" I had to laugh despite the seriousness of the situation. "My all-time record was four hours of hounding per knee pad."

"It's not funny."

It was. I could still remember her outraged little face when I'd pointed out that if she did enough damage to her knees, she'd never be able to skateboard again. She'd insisted that she had far too many mad skills to do anything worse to herself than collect a few scrapes and bruises, which were absolutely necessary badges of honor, and nothing to worry about.

"Things are different now," I said. "Not because I don't care about you and Noah but because you're an adult. I no longer have any more answers than you do, least of all when it comes to parenting. I never wanted to have kids, and I have zero experience with them."

"You didn't know everything back then either," CJ said. "But you still pretended like you did."

"I didn't have to know all the ins and outs of skateboarding, or whatever else you were planning to do, to know when you were about to risk your life."

CJ's face was taking on the expression I recognized as the warning sign that she was about to explode in frustration. With me? Or with herself, or life in general? I had no real idea, but I also didn't think now was a good time for the three sisters to be revealing any cracks in our bonds. Not with a house full of judgmental guests and a murder investigation hanging over our heads.

Fortunately for everyone, just then I heard someone coming in through the front door. Neither of us wanted to risk being overheard by the guests while we were acting like real sisters, the kind who sometimes squabble—or worse—instead of the nostalgic versions that the B&B's name invoked.

"Look," I said. "Can we table this discussion until the guests are gone and Mark's killer has been arrested?"

"Sure," CJ said in a falsely sweet tone as she grabbed the kibble bowl and headed for the pantry, presumably to feed Beam. "After ten years of waiting for you to show up for us, what's another twenty-four hours?"

* * *

I hurried out to the lobby to see who was there and found the sheriff's deputy, Evan Shurette, at the front desk with Em.

"Ah," said Em, "I was just going to call Jess so she could work out the details with you. She's a lawyer, you know."

Shurette gave me the sour look that apparently was routinely drilled into law enforcement during training as the appropriate attitude to take toward lawyers. I'd gotten the exact same reaction from police officers too many times in the past, even though I didn't handle criminal cases. I hoped the deputy didn't think I'd intentionally withheld my profession from him. I really hadn't meant to, but I never mentioned my law degree unless it was relevant to the conversation. Perhaps why I was such a terrible rainmaker for my law firm.

"What details need to be worked out?" I asked. "I thought we were just waiting for the sheriff to confirm the cause of death and for you to have enough information on our guests, so they can go about their business without any further constraints."

"It's gotten complicated." Before he could explain, he started sneezing violently.

Taylor, the tortie with the rainbow collar, was rubbing against his ankles. Em quickly scooped her up and carried her into the kitchen.

Shurette pulled a white cotton handkerchief out of an interior pocket of his jacket and blew his nose. "Sorry. Allergic to cats."

"Would you like some water or something?"

"No." He stuffed the handkerchief back where he'd found it. "I'm fine now."

"So, what got complicated?"

"The investigation." He glanced toward the stairs, presumably to confirm no one was lurking there listening to us. "While we were waiting for the sheriff to decide whether to consider this homicide or not, we turned up two prior suspicious incidents, and that kind of tied the sheriff's hands. He has to treat this as suspicious."

"We heard about Mr. Pleasant being run off the road," I said. "I assume that's one of them. There was another incident?"

He hesitated, probably trying to decide whether he should be sharing information with us, so I said, "We're going to hear about it from the grapevine anyway. Something as juicy as a murder attempt is going to make the rounds pretty quickly."

"All right," Shurette said, "but keep it among the three sisters. Your guests don't need to know. They don't live around here, so it doesn't really affect them."

"We won't tell the guests anything about your investigation," I agreed. "But they need to know that Mark died, and once they know about that, they'll likely check with their local connections for all the gossip. I can't stop them any more than you can."

"Fair enough." He glanced over both shoulders one more time to make sure no one had sneaked up on us before saying in a low voice, "It turns out, the victim had a late meeting in Lexington last week. Apparently after the road rage occurrence, he decided it wouldn't be safe to drive home at night, so he booked a room in the city and then spent the evening at the lobby bar. When he finally went to his room, there was an incident in an elevator."

"What kind of incident?"

"We're not entirely sure. Like a mugging, except he didn't get asked for his wallet. Pleasant claimed he was attacked for no reason whatsoever by someone wearing a hoodie that obscured most of his face. The hotel reported it at his request, but there wasn't any surveillance camera footage, and no further action was taken. Standard procedure when the victim won't go to the hospital for his injuries to be documented, and there's no property loss. We're taking a closer look now though, given what happened yesterday."

"I'm guessing the responding officer at the hotel assumed Mr. Pleasant had been drunk and fell, and then made up the story about being attacked because he was too embarrassed to admit the truth."

Shurette shrugged. "Probably. The guy was pretty impaired when the officer got there, and the hotel has a good reputation for safety. We hardly ever have to respond to calls there."

"But it looks different now that there's a pattern," I said.

Shurette nodded. "Bottom line, we need to consider his death a homicide, not an accident, until we can prove otherwise."

I'd long since come to that conclusion, and I thought Shurette had too. What wasn't he telling me? "And?"

Shurette looked at the stairs again, but this time I thought it was less because he was concerned about being overheard and more because he knew I wasn't going to like what he was about to say. "The sheriff assigned me to ask everyone at the B&B to stick around for a little longer, just until we have the official report on the cause of death."

As he'd begun to speak, I heard footsteps coming down the stairs.

"You mean the old man died?" Beck, coming to a stop at the base of the stairs with his brother right behind him, didn't seem concerned, but his naturally loud voice seemed to echo throughout the B&B. He could probably be heard as far away as the front porch and even in the Millers' ADA room around the corner. "And how long will the report take?"

"Yeah," Benn added. "How long are we stuck here?"

"Not long," Shurette said. "Normally we'd have enough information already, but it's the weekend. Everything takes longer to get back from the experts, so I'm thinking you'll need to stay until tomorrow. You were all planning to stay tonight originally anyway, weren't you? That's what everyone told me yesterday. I checked my notes before I came over."

Jack Dell came in from the front porch. "That was before we became murder suspects. We weren't planning to check out of the B&B, but we still had places to go, things to do. We didn't plan to sit in our room all weekend. And while the food here has been excellent, man does not live by breakfast alone."

Shelly and her daughter had apparently heard Beck's complaints and came down the stairs. "What's wrong?" she asked.

The Hammetts moved over to the fireplace, and Beck said in what would have been a grumble if he hadn't shouted, "We're all being blamed for the old man's death. And put under house arrest."

"Seriously?" Shelly looked to the deputy who nodded.

"I'm sorry. We just need a little time to get the preliminary report on the cause of death." His tone turned a bit desperate. "And you were planning to stay here all weekend anyway, right?"

"We were," Shelly said, coming down the last few steps. "I, for one, am just as glad we're confined to the B&B. Now my new friends won't have any excuse to avoid proving their claim to being the better bridge players." She turned to the Dells. "I don't suppose either of you play?"

"Sorry, never learned," Jack said, and his son added, "Me neither."

"Ah, well," Shelly said. "I'll just have to hope the Hammetts are really as good as they say they are."

"It won't take a whole day for us to prove our superiority," Beck said. "And we shouldn't have to pay for lodgings when we don't want to be here."

Em spoke up. "We'll comp the night's stay, of course."

"What about our meals?" Benn asked, more politely than his brother, but still annoyingly.

"We'll pick up the take-out tab," Em said in what undoubtedly sounded gracious to the guests, but I could tell that she was reaching the limits of her patience.

"I've seen the menus," Jack said, "and they look promising."

"I don't care what you think," Beck said. "My brother and I have refined tastes. And we have work to do that we can't do from here."

Shelly turned to her daughter. "I told you they'd try to wiggle out of the rematch."

"We're not wiggling out of anything," Beck shouted.

His brother laid a hand on his arm and took over. "It's just that we're very busy, and we'd counted on getting some work done this weekend. But as long as we're stuck here, we might as well pass some of the time with a few hands of bridge. Just until you realize how overmatched you are."

"It's settled then," Deputy Shurette said. "You'll stay until check-out time tomorrow. Voluntarily, as material witnesses. I can't force you to stay, but it wouldn't take much for me to start considering you as suspects. Eagerness to disappear would do it, and then I'd have to come up with charges I could bring against you. For littering or loitering or something. I'd rather keep everything pleasant though."

"Too late for that," Beck grumbled, this time quietly, suggesting that even he had some ability to restrain himself when the risk involved arrest.

Shurette pretended not to hear as he headed for the front door.

Jack gave Beck an annoyed look. "The deputy is just doing his job. No point in making it harder for him. The time will pass quickly as long as we keep busy." He waved the stack of menus he carried. "We found what looks like a really great place for regional home-style cooking, so we might as well enjoy our free lunch. If we order now, it should arrive around noon."

"Good idea," I said, gesturing for him to give me the menu from the restaurant he recommended. "Now that Jack has chosen the luncheon restaurant, we'll make more copies of the menu, so everyone can have one to decide what they want."

Em intercepted the menu headed for the kitchen, so I didn't have to figure out where there might be a copier.

As she left, Beck whined loudly, "How come he got to decide again? Shouldn't we take turns?"

"Jack is a professional chef, so I'm sure he won't steer you wrong, but if you don't find anything you like on the menu, we can make special arrangements for you."

He seemed to like the idea of being treated as "special," so while he continued to complain, it seemed more a matter of habit than any real irritation.

Shelly drowned him out with her excitement. "I've always wondered how my impression of a restaurant would compare to that of a professional chef. Maybe Jack and his son will give us some inside information on our lunch."

"I'd be honored," Jack said, "although my son doesn't like to talk directly about the competition. You could ask him about his plans for his own restaurant, though, if that would interest you. He loves talking about that."

Shelly squealed in delight. "So what do you recommend from the menu?"

"You probably can't go wrong with any of the simple regional specialties," he said. "I'd avoid the more complicated dishes, which are probably not made on-site. A lot of places buy them partially cooked and then frozen for the restaurant trade. I've heard that someone in town makes their own burgoo from scratch, and that's what I want to try. I'd like to compare a few spoonbreads too."

Em returned with copies of the menus and handed them out to all the guests there before leaving to deliver one to the Millers in their room.

While the guests pored over their options, I excused myself to prepare the kitchen table for when the food was delivered. I didn't plan to stay in there for long, though. I needed a break to come up with a new plan. I'd hoped that checking everyone's alibis and lack thereof would point to an obvious prime suspect, but I hadn't been able to rule anyone out. There were too many periods when both the victim's and the suspects' locations were unknown. Plus, to the extent the guests had alibis, they were unreliable, provided by family members who might lie to protect their loved ones.

If an alibi didn't rule anyone out, and the murder weapon was likely an unidentifiable floor or piece of furniture, then motive was likely the key to identifying the killer. Assuming the two prior incidents were connected to the murder, then the motive had existed before this weekend, so the killer had to have known

Mark before Friday. Except I had no concrete evidence that any of the guests—or anyone at the barrel company—had even met Mark before arriving at the B&B. As far as I knew, the co-op's board had chosen the judges—not from their own membership since we might have recognized them—from a pool of people who had experience in Kentucky's tourism industry and were familiar with Cooperton, but weren't directly involved in a business here.

So that was the next step in my plan: figure out who had known Mark before this weekend. But how was I supposed to do that without admitting that I knew why they were really here? And how could I believe their answers when everything about their stay at the B&B was a lie?

CHAPTER THIRTEEN

CJ was in the kitchen with Noah, giving him an early lunch. Grilled cheese again. He didn't seem particularly interested in it, instead staring into space as his mother worked around him. Definitely not the wiggly bundle of energy that CJ had been at his age.

I refreshed the buffet counter with plates, flatware, glasses, and napkins until Em arrived with marked-up copies of the menus to call in the orders. CJ disappeared into the pantry while Em made the call to the restaurant.

I watched over her shoulder—she'd dropped into the seat at the opposite end of the table from Noah, so for the moment, she was shorter than me, despite having outgrown me by the time she was twelve—as she placed the orders. The guests had put their names on their marked-up menus, so I could tell who had ordered which meal. Jack Dell had chosen burgoo and spoonbread for himself and his son, and the Readings had apparently copied that order exactly, right down to the sweet teas and an hors d'oeuvre-sized order of bourbon-barbeque ribs. The Millers had been a little more independent, ordering the burgoo, but skipping the spoonbread and ribs in favor of a chef's salad with local ham. The twins, despite their claim to a sophisticated palate, had chosen basic ham sandwiches with french fries.

Em disconnected the phone call and looked up at me. "Well? Are there any clues in their orders?"

"No." I sat next to her, but on the far side from Noah so as not to disturb his meal, although I doubted anything would disturb his seemingly single-minded attention on it. "I thought the choices might give us an idea of who they really are instead of who they're pretending to be, but it's not enough information to go on."

"Maybe their dinner preferences will be more revealing,"

Em said with what I thought was sarcasm but could just have been desperation for some answers.

"I wish we could just ask them who they really are and what interactions they'd had with Mark in the past. But the only way to do that is to admit that we know why they're here, so they can stop lying about it."

"We weren't exactly honest with them either," Em said. "Even if it was a lie of omission, they're not going to like thinking they've been played."

CJ emerged from the pantry, Beam at her heels. "So it's okay if they play us, but we can't play them in return? That's not fair."

Em said, "There's nothing fair about business. Especially when men are involved, and most of the tourism co-op's members are men. I bet they don't even follow their own rules about supporting the other members of the co-op. The men probably find ways to justify not referring business to the women in the group."

"Just because you hate the men you've worked with in finance doesn't mean that all males are evil." CJ looked over at her son, who had left the table and carried his book over to show it to Beam. The cat seemed fascinated by the pictures that Noah pointed to.

"Noah's different," Em said before glancing guiltily at me. "I mean—"

CJ cut her off. "I know what you mean. But as I was saying, you shouldn't take out your frustration with the business world on the tourism co-op. It may be dominated by men at the moment, but it was started by three women. And once we're members, we can work on making sure everyone is treated equitably."

"We shouldn't have to work at it," Em said. "It would be a lot easier just to kick out all the men. Or start our own group. No more stupid macho games."

"That's enough, you two," I said. "We can fight the battle of the sexes later. Right now, we need to figure out how to get the guests to tell us the truth about whether any of them had a reason to kill Mark before this weekend. Or else there's a real risk that the sheriff's going to decide one of us did it because it's the easiest solution, and the culprit will never be identified, and you'll lose your life's savings. We don't want any of that to happen, right?"

"Right," Em and CJ answered simultaneously, both voices filled with despair.

"I think we're going to need to come clean with the guests, admit we know why they're here, so they don't have any reason to lie to us about the judging. Then if anyone still lies, we'll have a reason to wonder if they're trying to cover up murder."

"There's got to be another way to get answers," CJ said. "If the inspection is canceled, the co-op might not give us a second chance, just reject us automatically."

"I'm open to other ideas, but coming clean is all I can think of." I turned to Em, who had always been a good long-term planner, even if she'd acted impulsively when she quit her job. "What about you?"

"My only suggestion isn't very practical," Em said. "I'd like to take the Hammett twins somewhere isolated and beat the truth out of them. I think they're the weak links. And my prime suspects. It's not that big a jump from metaphorical killings on Wall Street to a literal killing."

"I don't know about that," I said. "Wall Street's victims are invisible for the most part, and the Hammetts don't strike me as particularly introspective types who would think about anyone who was indirectly harmed. It's very different bankrupting someone you've never met and is just some numbers on a screen, versus slamming a person's head against a hard surface."

"I'd still like to beat the twins' heads against hard surfaces," Em muttered. "If not for killing Mark then for everything else they've undoubtedly done."

"What if we didn't tell the guests that we know about the inspection, just explained how bad it would be for our business if anyone suspected us of the murder," CJ said. "The Hammetts wouldn't care, but the Readings loved their B&B, and they seem kind. They wouldn't want us to lose this place over something that wasn't our fault."

"But they may not have any useful information," I said.

"And the rest of the guests are men," Em said darkly. "Well, except for Tanya Miller, but I've confirmed that she really is a part owner of Rackhouse Saddlebreds next door. That means she's a trust fund baby, sort of, and never had to worry about her family losing their business, so she might not understand why we're worried."

"I can start with the Readings if you two want to reach out to your local contacts to see if you can find out more about the guests' past interactions with Mark," I said. "If any of them hated Mark enough to try to kill him, not just once but three times, the feud might have generated some useful gossip."

"We can do that," CJ said.

"Meanwhile, I need to know what my limits are. I still think we need to confess to the guests, but you're right that it's risky. And it's your future on the line, not mine, so you two have to be the ones to decide, not me."

CJ and Em both looked down at Noah, who was obliviously running a finger along the text of another picture book, mumbling something unintelligible, as if he were reading to the cat. Beam watched with every indication that he was fully absorbed in the story. Or perhaps preparing to pounce on Noah's moving finger.

Em finally said, "I think CJ should decide. She's got even more on the line than I do. I can always go back to .." She took a deep breath as if to stifle a gag. "Go back to banking."

CJ sighed. "I trust you to do whatever you think best in the moment, Jess." She narrowed her eyes at me. "Just promise you'll make sure I'm not standing anywhere near the culprit when you figure out who it is, or I might do something crazy. Whoever dragged us into their fight with Mark is risking Noah's future, and I will do anything to protect him."

"I'd never let Noah's future be damaged by this," I said, although I didn't really know how I could protect him, especially when I didn't even know why he didn't behave the way I expected a toddler would. He and CJ could always come live with me if they lost the B&B, but she would hate living in a city, and I wasn't sure Pappy would take well to being transplanted. "I won't let you go all vigilante on the culprit."

CJ laughed. "Just in case, I'd better lock up my crossbow so I won't be tempted to use it. No point in proving our innocence in a murder investigation only to end up in jail anyway for assault."

"So it's okay with you that I come clean with the guests if I decide it's the only way to get answers?" I asked.

CJ glanced down at Noah one last time before saying,

"It's not okay, but there are lots of things we have to do in our lives, even if they're not okay. So do what you've got to do."

Em nodded. "Agreed. I really don't want to lose the B&B and have to go back to banking. Although I'd do that before I'd let my nephew be homeless. So do what you have to do."

"None of you will ever be homeless," I said, humbled by their trust in me. "Not while I'm alive."

* * *

At the last minute, I decided to start with the Millers instead of the Readings. Shelly and Candy might be more sympathetic to our situation, based on the shared experience of owning a B&B, but they'd never been Cooperton residents, so they were less likely to have interacted with Mark before this weekend. The Millers, with their ongoing strong ties to the horse farm next door, and thus to the town, might know more about any past conflicts between Mark and the other guests.

I found them out behind the house near the kitchen garden, where they had an unrestricted view of Rackhouse Saddlebreds' pastures and outdoor riding rings.

"It's an amazing view, isn't it?" I hadn't really had a chance to take it in until now. It brought back memories of growing up in similarly rural surroundings, although the farmers near my childhood home had been growing corn, not breeding horses.

Tanya turned to greet me, her expression one of intense longing. Not, I suspected, for the view itself as much as for the ability to ride again, to join the group working with their horses in one of the rings.

"We couldn't resist getting a look at the farm," she said as she schooled her expression into a less revealing one of simple admiration.

"There's no rush to come inside," I assured her. "I just wanted to let you know that the restaurant said lunch would be here between twelve and twelve-thirty."

"I, for one," said David, "am really looking forward to lunch. Pushing a wheelchair over grass is not as easy as it looks."

"It looks grueling," I said. "Would you like some help?"

He let out a startled laugh. "From you? Sorry, no offense intended, but you're too short to have the necessary leverage.

You'd be like the rich man trying to get into heaven or the camel going through the eye of a needle. But I do appreciate the offer."

"Ignore him," Tanya said, "he just likes to complain. I think he's secretly proud of the muscles he's put on in the last couple of years."

He smiled affectionately but didn't disagree.

"There's something else I need to tell you," I said, "and you're not going to like it as much as the prospect of lunch."

"We can handle anything," David said, squeezing his wife's shoulder.

"It's not that bad," I said. "It's just that we've decided to come clean with you about something, but I'd appreciate it if you didn't share what I have to say with the other guests until I can confess to them privately."

"All right," Tanya said.

"We knew who you were before you came here."

"Of course you did," David said, doing an admirable job of keeping up the pretense of being nothing more than a random guest. "We filled out a bunch of virtual paperwork when we booked the room, and that included our names and contact information."

"No, I mean we know that you're representatives of the tourism co-op, here to inspect the B&B. Not just you two, but all of the guests. Including Mark Pleasant."

Tanya wrinkled her nose. "I hate being lumped in with that man."

David shook his head. "I'll never understand how Mark got included. He was a disgrace to, well, to just about everything. To his profession as a tour guide, the town he lived in, even his religion. He claimed to be a good Christian, but from what I've seen, he broke at least half the ten commandments on a daily basis. I bet he's the one who broke his promise to keep the inspection a secret and told you why we were here. Probably demanded a bribe too."

"He didn't tell us anything," I said, although it was interesting that David thought he had. "Why would you think he would try to get a bribe from us? Had he done something similar before? Is that why you said he was a disgrace to his profession?"

The couple exchanged a glance. Tanya ended it quickly, but not before I'd noticed the silent warning she'd given her husband. What was she trying to hide?

Tanya waved a hand dismissively. "Oh, David always makes things sound worse than they are. Mark didn't do anything specific that we could point to as a reason for disliking him. He just had a knack for annoying everyone who met him. He was like grit in your eye, making everyone feel cranky from the moment he showed up, with the irritation lasting for hours after he left."

That was exactly how I'd felt around Mark. Like there was a constant, low-level irritant that I couldn't wash away, no matter how hard I tried. And he'd had the same effect on the twins, judging by their reaction to Mark's unintentionally bumping into Beck in the shuttle bus. The Hammetts were naturally aggressive, but they hadn't threatened anyone else in the group, at least not physically. Beck had threatened to clobber Shelly Reading at bridge, but I didn't think he'd meant it literally. On the other hand, when he'd turned to confront Mark on the bus, I'd really thought a brawl was about to break out.

"So how did Mark get chosen to be on the inspection team?" I asked. "It's pretty obvious that just about everyone disliked him, other than the people who booked his tours, I suppose."

"Oh, they hated him too," David said. "But remember that most of his career happened before people had access to review sites on the internet, and he marketed to people who were taking their first trip to the area. From what we've heard, he had virtually no repeat business."

"Pretty much the opposite of how we try to run things at Rackhouse Saddlebreds," Tanya said. "The farm's been around since the Civil War, and some of our customers' families have been regularly buying horses or getting stud services from us almost as long. We've always been in business for the long haul, not a quick buck. Unlike Mark."

"And I believe in long-term plans too," David said. "Although admittedly, my work in accounting was about ten-year plans, not hundred-year ones."

It struck me that the somewhat haphazard attempts on Mark's life suggested that the killer wasn't much of a planner, more of an opportunist by nature. The prior attempts on Mark's life had been so ineffective that it was hard to believe much planning had gone into them. Which sounded more like the

Hammetts than any of the other guests. The combination of big dreams and haphazard execution seemed to describe the twins. But as outsiders who only visited Cooperton occasionally, had they even known Mark before this weekend?

"Do you know if any of the other guests had a history with Mr. Pleasant before this weekend?" I asked. "What about the Hammett twins? They're not from Kentucky originally, so had they even met him before this weekend?"

"I never met the Hammetts before." Tanya looked at her husband, her expression questioning, rather than warning. "Did you?"

He shook his head. "I don't run in their circles any longer. The entrepreneurial big spenders, I mean. Mark didn't either, not really, although he tried. They might have met at some networking event. He loved showing up at those things uninvited."

I couldn't imagine attending that sort of gathering if I didn't absolutely, positively have to. "I thought Mr. Pleasant was retired."

"Not by choice," David said. "Wouldn't surprise me if he was trying to start up a new business, looking for clients or investors. He'd have seen the Hammetts, with their big-city money, as ripe targets."

"He was a fool," Tanya said. "Anyone could figure that out within moments of meeting him. Add to that the way the Hammetts seem to think all rural residents are idiots, and they wouldn't have given Mark the time of day."

"I don't know," David said, his tone almost apologetic about disagreeing with his wife. "He was good at worming his way into other people's businesses, finding their weak spots, and exploiting them."

"That's true enough," Tanya said lightly, although her grip on the arms of her wheelchair had tightened, and her knuckles were turning white. "I guess I've never really thought too deeply about either Mark or the Hammetts."

I thought David was going to say something more, but Tanya added, "I'd like to freshen up now before lunch arrives if you'd be so good as to excuse us, Ms. Walker."

"Of course. But call me Jess."

She nodded, and David said, "I should freshen up too

after all this exercise."

"When you do join the others for lunch," I said, "please don't forget that our advance knowledge of the inspection needs to remain between us for now."

"The secret things belong to the Lord our God," David said amiably. "You can count on us."

CHAPTER FOURTEEN

Shelly Reading called my name from the kitchen's French doors that opened onto the veranda. As I approached her, I could see Candy, a few inches taller than her mother, right behind her, holding two glasses of sweet tea.

Shelly said, "Are we allowed to sit out here, maybe have our lunch al fresco if the warm weather holds?"

I had no idea if the wicker seating was supposed to be for staff only, but I couldn't admit my ignorance, not without giving the women yet another reason to feel betrayed after I confessed about the advance knowledge of the inspection. Plus, having just the two guests out back on the veranda was an ideal opportunity for me to question them without anyone else overhearing us.

"We don't usually have guests eating lunch at the B&B, so there aren't any rules about it. You're certainly welcome to eat out here if you'd like. I can see about finding you a table so you won't have to hold the plates on your laps."

"Excellent," Shelly said. "And maybe a card table and chairs too, in case the Hammetts ever show up for a rematch. They said they had other plans this morning, but maybe this afternoon."

"I'll see what I can find."

Shelly stepped out onto the veranda itself and tugged her daughter along behind her, causing the ice cubes in the two glasses of sweet tea to jiggle and spill a few drops onto the deck surface. "We'll sit and enjoy the view for now, maybe take a walk around the yard."

"Before I go look for the table and chairs, there's something I need to tell you." Practice wasn't making it any easier to confess. "It's about the tourism co-op. We know you're here to do an inspection."

Both women turned to look at the horse couple, who had

apparently changed their mind about coming inside and had gone back to watching the activity over at the horse farm.

"Did they tell you?" Candy asked, handing one of the tea glasses to her mother. "No, wait. I know who it was. Mark Pleasant, wasn't it? You don't have to answer that. Of course it was him."

It was interesting that both the Millers and the Readings had such a low opinion of Mark that they'd immediately accused him of undermining their surprise inspection. I wouldn't have suggested it myself, but I didn't mind letting them continue to believe he'd been the one with the loose lips. He was beyond caring about his reputation, and it would distract attention from the actual person who'd let the information slip. The farm employee had made a mistake, nothing he should be punished for.

"You really didn't like Mr. Pleasant, did you?"

"No one did," Candy said. "And with good reason. Telling you about the inspection, presumably expecting he'd be able to hold it over your head for something in return, is typical of him. He cheated on everyone."

Shelly put a hand on her daughter's arm. "It's not nice to speak ill of the dead."

Candy's eyebrows rose so high they almost touched her headband. "Really, Mother? Like you didn't wish him dead almost daily for a solid year."

Shelly smiled at me confidingly. "She's exaggerating. I might have wanted Mark bankrupt and homeless, but not dead."

"That's still a pretty strong dislike," I said. "What did he do to you?"

The two women exchanged looks, and then Candy said, "Didn't he tell you? He usually liked to brag about his business deals."

"He didn't mention you at all in the short time I knew him," I said. "Was it something to do with your B&B?"

"Worse," the daughter said. "He was my stepfather."

Shelly had been married to Mark? Even if the dissolution of their marriage had been amicable—and I had a hard time thinking anything Mark was a party to would be amicable—it made Shelly a prime suspect.

"He wasn't abusive to Candy or anything," Shelly said. "I wouldn't have allowed that."

"He mostly just ignored me, but what I can't forgive him for is that when Mother filed for divorce, he made her give up her other child, the B&B."

"It wasn't that bad. Running a B&B is a lot of work, and I'm not as young as when I first opened it." Shelly looked at Jess. "Well, you know how hard the work is. Retiring was for the best really. Now I'm free to travel and play bridge whenever I want."

Out of sight of her mother, Candy rolled her eyes. I didn't need to see her reaction to know that Shelly was downplaying how hurt she'd actually been by having to sell the B&B. Shelly probably had years of practice at covering her real feelings about Mark and wasn't likely to give me any more useful information. Candy, on the other hand, seemed anxious to spill everything she knew about her ex-stepfather, as long as her mother didn't have to hear it. If I could have a chat with Candy in private, I might finally get some real insight into who had wanted Mark dead, and why.

* * *

I went looking for my sisters in the kitchen, so I could ask them whether the B&B had a card table, but the chefs were in there alone. They were taking the stacks of plates and flatware from the buffet counter to lay out individual settings at the table. As they continued to make minute adjustments to the placement, I told them that we knew about the inspection.

Jack just shrugged, and Jonny gave his father an annoyed look. "I told you having Pleasant on the team was a mistake. We should have refused to be part of the judging as long as he was included."

Yet another set of guests blaming Mark for our learning about the inspection.

"We needed a break from the restaurant," Jack said calmly, "and if we'd waited for the next opportunity to get a free vacation, it would probably be during a busier season, and we'd have had to turn it down."

"I suppose," Jonny said. "I'm just not sure getting a break, no matter how nice the accommodations are, is worth the price of being accused of murder."

"No one's accusing anyone of anything," I said.

"Maybe not out loud," Jonny said, "but you're thinking it.

The thing is, everyone hated Pleasant, so it's going to be hard to narrow down the suspects."

"Everyone?" I asked.

"Everyone who ever had any business dealings with him," Jonny amended.

"Does that include you two?"

Jonny just shrugged and waved the pepper mill in my direction to show me it was almost empty. "Do you have more?"

"We should. In the pantry." I nodded at the door. "Watch out for Beam, the orange cat who lives in there."

He grunted and took the pepper mill with him.

"Sorry," Jack said. "My son lets little things get to him. He needs to work on that if he's going to be happy as a chef. But to answer your question, yes, we knew Pleasant before this weekend. He came to our restaurant fairly regularly. Usually tried to wheedle a free meal out of us by threatening to tell his clients our food was terrible if we didn't comp him, but that's more the owner's problem than mine. I don't have anything to do with the money. I mostly stay in the kitchen while the owner deals with the finances and hobnobs with the guests. I don't have time for that sort of thing. I just want to cook."

"You still need the restaurant to succeed if you want to keep your job," I said. "You may not be directly involved in the finances, but you'd be out of work if the restaurant went bankrupt because of Mr. Pleasant's threats. Didn't you ever worry about that?"

"Not particularly. I get job offers just about every week, so I'm not dependent on my current one." He nodded at his son, coming out of the pantry. "And Jonny's planning to open his own place in Lexington once he's got a bit more experience. No need to have two similarly trained chefs in a small town like ours."

Jonny showed his father a jar of peppercorns. "What do you think? Will this do?"

Jack inspected it. "It's perfect. Someone here knows their spices."

"That would be CJ. She does most of the cooking. I'm just filling in while her arm's in a cast."

Jonny returned to fidgeting with the place settings, which reminded me that two of them weren't needed, at least not indoors.

"The Readings want to eat out on the veranda. I'm supposed to be looking for a table for them."

"They may change their mind when they hear that we'll be doing a live-stream for our social media, reviewing the burgoo, spoonbread, and dessert," Jack said. "They seemed interested in what we thought of the food. And if they're not interested, we'll plate their food and bring it out to them."

"What he means," Jonny said, "is that *I* will be the waiter if needed. Dad loves making me do the service. I worked for him during the summers after I turned sixteen, and he enjoyed the power trip. He made me into a bus boy and then waiter instead of doing actual cooking in the kitchen."

"It wasn't a power trip," Jack explained. "It was an important lesson. You need to know all aspects of the restaurant experience. Including what happens to the food after it leaves the kitchen."

If any of the guests were into power trips, I thought, it wasn't Jack, but Mark Pleasant, judging by the way he'd forced the sale of the Readings' B&B, and had insisted on me accompanying him on the trip to Hills' Barrels. That kind of game-playing could have been what got him killed. Jack might be willing to let the provocation roll off him, but I doubted the Hammett twins could resist taking any bait thrown their way. Shelly had given in before but could well have reached her limit and snapped if Mark had tried to pressure her again. Tanya Miller was passionate enough about Rackhouse Saddlebreds, and her husband seemed intensely protective of her, so I thought they would defend any threats against the horse farm, just as my sisters were prepared to defend the B&B.

I was confident my sisters wouldn't go so far as to commit murder to protect the B&B, but I couldn't be equally sure about any of the guests.

CHAPTER FIFTEEN

———

The Dells settled at the kitchen table to wait for the arrival of lunch, and I excused myself to resume my search for a folding table. I hadn't seen one in the pantry earlier, so I didn't bother to look there, just headed out to check the housekeeping closet on the second floor.

I'd barely entered the lobby when the Hammett twins came down the stairs. One of them asked, "Did we miss the arrival of lunch?"

"It's late," Beck said. At least I assumed it was him, judging by his annoyed tone. It would be a lot easier to tell them apart if they'd adopted distinctively different clothing, but while they weren't obviously matched like Shelly and her daughter, the twins seemed to have adopted a generic, aging-preppy wardrobe of khakis and sport shirts. They didn't even have the courtesy to each choose a different, preferred color of shirt, since yesterday the one I was fairly sure was Beck had worn a navy shirt, while his brother wore a paler blue. Today, probably-Beck's shirt was yellow, while his brother's was off-white.

I checked my watch, and it was only a quarter past noon. Not early for the promised delivery between twelve and twelve-thirty, but not yet late either.

"I'm sure it will be worth the wait," I said.

Benn nodded toward the hallway to the kitchen. "We heard voices as we came down the stairs."

Beck added, "Thought you'd started without us."

"We'd never do that," I said. "But while we wait for the delivery, I could use a moment of your time."

"Do you know what our time is worth?" Beck asked snidely.

"I'm sure your time is quite valuable, but I think you'll want to hear what I have to say."

Both pairs of eyebrows rose. Beck said, "You mean the police have realized they're violating our constitutional rights, so we can go now?"

They were wrong, of course. Most non-lawyers were when it came to understanding the Fourth Amendment and how it limited—or in this case, failed to limit—police behavior. As long as we weren't under arrest, there was no prohibition against the deputy politely asking us to remain within his jurisdiction, with the understanding that if we then left, it would be an indication of guilt that would get the police looking more carefully at our possible role in a murder.

But the twins weren't paying me for a legal opinion, and they probably wouldn't believe me anyway. I settled for saying, "This has nothing to do with the deputy. I wanted to talk to you about the real reason why you're here this weekend: the inspection for the tourist association."

The two men didn't reveal any surprise, merely looked at each other, both raising one eyebrow in silent inquiry.

After a moment, Benn turned back to me. "That's excellent news. Since you know about it, it doesn't qualify as a secret inspection any longer, so there's no point in doing our report."

Beck, however, wasn't as pleased. "Oh, great. So this whole weekend has been a waste of our time. We can't even cut our losses by leaving now, thanks to the old guy dying. The cops had better not keep us here much longer. "

"I'm sure they're doing their best." I had an idea. "In the meantime, you could think of it like a real-life game of Clue. You can try to solve the case before the cops do."

"We do like games," Benn agreed.

"Only if there's some skill involved," Beck said.

"There is," I told him. "The outcome will depend on logic and information, not the draw of cards. You're both witnesses to yesterday's events, of course, and you might even have run into Mr. Pleasant in the past, or know something about him that would help the police figure out who might have had a motive to kill him."

Benn started to say something, but Beck kicked his ankle and said, "How would we know anything about the old man? We'd never met him before we checked in here."

"Besides," Benn said, "even if we met him before, it would have just been in passing at some event or another, so how would that be useful to the cops? He was retired before we established our distillery here. No reason for us to know anything about him."

There was a ring of truth to what he said. The world was divided into two camps for them: People they could take advantage of, and people who couldn't do anything for them. Mark, no longer a local business owner, apparently fell in the latter category.

Still, I didn't entirely believe Benn. I couldn't explain why, beyond a gut reaction, but I was convinced that they were lying about not having known Mark before this weekend. And why would they continue to lie about it unless their prior knowledge of him was incriminating?

* * *

Before I could question the twins further, I heard tires crunching on the gravel driveway. The lunch delivery vehicle, I assumed. I sent the Hammetts off to the kitchen to let everyone know that lunch had arrived, went out front to greet the driver, and asked her to take the food into the kitchen. Then I went around the side of the house to let the Millers know that lunch had arrived, and the Dells were going to be doing a live review of the food that they wouldn't want to miss. While David prepared to push the wheelchair back across the grass, I asked if they'd seen my sisters, and they told me Em had been heading for the owners' quarters about half an hour earlier.

I found Em in the corner that was intended for use as an office once the renovations were finished. She was seated on a heavy metal toolbox that I recognized as once having belonged to our father. A moving box labeled "books" served as a table for her laptop, idle while on her phone call.

Noah was at the other end of the space, curled up on his bunk with Pappy, reading yet another book. I kept my distance, so as not to spook either child or cat, and waited for Em to finish her call.

Once she disconnected it, I asked, "Where's CJ?"

"She went into town. Apparently, she has a source who's much more likely to spill gossip in person than over the phone.

She owns a small gift shop and used bookstore in a renovated school building in the center of town, and she's very involved in the tourism co-op, providing meeting space for in-person meetings. She must know Mark and probably knows all the suspects. And she'll want us to succeed. The gift shop sells CJ's jams, and they're really popular, bringing in customers who then buy other stuff while they're there."

I nodded at the phone Em had just set down on the moving box. "What about you? Learn anything useful?"

"I'd let you know if I did," she snapped. "I don't need you interrogating me like I'm a hostile witness."

Considering Em's longstanding role in the family as the peacemaker, she'd sure become prickly since the last time I'd visited.

"Nothing that happened this weekend was my idea," I reminded her, keeping my tone calm so as not to escalate matters. "You and CJ asked me to visit, and then you asked me to make sure the B&B doesn't get hurt by the fall-out from Mark's death. That's all I'm doing, not trying to micromanage you."

"Right," Em grumbled, sounding even more irritated by the reminder that she had indeed brought the current situation—or at least my role in it—on herself. "The great White Knight Jess, riding to the rescue. But only when it's convenient for you. Where were you the last few years when we needed you? Where were you when CJ was pregnant and throwing up, or when I was getting concussions from smacking my head against glass ceilings?"

"I'm sorry," I said, even though I thought she would have hated it if I had tried to come to their rescue then, without waiting for an invitation. Then they could justifiably have disdained my actions as that of a white knight. But there was a germ of truth to her complaint, and she deserved an apology from me. "I should have visited more often. I didn't know you were struggling. You both always seemed so strong."

"We are," Em said, but without conviction. "It's just that sometimes even the strongest person gets tired."

"I know." I'd always been something of an irritant to CJ, who considered me a perpetual cloud over anything fun, while Em had seemed grateful for my help when their plans went awry. Now, she both wanted my help and resented it too. I understood, however belatedly, but I didn't know how to fix the situation.

We sat in silence for a long moment until, finally, Em heaved a long sigh. "I'm sorry. It's not really your fault that I'm angry with life right now. I shouldn't take it out on you. It's just that the Hammetts remind me a bit too much of some of the guys I worked with, the ones with more ego than actual knowledge or skill. They always, always, *always* got promoted over me, and then I'd end up bailing them out when they messed up big-time. I did eventually get the satisfaction of quitting right in the middle of a huge self-inflicted crisis, leaving them to fix the consequences of hiring incompetent jerks, but I'd forgotten that the whole world is populated with stupidly entitled men, and leaving banking didn't change that."

"For now. But I have confidence in you. Someday, you'll bring down the entire local patriarchy," I said and offered her a fist bump. "And you'll do it without bringing literal death to individual patriarchs like Mark or the Hammetts."

Em laughed. "See, that's why CJ always said you were no fun, never letting her do the risky stuff she really wanted to try. Now I can't even fantasize about bringing death to specific patriarchs, without thinking about how much you'd disapprove."

"Someone's got to be the party pooper," I said. "But back to the present for now. And please take this as a totally nurturing, collaborative kind of question and not an authoritarian inquisition. Have you learned anything useful about the guests?"

Em wrinkled her nose. "No. And that's probably why I got so annoyed when you asked. I've been calling everyone I can think of, and no one knows anything useful. They don't know the Millers or Readings personally, and most of them have never even heard of the Hammetts. They all know Mark and the Dells, and they all say the same basic thing. Mark was a jerk and probably somewhat shady in his business, while Jack Dell is his polar opposite, kind and generous and just a little tragic. Apparently, his wife died about a year ago from cancer, and both the husband and the son adored her. So did everyone else who knew her, and pretty much everyone around here did. She ran a popular cleaning business in town."

"And no one knew anything at all about the other guests?"

"Only the very basics. Tanya Miller was in a riding accident, which left her paralyzed, and her husband retired early to take care of her. No reason for them to have had any dealings with Mark. The Readings used to own a B&B a couple towns over, but the mother is retired now, and the daughter does some consulting for people who are looking to start a new B&B or buy an existing one."

"Did anyone mention that Shelly Reading was married to Mark, and he forced the sale of the B&B when they divorced?"

"No." Em frowned. "How could I have missed that?"

"The reason for the sale of the B&B may not be common knowledge," I said. "I got it directly from Shelly."

"That's a hell of a motive for murder." Em gave me a conciliatory smile. "You have my permission to swoop in and save me from myself if I'm ever on the verge of letting a man force me to sell my interest in the Three Sisters B&B."

"All you ever have to do is ask," I said. "Preferably before you kill the man who threatened to do that to you rather than after."

"I'll try to remember that through my rage."

"Not to bring up a sore subject, but what about the Hammetts? You said most of your contacts hadn't met them, but presumably some had."

"Only two people I talked to," Em said. "Ran into the twins at some charity fundraiser. Apparently, the Hammetts like to brag about their Wall Street careers, and how they're going to make Kentucky bourbon even more famous than it already is, but they don't spend much time here. It's like they have as little emotional attachment to their barrels of bourbon as they would to stock certificates, things that are meaningless in themselves but can be bought, held, or sold. It's all very distant and unemotional, not like how I'd expect someone to care about something that's a luxury. They certainly don't feel anything similar to what the owners of Rackhouse Saddlebreds feel about their horses, or the Hill family feels about its barrels."

"The twins claim they didn't know Mark before this weekend," I said, "but I think they were lying. I just can't figure out why. Or how they might have run into Mark in the past if they only pop into town briefly to do business. Mark had retired before the Hammetts established their headquarters here."

"I might have an explanation for how they could have run into each other," Em said. "The only property the Hammetts have in Cooperton is a small rack house for aging the bourbon. The actual creation of the bourbon happens at a large distillery that makes custom blends, using their customers' recipes. Mark used to take his clients on tours to that distillery, and back when the Hammetts were making plans to make their own bourbon, they could have gone on one of Mark's tours and met him before they were officially in business."

I nodded. "That makes sense. I can see Mark bragging about being best friends with the owner of the distillery or knowing all the inside information on other bourbon makers around here. It would have been a recipe for disaster: One side of the conversation claiming to be powerful when he was so blatantly weak, and the other side attracted to weakness they could exploit. And if something did go badly, well, the twins don't strike me as the sort who'd accept their own responsibility for failure, so they'd blame Mark for anything that went wrong."

"You know who could tell us if you're right about that?" Em said. "Reed Hill."

Before I could say that I'd already planned to talk to him about whether he'd been able to determine whether Mark's injury had happened at Hills' Barrels, someone knocked on the front door of the owners' quarters, startling us both.

CHAPTER SIXTEEN

"It's probably Shelly Reading," I said. "I'm supposed to be looking for a card table so they can play bridge on the veranda after lunch, but I keep getting distracted."

Em got up from the toolbox. "There's a closet in the hall leading to the Millers' room. You'll find a card table and folding chairs in there, although it's hard to see at first. They're on the right, behind some supplies that are hanging from hooks." She pulled the door open.

It wasn't Shelly or any of the other guests standing outside. It was Reed Hill.

"I was on my way back from the sheriff's office and thought I'd stop by," he said. "I've got some information about Mark Pleasant that you might want to know."

"If you're helping with our investigation, there's something you should know," Em said, ushering him inside. "At least, assuming you didn't already know that everyone on the tour was actually here to inspect the B&B for the tourist association."

"I didn't, although I probably should have guessed." Reed waved at Noah, who waved back. "I recognized them all as having links to the group, but they aren't actual co-op members as far as I know, so I didn't put it together."

"The Hammetts are, but it hasn't been announced yet," Em said, "What's your information?"

I interrupted, "Before that, why were you at the sheriff's office?"

"Dropping off our surveillance camera files for the time Mark and the rest of the guests were at Hills' Barrels."

"Does that include the interior?" Most businesses had exterior cameras these days, to monitor for break-ins and vandalism, but to have them inside was less common.

"Our insurer insisted," he said. "You might be surprised

by the lengths that criminals will go to get their hands on anything related to elite brands of bourbon, including the barrels they're aged in. Scammers have tried to order Hills' brand barrels to fill them with cheap stuff to pretend it was from one of the top-notch distillers we sell to. We refused to sell to them, which makes us a target for theft. We decided to upgrade our security after the great Pappy Van Winkle heist."

"The *what* heist?"

"Pappy Van Winkle," he said. "It's an elite bourbon brand. They lost about two hundred bottles of their most expensive label to theft organized by an employee. It got a lot of media attention, which of course led to copycat crimes and an increased number of attempts to enlist our employees in a theft. I have total confidence in my people—they're all loyal and would never risk their futures by helping thieves—but our insurance company insisted on the cameras."

Pappy—the cat, not a bottle of bourbon—meowed irritably, and Em excused herself to go see what he thought Noah needed.

I stayed near the door with Reed to ask, "Did you look at the videos before you gave them to the sheriff?"

"Not in any detail, just a quick fast-forward through the two hours Mark was on-site. As far as I could tell, nothing happened to him there."

"What about the restrooms?" I asked. "I assume you don't have cameras there."

"No cameras inside the restrooms, but there's one in the corridor. He did go into the men's room, but as best I could tell, there wasn't anyone else inside at the time unless they'd been in there waiting for him since well before he arrived, and that seems unlikely. If he was injured in there, it had to have been an accident, not an assault."

I didn't think his killer would have been lying in wait, at least not for long, or the absence would have been noticed. "Did the sheriff tell you they think someone tried to kill Mark before this weekend? More than once."

He nodded. "Yeah. That's another reason why I stopped by to talk to you. Especially since I found out why Mark retired. It really expands the suspect pool."

"And?"

"This has to stay between us," Reed said. "All I've got is rumor to go on, and I wouldn't want it to spread if I'm wrong."

Em had finished preparing a snack for Noah, which seemed to satisfy his guardian cat, so she returned in time to hear Reed ask for confidentiality. "We're good at keeping secrets."

"I know you are," he said. "Just wanted to be clear before I shared what I've heard. I do think the information is reliable since I got it from more than one person, and none of them have any reason to lie about Mark. But still, it's what you lawyers would call hearsay."

"Got it," I said. "Not enough to present in court, but it could be useful for an investigation."

"Exactly," he said. "I knew Mark used to be a member of the tourism co-op before he retired, but I didn't know until today that he may have been forced into retirement. Apparently, the co-op's board of directors found out that he'd been soliciting bribes from local businesses, both members of the co-op and non-members, to recommend them—or bad-mouth their competition—to the people taking his tours."

"That would explain the reaction of our guests when we told them we knew they were here for an inspection," I said. "They all assumed that Mark had told us about it."

"But he hadn't, and we hadn't paid a bribe," Em was quick to point out. "We found out totally innocently, and it wasn't intentional on the part of the person we overheard it from. I know we should have told the co-op as soon as we heard, so they could reschedule with different judges, but that would have taken time that we couldn't afford to wait. It wasn't like we would be doing anything for the judges that we don't do for our other guests. We brought in Jess, but we'd have done that anyway after CJ broke her arm since we needed someone to cook."

Reed held up a hand to stop her torrent of words. "You don't have to explain. I never suspected, even for a moment, that you'd pay a bribe or take one. I do, however, believe Mark would have offered to sell you the information if he thought you'd pay. Most likely, the reason he didn't try it with you is the same reason he never asked for money from me—he knew I wouldn't play along. For him to have gotten away with it for as many years as my informants said he did, he must have been really good at figuring out who might pay, and who would report him to the co-op."

Em frowned. "But why is it just a rumor? If the board knew he'd been taking bribes, why didn't they do more than just insist that he retire? They could have gone public with the information and kicked him out of the group, and that would have put a stop to it."

"From what I'm told, the board thought the district attorney wouldn't consider what Mark did to be a crime or at least not one worth prosecuting. Plus, having it widely known that a co-op member had been acting unethically would be a public relations nightmare. I'm guessing Mark promised to go quietly in return for letting the matter drop, and they figured it was their best option."

"That's what I'd expect an attorney to recommend if the board consulted one," I agreed. "Going the public, legal route would be expensive and time-consuming, in addition to potentially reflecting badly on the co-op and all of its members."

"It's the practical solution," Reed said, "but not everyone likes practical solutions. There could be members of the co-op who felt coerced into paying Mark, and then when he was caught, they expected him to be punished and were angry when he didn't suffer any real consequences. They could have decided to take matters into their own hands."

"Our guests all have businesses that could have interacted with Mark's tours. Or they used to, before he retired."

Em spoke up. "I'm not saying you're wrong, Reed. I can definitely see Mark soliciting bribes and eventually getting caught. But what I don't understand is, if the board knew about it, then why did they ask him to be one of the judges for our inspection? It's practically a tacit invitation for him to bribe us, either by warning us of the inspection or by selling us his vote."

Reed shrugged. "I'll admit that part of this weekend doesn't make sense, but with what you've said about prior likely attempts on his life, I'm convinced his death has to be related to something he did before this weekend. Unethical business practices are all I can think of. Maybe the board didn't hear the rumors and didn't force him to retire, but he sensed that the jig was up and got out while he could, just in the nick of time."

"Is there any way to find out for sure what the board knew?" I asked. "Who's in charge of it?"

Em laughed. "Spoken like a lawyer. Although I suppose

I'd have asked the same thing myself if I hadn't seen just how informally the co-op is run. It's not a money-making operation in itself—dues are just enough to cover some minimal overhead and group marketing—so there aren't any salaried employees, just volunteers. That means no one wants to be in charge. Someone has to fill the various offices for legal reasons, but they do it reluctantly and put in as little time as possible."

"So how do they choose the inspectors when new businesses apply to become members?" I asked.

Em shrugged and looked at Reed.

"We don't get that many new applicants," he said. "Usually, the board will send around a group text, asking for volunteers to get a friend to do the inspection, all expenses paid. One time, a member got a bunch of his friends to do the inspection of a restaurant as a group to make it more fun. The board loved getting a whole collection of inspectors handed to them, without having to do any recruitment themselves."

"Not even to check on the inspectors' qualifications?" I asked. Reed shook his head, so I added, "Weren't they worried that the reports would be unhelpful?"

"Apparently not," Reed said. "The thing is, most applicants are accepted without much fuss, as long as they have a local business. It's just a pass/fail inspection, nothing all that detailed. I've only ever seen one set of inspection reports come back negative. In that case, everyone who did the inspection agreed that the business was a disaster, likely to fail within months and give everyone else a black eye in the process. I'm not sure why they even bother with the inspections, other than for PR purposes, so the co-op looks more exclusive than it is. "

I glanced at Em. "Did you know this? That you're much more likely than not to pass the inspection?"

Before she could answer, CJ slammed through the door, forgetting about her cast and using the injured arm to shut the door behind her. She winced, but it didn't dim her enthusiasm. "You guys won't believe what I just found out."

* * *

"We've got news too," Em said. "Mark Pleasant didn't retire voluntarily. He got forced into it for demanding bribes to do what he should have been doing anyway, recommending and not bad-mouthing member businesses."

"Seriously?" CJ glanced in Noah's direction, who didn't seem to have noticed she'd returned. He was staring into space again, as if he were watching an imaginary friend doing something interesting. She turned back to us. "No wonder people wanted him dead. I'd want to kill him too if he tried something like that with us."

"Good thing he didn't then," I said. "It was hard enough keeping you out of juvenile court. I wouldn't want to see you facing adult charges."

Em asked, "So, what did you find out?"

"First, I need to confirm something." CJ addressed me, "You did say Mark's injury could have happened as early as about an hour before he arrived here, right?"

I nodded.

"I know where he was then, and he could well have been assaulted before he got here." She paused to draw out the suspense before adding, "All the judges got together at a popular barbeque place on the road to Lexington before taking separate routes here. And remember how Mark said he had a headache when he was registering here? That's an early sign of Talk and Die Syndrome, isn't it?"

"Yes," I said, although I wasn't as excited about the news as CJ was. No wonder she considered me such a Debbie Downer. "But there are other reasons for headaches. He said he was subject to migraines."

CJ waved her cast, dismissing the possibility. "I'm sure he was injured before he got here, and now we know where it could have happened. It's the only thing that makes any sense. Someone would have noticed if he'd been attacked here, and I'm sure Reed's factory is safe. You didn't see anything on the bus in between, so it has to have been before Mark got here."

"We don't know for sure that he wasn't injured here though." I couldn't help pointing out the gaps in her logic, even if it did make my sisters annoyed with me. The risk of being blamed for a man's death, whether intentional or not, was too high to allow ourselves a false sense of vindication. "All we know, beyond a reasonable doubt, is that we didn't hurt him, and everyone else here has denied doing it. But it still could have happened here, sometime between Mark's registration and his getting on the bus. We weren't watching him every second of that time. Although I think you're probably right about the barrel factory having a solid defense, thanks to their video cameras. Reed was just telling us he can't find any record of an incident there."

"Why are you taking the cops' side?" CJ demanded. "You're supposed to be backing us up with proof that it didn't happen here, not making the case against us. We can't let the B&B get a reputation for being unsafe."

"I'm working on it," I said calmly. I had a lot of experience dealing with CJ's flashes of irritability when denied something she wanted. Fortunately, her bad moods never lasted for long. Or at least she used to get over her irritation with me quickly. That might have changed, judging by how she'd resented my presence when I'd first arrived, before she'd needed me to help defend the B&B.

"We're all trying to help, CJ," Reed said soothingly. "We've got your back."

"I know. It's just that I'm under a lot of stress at the moment." CJ briefly glanced over at Noah, who continued to ignore us in favor of staring at his imaginary friend. "Sorry I took it out on all of you."

"It's okay," I said. "We understand."

CJ perked up. "Wait, I just remembered something else that might be useful. I didn't think it mattered until you said Mark had a history of bribing businesses. Apparently, the label is in financial trouble rather than the guaranteed success the Hammetts claim it will be. What if Mark tried to take advantage of that fact, perhaps threatened the twins with telling everyone about their precarious condition if they didn't pay him off?"

"I do think the Hammetts would be vulnerable to that sort of blackmail, and we know Mark wasn't averse to bribes," Em said.

I must have looked skeptical because she continued, "I know it sounds like wishful thinking when I say that a pair of jerky men who only care about money have a shaky business plan, easily threatened. The Hammetts are the very epitome of everything I hated about working in finance—too many men, and all they care about is money."

Reed gave her a self-deprecating smile. "Thank goodness I care about more than money, or you'd never let CJ slip me the occasional jar of bacon jam to take home with me."

Em gave him the same *cut it out* look she usually reserved for her sisters. "All I meant to say was that it's really likely that the twins' bourbon investment is going to fail. They're making the mistake of thinking that because they understand finance in general, they can apply what they know to any kind of business and succeed. Like they believed all they needed to do is slap a *Made in Kentucky* label on their bourbon and brag about how long it's been aging, and it will sell quickly and at a high price. It's a lot more complicated than that, or else others would have done the same thing before now, and the market would be crowded with startups."

"She's right," Reed said. "I've talked to dozens of people who were researching my barrels for a startup, and then they realized how hard it was going to be to succeed, and I never heard from them again. The Hammetts are in an even worse position than most since they don't have a real connection to this area, and they're not even trying to fit in. They're rubbing all the locals wrong, treating everyone like not-very-bright children.

"I do a good bit of business with the owner of the distillery they've hired to make the bourbon to their specs, and while he'd never say anything bad about one customer to another, his body language speaks volumes whenever the Hammetts come up in conversation. I wouldn't be surprised if the distiller opts not to renew the twins' contract when the current term ends. They probably won't even understand how bad that will be for their business. Bourbon buyers, especially the ones willing to pay top dollar, know that changing the distiller, even when the recipe stays the same, will change the product. And variability in the product is exactly what you want to avoid if you're marketing to an audience that is focused on quality."

"This is all useful information," I said. "I hadn't been able to see what motive they might have had for wanting Mark dead, but now I can. If the Hammetts had started to realize that no one here likes them, and then Mark came along and threatened to make things even worse, it could have been the last straw. They're probably used to destroying their perceived enemies financially, but given that Mark was retired, they couldn't ruin his business preemptively, so they escalated to a physical attack. But it's just a theory at this point. How do we prove it?"

"You're supposed to know that," CJ said. "You're the lawyer."

Not the right kind of lawyer, I couldn't help thinking. But I couldn't let that stop me. My sisters needed me. Even so, it took several long moments, while the others waited in anxious silence, for me to come up with a plan for proving the Hammetts' motive for murder.

Finally, I said, "First, we need to know if the rumors about the twins' bourbon startup's imminent bankruptcy are true."

"I'll talk to the owner of the distillery," Reed said. "I'll try to convince him it's not idle gossip, but important information to be turned over to the sheriff in a murder investigation."

"Thank you," I said. "Just remember that while the Hammetts do seem like the most likely suspects at this point, we need to keep an open mind. While Reed is talking to the distiller, we'll keep looking into the other possibilities. I probably don't need to tell any of you that time is of the essence, but I will anyway. The sheriff's office could decide to let all the guests leave any minute now, and then we won't be able to question them any longer."

"Got it," Reed said and headed out.

As I watched him cross the yard to the parking lot, I asked my sisters, "Are you sure we can trust him? He won't throw us under the bus if the factory comes under suspicion?"

"Of course not," CJ said immediately. "I can't believe you'd even think he'd betray us."

"No, Jess is right to ask," Em said. "I do think we can trust Reed, but Jess doesn't know him as well as we do. Most men would be tempted to blame Mark's death on us if it were necessary to divert attention from themselves or their employees. Reed's business is as much on the line here as ours is. And in some ways he has even more to lose if people think someone died at his factory. Hills' Barrels has been around for generations, and he'd be devastated if he was the one in charge when it was forced to shut down."

"I'd trust him with my life," CJ said. "Reed's always been here for us when we needed him, like a family member would be."

I heard the unspoken "unlike you" but didn't rise to the bait. CJ and I had some issues to work out, but it could wait until later. Solving Mark's murder couldn't wait.

"All right," I said, not fully convinced but willing to give Reed the benefit of the doubt for the moment. "While Reed is confirming the Hammetts' motive, we need to make sure that if Mark's injury happened before he got here, there aren't any suspects other than our guests, either at the barbeque place or between there and here. Could Mark have stopped somewhere along the route and been attacked? How long a drive is it from the restaurant? And when, exactly, did each of the guests leave there?"

CJ wrinkled her nose. "Ugh. I hate it when you get all lawyery and logical. The restaurant is about twenty minutes from here, and my source saw Mark in the parking lot, getting ready to leave about thirty minutes before Mark got here. So, yeah, he could have stopped along the way."

"And if he did stop," I said, "he could have been injured then, either by one of our guests who stopped with him or by a stranger."

"Or he just dawdled along the way," CJ said. "I'll ask around some more, right after I settle Noah in for a nap."

"There's really only one place between the meeting and here where he'd have been likely to stop for ten minutes or less," Em said. "A gas station with a convenience store. I worked on the financing when the place was remodeled, so I know the owner. Let me see if they have surveillance recordings from Friday."

"And you're sure there's nowhere else he could have stopped?"

"Not for just ten minutes," Em insisted. "Not anywhere he'd run into other people. It's pretty rural between the restaurant and here, more farmland than anything else. I mean, I suppose he could have stopped next door at the horse farm, but I can't imagine why. I can check on that too though."

"Good idea," I said.

"What are you going to be doing?" CJ still sounded irritated with me.

"I'll go find the card table for the Readings and use it as an excuse to mingle with the guests." It was a sign of how desperate I was to get answers that I was willing to network, given how terrible I was at it.

CHAPTER SEVENTEEN

CJ went to collect Noah while Em headed over to the dirt path that ran between the B&B and Rackhouse Saddlebreds.

I stepped outside but paused to take in my surroundings, so different from where I lived. Finally, feeling refreshed, I went around to the front of the B&B to go inside through the lobby to avoid interrupting the guests' lunch. The card table was right where Em had said it would be, hidden behind some hanging supplies in the hallway closet.

I carried it into the kitchen and found that all of the guests, other than the Hammetts, were still at the table, chatting and drinking coffee or tea and nibbling on cookies from a disposable tray that the take-out restaurant must have sent as a little bonus for the large order.

At my arrival, David Miller stood up and announced that he and his wife needed to return to their room to freshen up. "I need a shower after eating those ribs," he said. "Although it was totally worth it. The Lord has definitely filled this hungry person with good things today."

He wheeled his wife out of the room while Jonny Dell, at a look from his father, started clearing away the mess left from lunch, throwing out the trash and putting the reusable dishes and silverware in the sink.

I carried the card table over next to Shelly Reading. "Shall we go out on the veranda and set things up for bridge?"

"Not yet," she said. "There's no point. Jack and his son don't play, and the Hammetts are hiding—they insisted on eating lunch in their room, and Jonny took it up to them—so they won't have to admit they're afraid I'll trounce them again. If you want to put the table outside, just in case, that would be lovely, but I'm not holding my breath." She picked up her mug and waved it at me. "For now, I'm not done with my coffee, and it's too good to waste."

"Em is a real coffee aficionado, so she makes sure we have the best." I set the card table against the back wall, near the French doors to the veranda, and caught a glimpse of Candy outside in a wicker chair, scrolling on her phone. "I think I'll have some myself, and join you while I'm drinking it, if you don't mind me barging in on your conversation."

She and Jack both encouraged me to join them, so I filled a mug with decaf and settled in across from Shelly and next to Jack, who was at the head of the table.

"Have you heard from the sheriff about when we can leave?" Jack asked.

"Oh, no," Shelly interjected before I could answer. "You aren't leaving early, are you? I was hoping you'd still be here this evening for another entertaining and educational meal."

"Now that the inspection isn't a secret any longer, there's no real reason to stick around once the sheriff says we can leave," Jack said. "I'm not going to be able to relax here and enjoy myself with the shadow of Mark's death hanging over us, so I might as well get back home and take care of some work."

Shelly sighed deeply. "Leave it to Mark to ruin people's fun even after he's dead. I guess if everyone else is going to be depressed, then Candy and I might as well leave too as soon as we get the green light."

"We'd be happy to have you stay for the whole weekend, inspection or not," I said. "But I can understand why you'd want to leave. I'm sure the sheriff's office is doing their best, and you both told them everything you could think of that might be helpful."

They both nodded.

"Unless," I said, "maybe there's something you forgot to mention, and you thought of it later when it was too late. You can tell me, and I'll pass it along."

They looked at each other before shaking their heads.

"What about the meeting at the barbeque place before you came here?" I asked. "I didn't know about that until just a few minutes ago, and the sheriff's department might not either."

"Why would they want to know about our meeting at the restaurant?" Shelly asked. "It was hours before Mark died."

"It's still within the window for when Mr. Pleasant could

have suffered the injury that led to his death. He could have hit his head either there, or on the way here, and still been alert until he got on the bus to come back here after the tour."

"Really?" Shelly asked. "It could have happened that long before Mark died?"

"Up to four hours can pass between a head injury and death," I said, "and I'm told that your meeting ended about half an hour before you arrived here. That means he died almost exactly four hours after you were all getting ready to leave the restaurant."

"You think one of us attacked him at the restaurant?" Jack asked.

Candy came in from the veranda to refill her coffee mug. "Do we need alibis?" she asked, sounding more curious than worried.

"Not as far as I'm concerned," I lied, "but the sheriff will likely want to ask you about the meeting when he finds out about it."

"But we were all together the whole time," Jack said. "We can all alibi each other while we were at the restaurant, and none of us has any reason to lie for each other about this. It's one thing to go undercover to do a surprise inspection, but I wouldn't lie to cover up an assault by people I barely know." He turned to Shelly. "No offense intended to you or your daughter."

"No offense taken," Shelly said. "But a parent would lie to protect a child. You'd lie to protect Jonny, and I'd lie to protect Candy."

"Good thing that's not necessary," Jack said. "Jonny and I were together the whole time. Reminded me of when he was literally tied to my apron strings when he was a toddler. We haven't been out of each other's sight since we left home on Friday morning. And neither of us was alone with Mark at any point. I can confirm that categorically. I'm a little less certain about the others, but only a little. I can't recall any time when Mark was out of my sight at the restaurant, at the same time any of the other guests were also missing."

Candy gave her mother a questioning glance, and Shelly said, "My daughter and I may dress alike, but we aren't actually attached at the hip. We have our own lives. Even on vacation. I popped into the restaurant's gift shop briefly to get some barbeque sauce, and Candy was talking to Jonny about a possible future joint venture, so she didn't join me. I don't know where Mark was at the time."

"He left a couple times to go to the men's room," Candy said. "I can't recall if one of the absences was when you were in the gift shop or if anyone else left at the same time. I don't think so though. I just remember how everyone seemed to release a collective sigh of relief every time he left."

"That's my recollection too," Jack said. "And Mark seemed fine throughout the meal. No complaints of a headache or anything. He seemed full of his usual self-aggrandizing energy. So maybe he was attacked after we all left there, while he was on his way here. If that's what happened, I wouldn't have any way of knowing. We agreed to stagger our departures, so we wouldn't all arrive at the same time. Mark insisted on leaving first, and we didn't want to risk getting stuck behind him on the roads, so we waited in the parking lot for a full twenty minutes before leaving. By the time we arrived here, his car was parked out front and he was inside, getting registered."

Candy flopped down in the seat next to her mother. "Mark was a ridiculously slow driver."

"That's not an exaggeration," Jonny said from where he was handwashing the lunch dishes. "He always drove like an old man, but he's gotten even worse in the last year or two, ever since he retired, I guess. Like, he goes ten miles under the speed limit on a road where everyone goes well above it. I got stuck behind him once on the way to work for dinner service after visiting some friends in Lexington, and there was nowhere to pass." He gave his father an annoyed look. "Dad docked me for being late, even though it really wasn't my fault."

"I used to date one of his tour bus drivers," Candy said. "They hated how Mark would always be looking over their shoulder at the speedometer, complaining if they went even half a mile over the speed limit. Apparently, he was obsessed with keeping his insurance from getting any more expensive."

Shelly had been staring at her coffee mug thoughtfully but seemed to come to a decision. She looked up and said, "The reason he'd gotten worse recently was because he had a stroke. He probably shouldn't have been allowed to drive at all, but I'm sorry to say I didn't have the courage to report him to his insurer, and apparently no one else did either. I might be the only person who knew about it. He probably realized he'd lose his license if he got a ticket or was in an accident, so he overcompensated by going extra slow."

"I'm surprised he didn't get noticed by the cops anyway," Candy said. "He creates ten-car parades on the local roads where there's nowhere to pass. We got stuck behind him on the way over here from the restaurant, even though we left about five minutes after he did."

"That's why I told Dad to stop at the convenience store on the way," Jonny said. "I was afraid we'd catch up to him. A twenty-minute head start would have been enough for anyone else, but not for Mark."

"He could have stopped there too," I said, "and that would have thrown off your plan to avoid him."

"He didn't though, at least not when we were there," Jack said. "We were the only customers."

"We can vouch for that," Shelly said. "We were directly behind Mark almost the whole, never-ending trip over here, and he didn't stop once."

Candy added, "Unless you count the stop signs. There was hardly ever anyone in the intersection, but he'd still just sit there and wait forever, as if there was some rule about counting to a hundred before proceeding."

"I was so tempted to go around him while he sat at the first one, looking for nonexistent traffic," Shelly said. "But with my luck, I figured there'd be a cop hidden somewhere nearby, and I'd get a ticket while he sailed on oblivious to the chaos he'd provoked, just like he always was. So I distracted myself with thoughts of how lovely this weekend would be and held on to my patience while riding his tail all the way to Rackhouse Saddlebreds. I pulled over by the side of the road there to enjoy the view of the pastures for a few minutes and regain my calm."

It was theoretically possible that Mark had been assaulted by a stranger in the few hundred yards Mark had traveled between where the Readings had pulled to the side of the road and when he'd presented himself inside the B&B. Not very likely though.

Besides, if the Readings had been parked on the side of the road in front of Rackhouse Saddlebreds, I thought they would have also had a relatively clear line of sight to the driveway and front yard of the B&B. Would a killer have taken the risk of assaulting Mark out where passersby would be able to witness their interaction? I doubted it, especially since, no matter how unsuccessful the prior attempts on Mark's life had been, the perpetrator had at least taken enough care to avoid attracting any witnesses.

Bottom line, I felt reasonably comfortable ruling out the possibility that Mark's injury had involved an encounter with a stranger, somewhere between the restaurant and the B&B. I was equally convinced that it hadn't happened at the barrel factory either. Which meant that the killer almost certainly had to be one of the B&B's guests.

* * *

Jonny finished tidying up after the meal and returned to the table to stand behind his father, radiating impatience.

Jack rose and said, "Sorry we can't be more helpful. If you'll excuse us, we need to check in at the restaurant to make sure everything is running smoothly."

They left and I heard the front door open and close, suggesting the two men had gone out to the front porch to make their call.

Shelly said, "Aren't they a lovely family? Too bad you never met Mrs. Dell. She was lovely too."

"The perfect family," Candy said in a wry tone, suggesting she didn't believe it. "Makes me wonder what they're like when no one is looking. People don't always match their public image. Just ask Mother."

Shelly gave her daughter an irritated look, and Candy said, "Don't mind me. You'd think Mother would be the cynical one in the family, not me, but I've always expected the worst from people."

I would have liked to know why Candy thought the Dells might not be as perfect as they seemed, but it was clear that she wasn't going to say anything more while her mother was present. I'd already planned to find a way to talk to her alone later, but now I wanted to ask her about the Dells, as well as how badly Mark had treated her mother after the divorce.

Shelly stood. "Looks like the Hammetts aren't going to show themselves any time soon. Might as well go out on the veranda while we wait for an update from the sheriff. It's too lovely outside to stay in our rooms. Is it okay if we take our mugs out there with us?"

"Of course."

"Thanks," she said. "And perhaps we could set up the card table after all, just in case the Hammetts are brave enough to show their faces. I'm looking forward to clobbering the condescending brats again. Maybe I'll even suggest we switch to poker. I bet they think they're good at that too. And we can make them really suffer by taking all their—"

I interrupted before she could finish the sentence. "I don't want to hear about any illegal gambling on the B&B's premises."

"We would never do anything illegal," Shelly said smoothly. "I was just going to say we'd take away all their claims to being decent card players."

Yeah, right. There was definitely going to be illegal gambling on the B&B's veranda if the Hammetts showed up, I thought. But as long as they weren't too obvious about it, I was fine with the prospect of the arrogant twins getting a bit of a comeuppance. I doubted even the deputy sheriff would care about some not-so-friendly games of poker if it kept the guests from leaving.

"Then don't tell anyone I said this, because I really shouldn't be picking favorites among the guests, but I hope you take the twins for every bit of ego they possess."

"We will," Shelly said, and Candy, sounding more enthusiastic about poker than she'd seemed to be about bridge, added, "They won't even know what hit them."

My amusement evaporated as her phrasing made me wonder if Mark had seen what or, more accurately, *who* had hit him.

CHAPTER EIGHTEEN

I got the table set up for bridge and then headed back to the closet where it had been stored to collect some folding chairs. As I approached the closet in the hallway, the Millers emerged from their room, with Tanya talking in an urgent but low tone that prevented me from hearing the words. She didn't seem to notice me, but David apparently did since he stopped in the doorway and tapped her on the shoulder to get her attention. She stopped talking and looked at me.

"I didn't mean to startle you." I gestured at the nearby closet door. "Just grabbing some chairs for the card players."

"We were just in our own little bubble," David said. "We got used to how quiet and private it is over here. You've done a really nice job setting up this space, so it feels very homey and still has all the extra amenities Tanya could possibly want."

"Thank you." I made a note to pass the compliment along to my sisters, the ones who deserved the praise. "As long as I'm here, do you need anything?"

"Actually," Tanya said, "we were going to ask if you thought the sheriff would mind if we went next door to the horse farm for a while, as long as we don't go any farther."

"I don't see why it would be a problem. You could be back here in just a few minutes if he has more questions for you."

"The thing is," David explained, "we'd need to take the van because the path between here and there isn't really ideal for traveling by wheelchair. And we don't want it to look like we're trying to run off or something."

I hesitated, not sure I was the right person to ask.

Tanya hurried to add, "You'll be able to see our van the whole time we're gone. We'll make sure to park out front where it's visible, not on the far side of the farm where the main lot is. I still have some family privileges, and now seems like a good time to take advantage of them."

"Perhaps you should check with the deputy first," I suggested. "I have his number in my phone."

David squeezed Tanya's shoulder. "Never mind," he said. "We can go back out by the fence and appreciate the view from there."

"We wouldn't want to interrupt the deputy when he's got more important things to deal with than my homesickness," Tanya said. "I can wait a little longer to go over to the farm. Surely the preliminary work will be done soon, so they'll know there's nothing more we can add to what we've already told them."

"There is one thing you might not have discussed with him," I said. "I just heard that all of you—including Mark—met at a restaurant before coming over here, and that's within the window for when his injury could have occurred. I expect the police will want to trace everyone's movements from then to the time he died."

Tanya glanced over her shoulder at David as if seeking reassurance. Was her anxiety just about the delay in visiting the horse farm or about something more serious?

"We thought they were focused on the hour or so before Mark died," David said. "The deputy didn't ask us anything about the meeting during our interview. Or about what happened during the drive here."

"Should he have asked?" I said. "Did you notice anything he needs to know about?"

"I didn't mean it that way," David said. "I was just surprised by the timeframe. I hope the deputy isn't detaining us just so he can ask about what happened before we arrived here. If anything happened to Mark when he first got to the restaurant or on the drive here, we wouldn't know. The place wasn't as accessible as the owners claim, so we had to go the long way around to get to and from the room where we ate. It made us a few minutes late, so we were the last to arrive, and then we had to use that alternate route to leave, and no one came with us. So we can't tell the police anything that the others didn't also witness."

Tanya added, "All I know is that Mark seemed his usual annoying self during the meeting. It's hard to imagine he'd suffered a serious injury before or during the meal, given the way he dominated the conversation. He spent a good fifteen minutes explaining to the whole group why I should never have been asked to do the inspection since I'm in a wheelchair. He acted like he thought he was a stand-up comedian, there to entertain us. He wasn't funny, but I'll give him points for being energetic, jumping up from time to time to do an impression of how clumsy I am with my wheelchair."

Mark really had been a piece of work, I thought. Not that it would justify killing him. But it meant there was an almost endless supply of people who might have hated him enough to attack him, if not necessarily to kill him.

"What about on the drive here after he left the restaurant?" The Readings had said he hadn't stopped on the way, but they could have lied, especially if they were covering up the fact that one of them had been the one to cause Mark's fatal injury.

"We didn't see him leave since we had to take a detour to get out of the restaurant," Tanya said. "And then, well, I was seriously considering dropping out of the inspection, so I wouldn't have to spend the weekend around Mark. We sat in the van and discussed it for a while, before David convinced me to give it a chance, and promised we'd leave the next time he insulted me. It took rather a long time to get to that decision, so we left well after the others. I didn't see any of them on the road, as best I can recall. Of course, as a passenger, I don't pay all that much attention."

"No, you're right," David said. "I didn't see any of the others along the way either, and I was paying attention."

"There's really only one place any of them might have stopped," Tanya said. "There's a convenience store about halfway here, and the rest is all farmland. But I think he got banned from there a couple years ago for being a jerk."

"I wouldn't put it past him to ignore a ban," David said, "but I doubt he stopped anywhere along the way. He drove like a little old lady, so if he'd stopped, even for just a few minutes, some of the other guests would have arrived before him, and I heard he was the first to check in."

"He's lucky he drove so slow, actually," Tanya said. "I don't know if you heard, but someone tried to run him off the road a little while ago. He probably would have been hurt a lot worse than he was, except he was going so slowly that the impact was pretty minor."

"Where did you hear about the incident?" It seemed odd that she'd known about it. Who would have told her? Not Mark, and not the police who'd dismissed it out of hand. The only other person who would have known about it was the person who had tried to run Mark off the road. But would the Millers have risked their specially equipped van to get rid of him? Or did they have another, less expensive and less identifiable vehicle they could have used, one that David drove when the van wasn't needed?

"I hear lots of things at work," Tanya said. "Both in the courtroom and in the hallways. When it's hearsay and ex parte, I do my best to forget both the information and who gave it to me. I seem to have succeeded in forgetting who told me about Mark's police report, even if I couldn't forget about the incident itself."

"Do you have any idea why someone might have tried running Mark off the road?" I asked. "Because you seem to believe it really happened and aren't dismissing it as just an accident, like the police apparently did."

"Perhaps I was more inclined to believe because I was aware of how disliked Mark was by the local business community," Tanya said. "Mark did a lot of unsavory things, from what I've heard."

"So you knew about his history of soliciting bribes?"

"Not firsthand, but yes, I heard enough complaints that I came to believe it was true, even if it couldn't be proven in a court of law."

David nodded. "I heard about it too. We don't visit the farm so often any more, but back when we did, there were stories about how Mark would bring his tours there, always with his hand out, backed up with threats to divert the visitors to other horse-related businesses if his demands weren't met."

"It was never anything worth killing over," Tanya added quickly. "The farm could afford to pay him if we'd wanted to, but it wasn't necessary. He benefited more from the tours than we did. I mean, I was glad when he retired, so he wouldn't harass us any longer, but I didn't want him dead then or now if that's what you're thinking. I don't have the time or energy to hold a grudge."

"You're a better person than I am," I said lightly. If anyone tried to hurt the B&B, which would hurt my sisters and nephew, I would go to my grave holding a grudge against that person. Maybe not to the point of murder, but I wouldn't be as calm about it as Tanya appeared to be. Perhaps why she was more suited to be a judge than I was. "I'm sorry to have brought up unpleasant memories. I should let you enjoy the lovely spring weather."

"The horses seemed to appreciate the sunshine this morning," Tanya said, and I could hear the yearning in her voice to get a closer view of the animals.

I reached for the closet door. "You know, now that I've thought about it some more, I think it would be fine if you go ahead and drive next door for the afternoon. You can blame me if the deputy doesn't like it. Tell him I encouraged you to go, and that I was watching to be sure your van was parked out front the whole time."

The longing on Tanya's face turned to anticipation, but before she or David could respond, I heard someone in the lobby demanding to know where the owners were.

* * *

"Enjoy your visit to the farm," I told the Millers and hurried in the direction of the drunken-sounding commotion. Collecting the folding chairs could wait.

"There you are," Beck said. At least, the sneer on his face and the loudness of his growl suggested it was him, not his twin. "We've been waiting for service for hours. Guess it's a good thing we're not going to be filing a report on our stay, huh?"

"Good thing," I agreed cheerfully, which seemed to confuse him. He didn't scare me. I had plenty of practice mollifying probate court judges who were more abusive than he was, and unlike him, they had the power to put me in jail for contempt if I said the wrong thing. Besides, I suspected that an unreasonable, nitpicky report from the Hammetts would actually reflect worse on them than on the B&B and might even lead to reconsideration of the decision to let them be a member of the tourism co-op. "What can I do for you?"

"Shelly Reading is hiding from us, so we can't show her how real winners play bridge," Beck said.

Benn added, "We tried knocking on her door, and either she's not there or she's stone deaf."

"Did you look on the veranda out back? She was planning

to take a walk and then wait for you to join her out there," I said. "I was getting some chairs for the card table when you interrupted me."

"Well, hurry up." Beck headed for the kitchen to access the veranda.

Benn followed for a few steps, then stopped to say, "I assume you'll come find us when the deputy finally realizes he's wasting our time and lets us leave."

"That could be awhile," I said. "The sheriff's office is small, and they have to cover a lot of ground looking for witnesses and suspects. I believe they're currently checking out what happened at the restaurant where you all met before coming over here." Or they would be, once they learned about it.

Beck, who had stopped as soon as his brother spoke, snarled, "That's stupid. The meeting had nothing to do with the guy's death hours later. They should be looking at what happened at the barrel factory. The management there was pretty incompetent. I wouldn't be surprised if people get hurt there on a daily basis."

I bristled at his criticism of Reed but didn't rise to the bait. Especially since I didn't really know Reed well enough to have formed an evidence-based opinion of his management style.

"The police have to consider all the possibilities. It's at least theoretically possible that Mr. Pleasant was injured around the time of the meeting at the restaurant and didn't succumb until later," I said. "Perhaps you saw something useful at the restaurant, and it would speed up the investigation if the police knew about it. Just think how great it would be for your local reputation if you're the ones who provide the key to identifying and convicting a murderer."

That seemed to get their attention. Their faces lit up with enthusiasm, and Beck came back to stand next to his brother. "Is there a reward?"

Of course he'd want money for doing the right thing.

But it was still a little surprising that he was so eager to help. He and Benn were the guests I would most like to see dragged away in handcuffs, but his interest in getting a reward, which would only be paid if the culprit was convicted, seemed genuine. Did that mean he and his brother were innocent of the crime, or were they were truly sociopathic and would manufacture evidence to convict an innocent person just to get a reward?

Unfortunately, both scenarios struck me as equally likely.

"I haven't heard of a reward," I said, "but the sooner the sheriff has a solid lead, the sooner they'll let you go home. I would think that would be incentive enough, considering how much you want to leave."

Beck shrugged. "We can wait a little longer. More time to revel in wiping the smirk off the old biddy's face when we show her how real players play the game."

"Besides," Benn said, "We don't know anything useful for the investigation. We never met Mark before we gathered at the restaurant, so we couldn't say if he'd been acting strangely then, due to an injury. He seemed as normal as anyone in this hick town. We had some business calls to make after the meeting broke up, so we headed over to the bar to take care of our work and then reward ourselves with a drink. We left well after everyone else, so we didn't see any of them on the way here."

"You know," Beck said with an unusually thoughtful expression on his face. "Maybe we did see something that could get us the reward. I'd forgotten about it until now, but right after everyone left the table, the lady in the wheelchair and her husband started to go in the wrong direction for the exit. The dead guy went over to redirect them, but they didn't appreciate his help. Acted like they wanted to punch him, except they knew we were watching, so they had to be polite."

Benn nodded. "That's right. The wheelchair lady kept gesturing for him to go away, and it really did look like if she weren't crippled, she'd have taken a swing at him. Might have anyway, except her husband was hovering over her like a nanny, a hand on her shoulder, keeping her in place. But we couldn't actually hear what they were saying."

"More like we didn't care what they were saying," Beck said, grabbing his brother by the arm and tugging him a step toward the kitchen. "Come on. We've said our piece, and she can pass it along to the cops. After she gets the chairs."

Benn gave me what I thought was an apologetic look and then let himself get dragged away. He ruined his impression of a decent human being by looking over his shoulder and saying, "Well? Why aren't you getting the chairs?"

Maybe it wouldn't be so bad if an innocent person—or an

identical pair of them—was blamed for a crime they hadn't committed. Especially when they'd probably gotten away with plenty of other crimes before now. I knew full well that the legal system seldom handed out poetic justice, but I could dream.

CHAPTER NINETEEN

I grabbed four folding chairs from the closet and took them out to the veranda where the Hammetts and Shelly Reading were talking trash to each other. Candy stayed out of it. Despite being in her thirties, her expression and body language looked like those of a teenager, who was forced to spend time with her parents in public and thought everything they did was embarrassing.

I invited her into the kitchen to help me collect some beverages, and she agreed with obvious relief. While I collected glasses and napkins, and Candy inspected the beverage options in the commercial refrigerator, I asked, "Don't you like bridge?"

She shrugged. "It's okay. I'm just not as cut-throat as Mother is. She has a couple other partners for competitions, so I only play when there's no other option."

"You must be a good player since you helped to beat the Hammetts."

She shrugged. "They're not very good. Just enough to make it interesting for Mother. And we got a bit lucky last night with good hands." She settled on a can of ginger ale, along with the pitcher of sweet tea. "Do you have lemons?"

"Of course." I grabbed one from a basket on the counter and prepared to slice it. "I didn't really ask you in here to help. I'd been wondering about something from earlier, when your mother said she didn't mind being forced to sell the B&B. It looked like you didn't agree."

"She definitely minded, but she's always been practical too, and that leads her to put a good face on things she can't change. She tried really hard to get past all the things Mark did to hurt her, even the forced sale of the B&B, but he would never let the subject drop, so the pain kept coming to the surface again. Every time he saw her, he had to remind her that he'd gotten half the proceeds from her beloved B&B, and she'd gotten nothing he cared about. Nothing at all, really."

"That doesn't seem fair."

"Mark didn't exist in a fair universe. I mean, I understand why the judge might have thought selling the B&B was the right thing to do. After all, Mark didn't have any assets to divide—the tour company barely broke even and didn't have any vehicles or equipment that could be sold. He claimed he'd worked, unpaid, at the B&B throughout the marriage, which was a lie, but there was no way to prove he was lying."

"It's very hard to prove a negative." I'd tried, unsuccessfully, to do it a number of times when heirs had lied about having spent a lot of time caring for a sick relative in return for the promise of an extra share of the estate. "Like trying to prove that Mark couldn't have been injured either at the restaurant or on the trip here. It would be really useful if the sheriff could be sure nothing happened to him before he checked in here."

"I wish I could help, but all I can tell you is that Mother and I were together all the time, except for the few minutes when she did some shopping, and I stayed with the rest of the group. Including Mark. I made sure he never got the chance to be alone with Mother, not because I thought she'd kill him, but because I was afraid he'd hurt her. Emotionally, not physically. And she'd just let him do it." She smiled wryly. "Of course, you only have my word for it, and she's my mother, and we're best friends too most of the time. I would definitely lie to protect her if she'd killed someone who deserved it as much as Mark did."

I thought I'd probably do the same if I suspected one of my sisters had killed Mark. Which was why we needed extremely persuasive evidence against the actual culprit, or no one would believe us.

"So who do you think killed Mark?" I asked.

"I hate to say it because the other guests are so nice, but it's got to be one of them." She laughed. "Well, the Dells and the Millers are nice, not the Hammetts. But the thing is, they all spent some time alone with Mark on Friday, either at the restaurant or on the tour. It was like he had set out to use this weekend to harass each and every one of us. He tried with Mother, but I blocked him, so he moved on to the others. I saw him catch the Millers at the restaurant when they were trying to leave after lunch. And he argued with the Dells in the parking lot."

"What about the Hammetts?"

"I'm not totally sure where that confrontation happened," Candy said. "But I made a point of keeping an eye on where Mark was, so I could steer Mother in a different direction. There were a couple times I didn't see him anywhere, and the Hammetts were missing then too."

Not exactly overwhelming evidence of their guilt, but it didn't absolve them either. "There's just one thing I really don't understand. If things were so bad between your mother and Mark, why did you let her do this weekend's inspection when he was part of the team? And why would she even want to?"

"We didn't know he'd be part of it until we got to the restaurant. I don't think anyone else did either. We weren't given the other names, just told to meet up at the barbeque place, and tell the maître d' that we were there for the co-op's meeting. He was the last to arrive, except for the Millers, and I remember looking around the room and thinking that he must have felt like he'd been ambushed when he saw who was waiting for him. Except of course, he didn't have that kind of self-awareness. But it left me wondering if someone had intentionally chosen the people who hated him the most to work with him on the inspection."

"Even the Hammetts?" I said. "They said they hadn't even met him before Friday."

Candy raised her eyebrows. "They're lying. Mother and I were seated across from the Hammetts when Mark arrived. The door was behind us, so I didn't see him at first, just the matching furious expression on the twins' faces. One of them grumbled, "Oh, hell, not him," so I turned around to look, and it was Mark. Probably the only time all weekend that I've agreed with the twins. *Oh, hell, not him* was my reaction too."

"From what I've heard, that was everyone's reaction, once they got to know him." I filled a small glass bowl with lemon slices, taking my time to make them look pretty, so I'd have an excuse to delay taking them outside. "So anyone chosen for the inspection team would hate him."

"But no one hated Mark as much as the people sent to inspect the B&B," Candy said. "I don't know the details of the Hammetts' experience with him, but they could have been included because of the way, as we've seen, they'll lash out at the least little provocation. The rest of us aren't as hotheaded, but we all hated Mark, deeply and intensely, and with good reason. Everyone knows that Mother's divorce was bitter, so it would be easy to guess that there would be fireworks if she was forced to work with him for a whole weekend."

"What about the others?" I asked, fidgeting unnecessarily with the lemons. "Why do they hate Mark so much?"

"You know Tanya is part of the family that owns Rackhouse Saddlebreds, right?"

I nodded.

"Well." She glanced at the French doors, closed between us and the veranda. "Did you know that Mark slipped and fell while doing a tour there? Or at least he claimed he did and filed a lawsuit against them. It got settled by their insurer for a fairly small sum, but Tanya always thought he'd lied about it all and should have been charged with fraud. Then there was the incident at the restaurant where the Dells work. I don't know the details, but there was some kind of scuffle, and he got permanently banned. Then he went to the press and claimed to have been kicked out because he had insulted the Dells' cooking. I doubt anyone believed him, but I heard that the restaurant's owner had considered firing the son, and if anything could make Jack Dell see red, it's a threat against his family."

"I didn't know Mark well, but I can't help thinking there must be other people who hated him just as much as the Dells and the Millers," I said. "Wouldn't you have been able to come up with examples of problems with just about anyone else around here who'd been forced to work with Mark?"

"I can't think of any," Candy said. "I mean, everyone disliked him but most tolerated him."

"What about Reed Hill?" My sisters were convinced he was a good guy, and I wanted to believe it, but I couldn't risk the B&B's future without being absolutely sure about Reed. "Do you know if he's had any issues with Mark in the past?"

"Not that I'm aware of," she said. "Well, I know that Mark tried something once at a political fundraiser, and Reed just laughed at him for being such an idiot. The story went around town, and it was so humiliating to Mark that even he noticed that he'd been put in his place. I could imagine Mark wanting revenge against Reed, but not the other way around."

That fit with the two men's personalities to the extent I'd been able to observe them. But then it struck me that I might be agreeing a little easily. Candy was telling me pretty much exactly what I wanted to hear—that the Hammetts, whom I disliked, had lied about knowing Mark and never being alone with him, making them solid suspects, and that Reed Hill, whom I liked, was much less likely to be a killer.

Given that she was reinforcing what I wanted to be true, perhaps I should be looking for holes in what she said. After all, Candy could simply be spinning the story that she thought would keep me and, more importantly, the sheriff from looking too closely at her mother's motive and opportunity.

Before I could think of a follow-up question, Beck's loud, irritated voice reached us through the kitchen windows. "Where's our drinks?"

My host duties had to take precedence over the murder investigation.

*   *   *

Once the bridge players had their drinks and their fourth player, Candy, I headed for the owners' quarters to see what my sisters might have learned. On the way, I remembered I was supposed to be keeping an eye on the Millers' visit next door, so I could vouch for them. I detoured briefly over to the fence to confirm that I could indeed see their van parked in plain sight in the driveway of Rackhouse Saddlebreds.

Reassured that they hadn't made a run for it, I continued over to check in with Em and CJ. Noah was napping in his bunk bed while my sisters had settled on a pair of trunks about ten feet from the front door and were staring at their phones. The last time I'd seen them both looking that dejected was when they'd found a stray kitten, and our parents had told them they couldn't keep it since they'd already adopted the three previous ones they'd brought home. I'd found it a good home, and somehow, I'd become the bad guy for giving it a loving family while my sisters had still harbored hopes of being able to win my parents over and keep it. Not unlike the way they were probably going to blame me for the current mess if our investigation wasn't any more successful than the sheriff's.

I closed the door behind me, startling them out of their

despondent distraction. "So you haven't learned anything useful?"

CJ set her phone down on the trunk beside her. "It's like the whole town is shunning us. No one will even answer my calls."

"Or mine," Em said, "I don't think they're mad at us exactly. They just don't want to get involved."

"The only person who'll talk to me is Lucas, the shuttle driver," CJ said. "And all he's got is bad news. He's worried the bus company will blame him for Mark's death, so he's been trying to find out the status of the official investigation. He's got cousins in the state police force, and they're all telling him they're getting shut out of the investigation by the sheriff, who wants to run everything himself, even though he doesn't have the right resources to do it. Lucas thinks the case will go cold, and all the evidence will be mucked up before the sheriff admits he isn't up to the investigation and calls in the state police. Then it will be too late for the truly qualified officers to do anything."

Em added, "Leaving the case unsolved is almost as bad for us as getting charged with murder. Either way, people will think we did it, and no one wants to stay at a B&B that's even distantly associated with death, especially of the intentional kind. Unless it's the Lizzie Borden house, I suppose, but I'd rather not go all gothic with this place."

"Definitely not gothic," CJ said. "Noah's got enough challenges already without growing up in shadows."

Em said, "That's not going to happen," and then turned to me. "I'm sure Jess has some new information that will crack the case wide open."

"Not really." This conversation was likely to take awhile, and there weren't any other convenient trunks to use as a chair, so I dropped down to sit on the floor in front of them. "Candy had an interesting observation though. She said that when she got to the restaurant and saw who else was on the inspection team, it felt like someone had gathered all of Mark's worst enemies in one room. She didn't go so far as to say it was intentional, but what if it was? That person would have to be one of the guests since they'd want to see how their little scheme worked out."

"I can see someone doing it as a prank," Em said, "but we're talking about a murder here."

"Things could have gotten out of hand," I said. "Whoever

set it up could have just wanted to see Mark squirm. They could have thought that people who hated him intensely, but were forced to pretend they didn't even know him, would still have made the weekend miserable for him. Not just a single quick confrontation, but over and over again for forty-eight hours. Except someone snapped and killed him."

"Okay," Em said, "but you'd have to hate someone a lot to go to all that trouble, even if it was just supposed to be a prank. And you'd have to not care about the collateral damage. Mark wasn't the only one who would suffer from the forced proximity to his enemies. The other guests would suffer too. And us."

"It's the only theory that makes sense," I said. "I've confirmed with multiple sources that Mark didn't stop along the trip here, so it had to have happened either at the restaurant or here or at Hills' Barrels. It defies logic to think that some other enemy of his just happened to run into him when he was surrounded by other people who hated him, and that stranger managed to attack him without anyone else noticing. Our guests all have motives, and they all had the opportunity to attack him. I've confirmed that each pair was alone with Mark at some point on Friday, even if they've all denied it. There isn't really a murder weapon, per se, since he most likely hit his head on something during a scuffle. The killer didn't need to bring a weapon with them or dispose of anything afterward, like a gun or knife or poison."

"Even if we narrow down the options to the three pairs of guests, that's not good enough," CJ said despairingly. "Unless we can pin it on one of them definitively, we're going to lose the B&B and ruin Noah's future."

"I'm not giving up," I said. "If it's true that someone set this up, putting Mark into a fraught situation with his enemies, then we need to know who picked the inspection team. Do either of you know anyone at the tourism co-op who could tell you how the judges were chosen?"

Em answered, "We don't know anyone there personally. We could call the office, but it's Saturday, so it's closed. The association only has a few office hours on Tuesdays and Thursdays. The rest of the time, you can only leave a voicemail message, which is eventually checked by someone on the board. But not on Fridays or weekends when, not surprisingly, everyone is extra busy working with tourists."

"Then I think we're done with asking questions of the guests and trying to figure out who's lying," I said. "I think it's time to get proactive."

CJ gave me a suspicious look. "Proactive how? We can't go violating our guests' privacy by snooping in their rooms."

Em snorted. "I'm pretty sure Jess has already done that. There's no way Taylor got into a room upstairs on her own, and she's good about avoiding guests who might not appreciate her presence. If you saw her in a room, Taylor must have followed you into it, Jess. Probably thought you were the housekeeper we hire occasionally, who keeps cat treats in her pocket."

I started to explain why it had been necessary to inspect the rooms, but Em held up a hand. "I'd really rather not know for sure. The only thing the instructors emphasized in our training more than thinking of our guests as family was that we should never, ever violate the rules of hospitality, or we'd be cursed forever."

CJ jumped to her feet. "I knew this was a mistake. Ever since you got here, Jess, things keep getting worse. When the tourism co-op finds out we breached our innkeeper's oath, we'll be banned forever."

"You didn't do it," I reminded her. "I did, and I'm not really an innkeeper. Besides, I didn't do anything too invasive, just checked the rooms in case there was anything obviously incriminating that they'd left out where housekeeping could see it. Something they'd known could happen. And I intentionally didn't tell you about it, so you'd have plausible deniability. If anyone finds out after I've gone back to DC, you can tell people you kicked me out of the B&B partnership when you found out what I'd done, so it will never happen again."

There was a long silence while CJ paced and Em looked down, presumably considering whether to accept my explanation.

"I'm not the only one keeping secrets," I said. "You two haven't exactly been honest with me. You made it sound like the odds were against your passing the inspection without my help, but Reed said that almost all the applicants to join the co-op pass the inspection. You must have discussed it with him when you applied, so you'd have known the odds were heavily in your favor."

CJ kept pacing, and if it was possible to stomp quietly,

that was what she was doing.

Em shrugged. "We might have exaggerated a little. Sure, it was likely we'd pass the inspection, but it wasn't a guarantee. Even if only one percent of applicants were rejected, it was still too much of a risk when Noah's future is on the line."

CJ finally flopped down on her trunk again. "Okay, so we're all big, fat liars. But we still have to work together and somehow trust each other for the rest of the weekend."

Em sighed. "We all had good reasons for what we've done. But the truth has come out now. No point in dwelling on past mistakes. We need to move forward to identify the killer. But how?"

Both sisters looked at me expectantly.

"I have an idea," I said. "I'm not sure you'll like it because it involves treating our guests like the enemy."

"No more invasion of privacy though, right?" CJ said, still unwilling to drop the issue. "Because I won't risk doing any more damage to the B&B's reputation."

"Does lying to them count as invasion of privacy?"

CJ cheered up. "No, that's fine. It's practically required for any kind of work with the public. In a benevolent sort of way, like when you tell someone you love their ugly sweater."

"All right," I said. "So what we need to do is—"

Just then, Beck barged through the front door of our private quarters to say, "Deputy Dawg is here and looking for you. And he's not happy."

CHAPTER TWENTY

Em stayed behind to keep an eye on Noah, who somehow managed to sleep through Beck's loud insistence that all three of the owners had to come back to the B&B, or the deputy would blame him for not getting everyone.

"I'll explain," I said, and CJ and I headed out, leaving Beck to follow. I expected to find the Readings on the veranda, but it was unoccupied, the table and chairs overturned. It seemed unlikely that the deputy would have engaged in a scuffle to get everyone inside, so the upheaval was more likely the result of a poor loser's temper tantrum. And I knew which set of bridge partners was the more likely to behave childishly if they lost. But it didn't tell me where the Readings and Beck's brother had gone. "Where is everyone?"

"The lobby, of course," Beck snapped before trotting off ahead of us, as if he thought a few seconds' difference would matter.

I could feel CJ was tempted to race him—she could never turn down a dare—but she'd matured enough to keep her pace down to a quick walk that my shorter legs could keep up with. Inside, we found that all of the guests except the Millers, who were presumably still next door at the horse farm, had indeed assembled in the lobby. The Dells were leaning against the front desk, engaged in a whispered but decidedly annoyed conversation with Benn Hammett, while the Readings were seated next to each other on the sofa, with Shelly looking happily smug, confirming that she had not been on the losing end of the card games. Deputy Shurette stood just inside the front door, effectively blocking the exit closest to the parking lot, although I wasn't sure if he was doing it intentionally.

Beck announced, "The B&B's owners are here now. Except the one babysitting the brat." He flopped onto a wing chair while his brother hurried over to sit in the one next to it. "Let's do this, so we can all leave and get on with our lives."

The deputy ignored him and turned to me. "Isn't there supposed to be another pair of guests? The woman in a wheelchair and her husband?"

"They're next door, visiting family," I said. "I can get them if you'd like."

"No, that's all right," he said. "I'll stop by there when I leave."

"Hey," said Beck. "How come they got to leave and no one else did?"

I decided the deputy had the right idea for dealing with the brothers and just ignored Beck's question. Instead, I asked the deputy, "So, how is the investigation going?"

For a moment, his face revealed frustration. "I can't release any information yet." He turned to address the guests in the lobby. "But on behalf of the sheriff's department, I'd like to thank you all for your patience and cooperation. We were finally able to organize a forensics team to inspect the shuttle bus and the decedent's room. They'll be here in a few minutes, and they'll also be taking fingerprints from all of you."

The Hammett brothers exchanged a few words in a tone that was too low for me to hear, and then Beck demanded, "Why are you treating us like suspects? We're just witnesses. Not that we saw anything useful."

"The prints are just for elimination purposes, and we'll destroy them when the case is closed."

Unfortunately, I thought, at this rate, the case might never be closed.

Jack Dell said, "Knock it off, Beck. The deputy's just doing his job, and the sooner he finishes, the sooner we can leave. My son and I have nothing to hide, so we'll go first."

"Thank you," Shurette said. "We'll set up a fingerprinting station on the front porch as soon as the forensics team gets here."

Shelly said, "This is exciting, being in the middle of a real live CSI scene."

Candy muttered, "Except with our luck, we'll end up being the killer's next victim rather than the exonerated suspect."

Shurette ignored them too. "Thank you all again. We'll try to make this as quick and easy as possible for you. You'll be glad to know that we have digital printing systems, so you don't have to worry about getting ink all over your fingers."

"If we let you take our prints," Benn said, sounding reluctant but not as confrontational as his brother, "then can we leave?"

"You were planning to spend the whole weekend here anyway, from what I've been told," Shurette said. "So we'd appreciate it if you'd stick to the original plan. We'll have a preliminary report from forensics by noon tomorrow, and until then, we want to be sure we can reach you if we have any follow-up questions. If you insist on leaving, we can't stop you, but it will raise some questions in our minds about why you felt the need to leave ahead of schedule."

The Hammett brothers exchanged glances, and then Benn shrugged. "For the record, we think you're wasting our time, but I suppose we can get some work done in our room. The wi-fi here is adequate."

"But we expect to leave on the dot of noon tomorrow if not sooner," Beck added. "That's when check-out is, and I'm not paying any surcharges. Or sitting in my car while you guys figure out how to do your job."

"We might need an extra hour or two after we get the report," Shurette said. "We'll need time to process it and make sure we know where our investigation is leading us. Then you'll be able to go home."

CJ offered, "We can extend check-out to two p.m. No charge, given the circumstances. I'm sure everyone wants to help the police close this case, including us, and we're all willing to make some small sacrifices along the way."

No one else raised any objections, so I had a clear deadline for my own investigation. I had roughly twenty hours to unmask the killer. And a solid half of that time was at night when I was fairly sure my sisters would insist that the guests couldn't be disturbed for fear of violating their innkeeper's oath.

It was probably a good thing that at least one of us wasn't a real innkeeper. My oath of fealty was to the Constitution and state laws, not to any rules of hospitality.

* * *

Deputy Shurette ended the meeting by thanking everyone

for their time and then saying, "Now, if you'll excuse me, I'd like to talk to the sisters in private."

That didn't sound good. Until then, I'd gotten the impression that everything was going smoothly from his point of view, but his need to speak with us seemed to contradict his reassurances to the guests.

"Let's go into the kitchen," I suggested. "I don't know about you, Deputy, but I could use a drink. Would you like something? We have sweet tea and soft drinks in the fridge."

"No, thank you," he said stiffly. "This won't take long. I just wanted to thank you for your cooperation and ask one more thing of you."

"You want to print us for elimination purposes." I'd been expecting that request and had even run through my options. I wasn't a criminal defense lawyer, but I knew that prints, taken with a promise to destroy them later, tended to linger in the system. Mine were already on record somewhere, taken as part of the bar examination process. I was more concerned about my sisters' prints, especially CJ's, which could lead to her juvenile record. It was for minor matters, and supposedly sealed, but the sheriff didn't strike me as an icon of ethical behavior. Unfortunately, while invoking CJ's right against self-incrimination was the preferred legal approach, I didn't think it was the best one from a practical point of view. The Fourth Amendment only protected people from having to answer questions in court, not from public opinion. If CJ refused to be printed, on advice of counsel, it would undoubtedly get around the grapevine within a few hours, and the B&B's reputation would be destroyed.

"That's right," he said earnestly. "We need to know if anyone was in the victim's room who didn't belong in there."

"Normally I'd refuse on principle," I said. "But in the circumstances, I'll agree. We've obviously left prints all over the B&B, and you'll find mine near Mr. Pleasant's seat on the bus, because he insisted I sit with him."

Relief softened his face. He must have heard that I was a lawyer and expected some resistance to his request.

"Thank you," he said. "The team will take the guests' prints first and then yours. I'm heading next door now to get the Millers."

"We'll be here when you get back."

"Your other sister too?"

"Of course. She's just out in the owners' residence with her nephew."

The deputy left, and CJ said she wanted to check on Noah and would let Em know what the deputy had said.

"While we wait for our turn to get our fingerprints taken," I said, "we should discuss how we're going to trap the killer."

"I'll come right back with Noah and Em," CJ promised and dashed out the back door.

I started a fresh pot of coffee and then checked to be sure none of the guests had come back inside the lobby where they could overhear our planning. When I returned to the kitchen, Em was pouring herself some coffee, and CJ was setting Noah up at the far end of the table. Belatedly, I thought of the old adage that little pitchers have big ears and realized it might not be wise to discuss our plans to lie to people in front of a toddler. I didn't think Noah would tell anyone other than perhaps one of the cats, but it worried me that I wasn't exactly being the best role model for him.

CJ might have been right to keep him away from me. She didn't seem too concerned about his overhearing our plans though. She got him settled in with a snack and a new picture book, and then moved over to the opposite end of the table where Em and I waited for her. CJ gestured for me to take the seat at the head while she and Em sat on either side of me.

"Well?" CJ asked. "What's your plan?"

"The first step is just to convince the guests that we have inside information and will use it to help the killer get away with it. The deputy's insistence on talking to us separately will be useful for that. We need to let each of the guests know that we've been cleared of suspicion, but we hated Mark as much as everyone else. Oh, and that we lied when we said we didn't find out about the inspection from him. He'd actually threatened to write a terrible report if we didn't pay him, so we're glad he's dead and would be willing to help make sure the case is never solved."

"What's the second step?"

"Let's see how the first one goes before we lay out the next step," I said, buying myself some time to actually figure out all the details. "We've got until noon tomorrow to sort everything out, so for the rest of today, we just need to get the guests prepared to confess to us. Maybe one of them will surprise us with something incriminating today. If not, we'll ratchet up the pressure tomorrow."

"Got it," Em said thoughtfully. "We convince them we're allies with inside info."

"And we introduce a new suspect they can blame. I'm thinking a new girlfriend, someone who might know too much or be a suspect herself."

"Okay," Em said. "But how are you going to do that?"

"Not me," I said. "*Us.* Everything's better in threes, right?"

"Right," CJ said immediately, although Em, as usual, continued to reserve judgment. And she was the key to the success of my plan.

"I'm counting on you to convince them, Em," I said. "You're a good actor, better than me and CJ, and you read your audience well. You can tailor the story for each guest, so they'll believe it. If they're upset about the fingerprints, like the Hammetts were, you can say it was just for show, so no one would know the police were already closing in on a suspect that's not one of the B&B guests. You think it might be Mark's new girlfriend, and you hope she gets away with it because Mark deserved to die for ruining so many lives."

Em nodded. "I can do that."

"What about me?" CJ asked.

"Keep digging into who suggested this particular team of judges. If we can find that out, we really will have inside information."

"But that's boring," CJ said. "I want to shake the truth out of someone."

"You'll get your chance tomorrow if it's not resolved by then," I said. "But if you're busy playing the bad cop with the guests while Em is being the concerned confidante, I may be the only one available to watch over Noah. Is that going to be a problem?"

CJ looked at Noah for long moments, and Em reached across the table to put a hand on the cast-free arm. "Jess didn't do so badly with us when we were his age."

"Yes, but Noah.... he's different."

"Jess will be able to handle it," Em said.

CJ tore her gaze away from Noah. "If we do this, you promise you'll be kind to Noah? Not try to be the mean mom like you were with us?"

"I promise."

CJ sighed and then apparently had a happier thought. "If we figure out who the killer is and they make a run for it, can I chase them down on my motorcycle?"

I didn't have to be the mean sister this time, thanks to Em who answered for me. "No motorcycles until you have two fully working arms again. And no tackling anyone either, not when you might land on your cast and break it. But you can trip the killer if you can do it without falling yourself. And you can chase them on foot."

"I do love running, and I'm really good at chasing people into dead ends," CJ said with glee. "Let's do this."

CHAPTER TWENTY-ONE

Em and I went back to the owners' quarters to get her ready to feed misinformation to our suspects while CJ stayed in the B&B to keep an eye on Noah and the front desk.

Em was quiet on the way over, but once inside, she asked, "Do you really think we can do this? That *I* can do this?"

"Of course you can. You were brilliant in all the school plays."

"Tricking a killer is a lot different from acting in a play," Em said. "For one thing, I'm going to have to make up all the lines on the spot."

"And you'll do it brilliantly," I said. "You've been playing a part for your entire career in banking, ad-libbing all your lines. You wouldn't have lasted as long as you did if you hadn't been pretending to be the person the men in banking wanted you to be."

"Men are easy to fool. Just tell them what they want to hear."

"For most people, doing that isn't as easy as it sounds," I said. "You're good at figuring out what people want to hear. You can use it to make the guests believe you when you're setting them up."

Em narrowed her eyes at me. "You never trusted me when we were kids. Are you sure you're not just manipulating me now, telling me what *I* want to hear so I'll do what you want?"

When did Em get so unsure of herself? Could I have prevented it if I had been around more? Or had I sowed the seeds of self-doubt when we were kids, and they'd just grown worse over time? "I never meant to make you think I didn't trust you, now or in the past. I was just trying to help you be your best. But I can see how it would look like I doubted you at times, even though I didn't."

"You were always so bossy."

"I was just a kid myself, and it was the only way I knew how to interact with you and CJ."

"Maybe," Em said. "But we're all grown up now, so how come you're still giving us step-by-step instructions like we're children? Do you remember when you laid out like ten steps for us just to put the silverware in the dishwasher?"

"That was kind of overkill," I admitted.

"So for all of our early years, you were there telling us what to do, and then all of a sudden, you abandoned us," Em said. "We missed—I missed—having someone there to make sure we didn't mess up too badly. You were always the family fixer, and then you were gone, and somewhat to my surprise, I didn't know what to do without you. CJ felt even more adrift than I did."

This was the first I'd heard that they'd cared that I'd left. "I didn't think you'd miss me. It's not like we hung out together by choice. You always complained that you didn't need a constant babysitter. And you were right. You didn't really need me most of the time. And when I left, you still had Mom and Dad."

Em shook her head. "Not really. They were hardly ever around. It's why you stepped up to watch over us, after all."

"That was when you were toddlers," I said. "By the time I went to college, you were old enough to take care of yourselves for the most part. Besides, I thought you'd be glad to be free of being bossed around."

"We were at first," Em admitted. "But then CJ got herself arrested for some silly little prank, and that's when we realized you weren't around to fix everything for us."

"But you managed," I said. "And without CJ ever spending a single minute in juvenile detention. That's because you're both smart, talented women, and you were smart and talented even as kids."

"What didn't kill us made us stronger, huh?"

"Exactly."

"I hate that saying," Em said mildly. "Let's just hope that after this weekend, we all end up stronger and not dead like Mark."

"We will," I said with more confidence than I felt.

I didn't think we'd end up dead or even injured unless CJ forgot she wasn't supposed to tackle anyone while wearing a cast.

I'd pull the plug on the plan if things got that bad. But for now, I was more worried that my plan wasn't as detailed as I would have liked rather than that it was inherently dangerous. We were going to have to make decisions on the fly, which wasn't ideal with so much riding on the success of our scheme. With more time, I could have given Em a script and CJ something equally useful for her role, and then I'd have been totally confident about identifying the killer.

Unfortunately, we weren't putting on a school play, and there wouldn't be either rehearsals or do-overs. If we couldn't identify the killer by the end of Sunday's luncheon, my sisters would lose the B&B and all the money they'd put into it. And that wasn't even the worst case scenario.

* * *

CJ sent a group text to let Em and me know the techs were ready to fingerprint us. When we left the owners' quarters, we saw that most of the guests had gathered on the back veranda. The Readings and Hammetts were settled around the card table with a new game underway, and the Dells were seated in the wicker chairs, texting.

Em and I detoured around the house to the front porch, where we were printed more efficiently than I'd expected. That done, Em headed through the B&B to the veranda to set our plan in motion while I stayed in the lobby to take over at the front desk, freeing CJ to focus on finding out who had suggested the members of the inspection team.

Noah was happily reading a book on the floor behind the front desk with the tortoiseshell cat, Taylor, curled up with him. They didn't acknowledge me, but neither did they shy away. That was encouraging, right?

"Have you seen the Millers lately?" I asked CJ.

"They went next door again."

"What did the deputy think of that?"

"He said it was okay, as long as they kept their van parked where it could be seen from the street. I think he was afraid to get into another confrontation with them and decided it wasn't worth making a fuss over their being next door."

"Another confrontation?"

"I forgot," CJ said. "I meant to tell you that the Millers

were the last to be printed because they kept changing their minds about whether to agree to do it. As far as I can tell, they were the only ones who made a fuss."

"That's odd," I said. Tanya was a judge, so she must have been printed before, but perhaps she'd objected on principle or to protect her husband. Still, it was a little surprising she'd been so public about the matter, instead of just taking the deputy aside and explaining her concerns. "I'd have expected the Hammetts to complain, not the Millers."

"From what I could hear, the twins were sarcastic and rude, but they insisted on going first, saying they just wanted to get it over with."

"Did the Millers say what their concerns were?"

"Something about the wife not being able to use one of her hands because of nerve damage from the accident."

"That's understandable if they've never been printed before or last did it a long time ago," I said. "I did it for the bar exam and then again during a continuing education program on the arrest process, both times with digital equipment. If you can't do it yourself, the forensics team can help you. It's actually easier in a way if you don't have control of the hand, so you're not fighting against the other person's control."

"That's basically what the deputy said."

"It's still interesting that Tanya is the only one who had any qualms about having her prints taken. She's my least likely suspect since she's the only guest who literally doesn't have the ability to have attacked Mark physically. She doesn't even control her own wheelchair, so she couldn't have run him down with that. Plus, she hasn't been able to drive since her accident, so she couldn't have been the one who ran him off the road in the past."

"Tanya could have ordered David to do it on her behalf, and I can't see him saying no to her," CJ said. "She seems a lot more strong-willed than her husband is."

"It would make sense that David would resist being printed if he's the killer, but he had to know that his reluctance would make him seem guilty. His wife has a superficially reasonable excuse, even if it doesn't hold up, but what was his?"

CJ shrugged. "He didn't make a lot of sense. Just a whole bunch of quotes about his word being his bond and having faith in one's fellow man. Like he thought he could wear down the deputy by the sheer volume of biblical verses."

"But the deputy didn't give in, did he?"

"No." CJ glanced over at Noah, who continued to seem oblivious to the adults in the room. "Shurette may be new to police work and he's definitely never investigated a murder before, but I'm starting to think that's a good thing. He hasn't had time to develop any bad habits or get worn down by incompetent colleagues. He was persistent in trying to persuade the Millers to be printed, and I'm pretty sure that unlike the deputy, the sheriff would have just let them skip it. Probably on the theory that they couldn't possibly be the killers since Tanya doesn't have the physical ability to assault anyone, and David, a God-fearing man, doesn't have the psychological ability to do it."

"It's definitely bad practice to make that kind of assumption," I said. "I'm inclined to agree the Millers are unlikely killers, but so are the rest of the guests except maybe the Hammetts, who definitely have tempers and can be aggressive. We'd be as bad as the sheriff though if we jumped to the conclusion that the killer had to be one of the Hammetts."

CJ's phone, the one currently receiving calls forwarded from the front desk's number, pinged and she checked the text. She typed in a response before explaining, "It was from the Hammetts. They're hungry. I told them I'd bring some menus out there for ordering dinner." She jumped to her feet. "I guess now's as good a time as any to find out how you and Noah get along without me. You shouldn't have to actually do anything with him. He'll be fine as long as he's got a book, and there are more in the bottom drawer of the desk here if he finishes his current one. Text me if you have any questions."

I was surprised CJ suddenly seemed so comfortable leaving Noah in my care, although there really wasn't any other option. Em needed to engage with the guests and convince them we had inside information, and I needed to be available to back her up. Someone else had to deal with ordering dinner. Besides, Noah still wasn't acknowledging my existence, so he wasn't likely to care that I was the one watching over him. At this rate, I was never going to have the chance to get to know him before I left for home.

* * *

I settled in at the front desk with my cell phone close at hand, waiting for CJ to return or Em to report in. I didn't hear anything from them though, and an hour later, I was the first to reach out because Noah had finished his second book and wasn't interested in a third.

CJ came to see what he needed and sent me back to the kitchen to deal with the chaos there since, as she described it, most of the guests, including the Millers who'd returned from next door, had come in from the veranda to argue over their dinner options. The only one missing was Candy, who'd stayed on the veranda after her mother went inside. What had started as a pleasant conversation had quickly devolved into angry accusations. Apparently everyone was on edge, but CJ didn't know who Em had talked to yet, so she couldn't tell if they were upset by what Em had told them, or if they were naturally restless from being unable to come and go from the B&B as they pleased.

When I entered the kitchen, Beck was yelling at Jack Dell. "Who made you God and gave you the right to tell us what we have to eat? You can go ahead and have your stupid burgoo again, but we're having rolled oysters. Everyone's been telling us we should try them, and this seems like as good a time as any." He turned to Benn. "Right, bro?"

"Right," Benn agreed, abandoning his spot next to Jonny, who'd been poring over a menu with him. I thought he gave Jonny an apologetic look before hurrying over to stand by his brother's side, but I could have imagined it.

Shelly Reading was avidly watching the argument as if it were a television show, and the Millers were quietly comparing two menus and pretending not to be aware of anyone else in the room. It wasn't a convincing act though. They'd have had to be totally deaf not to hear Beck's shouting, and even then, they could probably have felt the sound vibrations through the floor.

"Fine," Jack said, with only mild irritation. "We thought it would be interesting to compare how this other place did the same dishes we had at lunch, but no one has to do it except me and my son. It was just a suggestion. Go ahead and make your own choices. But don't blame us when the food is terrible. You'd do better getting rolled oysters in Lexington. Small-town restaurants don't have all the purchasing resources that a big city has, so their menus can be a trap. They offer things they feel obliged to have available just to satisfy tourists, but if they can't actually source the ingredients fresh, the results are mediocre at best. The locals know which things not to order but outsiders don't."

"That's ridiculous," Beck said. "We're living in a global economy. You can get anything anywhere. And we're not outsiders. We have a business here."

"Whatever," Jack said. "Jonny and I are having another take on burgoo and spoonbread, both of which are easily made fresh here, if anyone else wants to join us in an impromptu comparison."

Shelly Reading said, "Ooh, that sounds like fun."

Beck snorted. "You're just saying that to spite us."

She smiled sweetly. "I don't need to spite you more than I already did at the card table."

Beck took a step toward her, assault clearly on his mind, but fortunately his brother grabbed him and held him back.

It was definitely time for me to intervene. "You're all welcome to choose your own meals. We'll order from as many different places as necessary. No need to get upset."

"From the moment we got here," Beck said, "there's been one upsetting thing after another. And we can't even leave to get away from all the stupidity. We're stuck here with nothing to do."

Shelly said, "It's not that bad, as house arrest goes. We're in a lovely B&B, with gracious hosts, when the police could have stuck us in some bland, boring place like the motel next to the restaurant where we met on Friday." She shuddered.

"They wouldn't dare," Beck said. "Who cares, anyway, that some old geezer tripped over his own feet and died?"

Shelly snapped, "Someone should have taught you manners before now." She stood, grabbed a handful of menus from the table in front of her, and announced, "I'm going to my room since some people can't be civilized. They're terrible losers and even worse conversationalists. I'll probably go with whatever Jack suggests, but I need some peace and quiet to decide. You can let Candy know where I am when she's ready to come inside. We'll text the front desk when we've made our choice."

"Good idea," Tanya Miller said, abandoning the pretense of not hearing what the others were saying. She gestured toward the table, and her husband grabbed some additional menus before pushing her out of the kitchen in Shelly's wake.

Beck circled some items on the menu he held and turned it so his brother could see it. When Benn nodded agreement, Beck slammed the paper down on the table. "We already made our choice. We'll be in our room until dinner, trying to get some work done since there's nothing else to do. When our order arrives, you can deliver it up there."

They stalked off, leaving just the Dells at the kitchen table. Jack marked a different restaurant's menu with his and his son's dinner choices and handed it to me. "I suppose we should eat in our room too. No point in messing up the kitchen just for us. We wouldn't want to be more of a burden to you than necessary."

"It's no trouble having you down here," I said, partly out of hospitality and partly because it had dawned on me that with the guests scattered all around the B&B, it was going to be difficult for Em to engage with anyone she hadn't already primed to incriminate themselves..

"No, no," Jack said. "We don't mind eating in our room. But don't worry, we'll come down to get the food if you let us know when it arrives. You don't need to deliver it."

"Thank you."

As they left, I texted my sisters to let them know the guests had all gone to their rooms, arranged for us to discuss Em's progress, and work out the details for the next phase of my plan.

CHAPTER TWENTY-TWO

"You'll never guess what I found out," Em said half an hour later, the last one to arrive in the kitchen after my text.

Noah was already ensconced in his usual seat at the far end of the table with a new book, and CJ was hovering, absently rubbing at what would be her wrist if it weren't covered with plaster.

Em made a beeline for the coffeemaker. "I was just talking to Candy. She's always so quiet when her mother is around, but get her alone, and you can get all sorts of information out of her."

That had been my experience with her too. "Like what?"

"Like the Hammett brothers admitted during the bridge game that Mark had threatened to ruin their reputation locally if they didn't hire him for some sort of vague public relations role. They refused initially then started getting calls from some companies they were doing business with here, asking if a rumor about their insolvency was true. So the Hammetts paid Mark what was supposed to be a one-time bribe, and the calls stopped. But they were concerned that Mark would be back for another payment before long."

"Interesting," I said. "Who else have you talked to so far?"

"Everyone except the Hammetts themselves and Shelly Reading, but I'm sure Candy will tell her mother about our conversation," she said. "I wish you'd been with me. You might have noticed something suspicious in their reactions that I missed. I think they all believe me about our being cleared and having inside information though."

"Before you talk to the Hammetts, we need to adjust our plan a little. I'd been counting on everyone having dinner together tonight, like they did at lunch, but now they're all mad at each other and insisting on eating in their rooms. Originally, I didn't think we'd have to worry about anyone trying to skip out on the deputy until after we put some more pressure on them tomorrow, but now I'm wondering if eating in their rooms is just an excuse so we won't notice if they make a run for it."

"Isn't that sort of what we want? Prove their guilt by triggering them into running away?"

"We're going to need something really solid, like trying to get us to cover up their guilt," I said. "With the Hammetts, in particular, running could be explained away as just the result of their usual impatience and arrogance, thinking the rules don't apply to them. We'd still need to get a confession out of them. I'm also concerned that if the Hammetts decide to leave just because they're impatient, not because they killed Mark, then the real culprits could see it as an opportunity to escape while we're busy with the Hammetts. The thing is, we're outnumbered—sometimes three isn't the perfect number—and I don't know how we can keep an eye on everyone overnight."

CJ immediately said, "I bet Lucas, the shuttle driver, would help. He doesn't have classes on the weekend, and his boss has suspended him until he's cleared of involvement in Mark's death. I'm sure he would help us stake out the guests if it would expedite clearing his name."

CJ seemed to know a lot about this Lucas for having only met him on Friday.

"Are you sure Lucas wasn't involved in Mark's death?" Em asked, echoing my concern. "You hardly know him."

"I know enough to be absolutely sure he didn't do anything to Mark," CJ said. "Why would he? Mark couldn't affect the only thing Lucas cares about, his engineering degree. I suppose Mark could have threatened to get Lucas fired, but it's not like he plans to drive the shuttle for the rest of his life. He's just doing it while he's a grad student. He can find another job if he's fired for being rude to a passenger or whatever other lie Mark could have told, but not if he's been blamed for a passenger's death."

"Typical guy," Em said, "always looking out for themselves first. If he agrees to help, how do we know he's not working for his law enforcement buddies, trying to trick *us* into incriminating ourselves?"

"So what if he is?" CJ said. "We didn't do anything wrong, so there's nothing for us to confess to. Besides, he's got as much motivation to get to the truth about Mark as we do. More than anyone else I can think of asking to help us."

"What about Reed Hill?" Em said. "He's in the same position we are, with a cloud over his head until this is resolved. And we've known him forever. Reed was there for you when your husband died. Unlike most men, he doesn't betray his friends. Or in your case, his brother's best friend's widow."

CJ nodded. "I'm sure Reed would help us if we ask. But I still think we should bring Lucas in too. We could use all the help we can get."

"I agree," I said, although it made me a little nervous that, for once, CJ and I were on the same side of a family disagreement. It always used to be me on one side of an argument and CJ and Em on the other. "With five people—the three of us and the two of them—we can have one person assigned to each pair of guests, plus one person at the front desk to coordinate information."

"All right," Em said. "But I'm holding you responsible for Lucas's trustworthiness, CJ."

"That's fair," I said. "CJ, please call Lucas, and Em, would you call Reed? Just ask them to stop by around six, if possible, without getting into the details of why. If they're truly our allies, they shouldn't need to know why, and if they balk, we'll know we can't trust them. But assuming they agree to help, I'll lay out the details of our plan for everyone when they get here."

And in the meantime, with luck, I'd actually figure out the rest of the plan.

*　*　*

Em volunteered to take Noah outside for some active play time while CJ and I waited in the kitchen for the guests to decide on their take-out orders. CJ's phone was still the one programmed to receive forwarded calls from the front desk, and the pings started as soon as Em left, alerting us of texts from the guests.

CJ laughed. "Considering how resistant everyone was to cooperating for their dinner choices, they all ended up with the

same restaurant and pretty close to identical meals except, of
course, for the Hammetts. I'll call in the orders now, to be
delivered by six, unless you want me to make it six-thirty in case
Lucas and Reed are running late. We wouldn't want someone
trying to escape while we're distracted by the deliveries."

I was fairly certain the guests wouldn't try to leave until
after they were fed—no one turns down a free meal—but they
might run out of patience if the food was unduly delayed.

"No. Go ahead and place the orders for six. Then I'll need
you to be outside to coordinate the arrivals and departures. "

"Sounds like fun." CJ placed the orders and then texted
the guests to let them know when to expect the delivery. She put
down her phone and said, "I've been thinking, Jess, and I should
have said this before. No matter what else happens this weekend,
I want you to know I'm glad you came out to visit. I haven't been
as grateful to you as I should have been. I do understand that
you're busy and have more important things to do than cooking
breakfast for strangers."

"I have to admit, I probably wouldn't have come if I'd
known that's what you wanted me for," I said. "I thought I was
invited to get to know my nephew."

"That was the original intent, along with needing you to
be the third sister, so we'd live up to the B&B's cozy name while
the inspection team was here," CJ said. "You were supposed to
just be sort of cosplaying, not doing any real work. But that was
before I broke my arm."

"And before a guest died," I said. "I figured that much
out. But I don't understand why you're being so protective of
Noah, even keeping his aunt at arm's length. Was I really that
mean to you when you were that age? I would have expected you
to be leading him off on adventures, going skydiving or
something, not encasing him in metaphorical bubble wrap."

She looked down. "Noah isn't like me. Or his father. He
gets overwhelmed easily."

"I noticed that. Is there a problem?"

A tear ran down her cheek. "Nothing I can't handle. He's
going to be fine. I'll make sure of it."

"Why wouldn't he be?"

She brushed away the tear impatiently, but a second one
fell to replace it. "He had his most recent pediatric check-up a

month ago. I'd known there was something different about him for a while. He wasn't hitting some of the social milestones I'd read about, and he was way ahead on other things, like starting to read so young."

"Everyone develops differently," I said. "You started walking and talking really early while Em took her time, as if she wanted to be sure she could do things perfectly before even trying them."

"Yes, but Noah's differences are more than that." CJ crossed the room to get a paper napkin to use as a tissue. "He's officially been diagnosed as being on the autism spectrum."

So that was why he hadn't spoken to anyone except the cats. And why CJ was being overly protective. It all made sense now.

"Okay, but why didn't you tell me right away, instead of trying to hide it?"

"I didn't want you to judge Noah for being neuroatypical," CJ said. "Or judge me, like I caused him to be atypical. I'm tired of people asking me what's wrong with him, when there's nothing wrong. I wanted you to get to know him for who he is before you put a label on him. Except then things got out of hand this weekend, and he can only handle one bit of chaos at a time, so there was never a chance for you two to interact without distractions."

"We're running out of time before I go back home."

"That's why I'm telling you now. So maybe you'll consider coming back again sometime when there isn't a murderer on the loose," CJ said. "It's going to take a lot of therapy and family support to keep Noah from withdrawing too far away from the world and to give him the tools he'll need. I don't know if I can do it. Especially if I lose the B&B and have to get a more traditional nine-to-five kind of job."

"You aren't going to lose the B&B," I said. "And even if you did, Em and I would make sure Noah gets everything he needs."

"But Em deserves to have her own life, not get bogged down with my problems. You do too. We can't expect you to be the family fixer forever."

"Once a fixer, always a fixer," I said. "But it doesn't have to be a full-time job for me. You don't need that much help as an adult. Once the B&B's reputation is cleared, you'll be fine, and I'll go home. But I'll visit more often, so I'll know if you're hiding anything important from me."

"You make it sound so easy."

"Not easy, but we can handle this. *You* can handle this. Just consider Noah's therapy an adventure. You're good with adventures. And Em and I will be standing by in case you fall and scrape your knee or break an arm."

She laughed. "Raising Noah is not exactly the kind of adventure I've got experience with. I wish I could just take him skydiving or build him a skateboard park in the backyard, and that was all he needed from me."

"Broken bones are so much easier to fix than intangible things."

"Noah doesn't need fixing," CJ said hotly. "He's perfect."

"I know," I said. "I didn't mean it that way. I was thinking of the social expectations he was going to bump up against, and how frustrating that would be for him, and you won't be able to fix that for him."

"I'm sorry," CJ said. "It's a bit of a hot button for me. Which just goes to show you how incompetent I'm going to be at helping Noah interact with the world. I'm terrible at peopling myself. I mean, look at how badly I messed up our sisterly reunion, resenting you for being gone so long instead of being happy to see you again."

I shrugged. "You're not terrible at anything except believing in yourself. It's normal for family to be difficult sometimes. But we've taken the first step. And we'll have plenty of time after this weekend to continue mending our relationships."

"I hope so," CJ said. "But first we need to make sure that future reunions don't happen in a visiting room at the state prison."

* * *

The guests were all safely ensconced in their rooms, awaiting their meals, when Reed arrived and joined me and CJ in the kitchen. Em was taking a quick break in the owners' quarters.

Reed tossed a huge paper bag onto the table. "I was starved and not in the mood for any of the breakfast foods that fill

your pantry and freezer, despite how great they are, so I stopped
to pick up sandwiches."

CJ thanked him, grabbed one of the sandwiches, a stack
of napkins, and Noah, and headed out to the front porch to wait
for Lucas and the delivery vehicles.

"Em tells me you need my help to catch Mark's killer."
Reed upended the paper bag to scatter three more sandwiches, a
large container of salad, and several single-serving packets of
chips on the table. "So you don't still think I'm responsible for his
death?"

"Em and CJ convinced me you're innocent," I said from
the refrigerator, where I retrieved a pitcher of sweet tea.

"I wouldn't go quite that far." He dropped into the chair at
the head of the table. "But I've never killed anyone. And neither
has anyone at Hills' Barrels. At least not on the job."

"We're pretty sure one of the guests killed Mark." I
settled next to Reed at the table while I went over what we knew
about the timeline on Friday, and where each of the guests was
along the way and their motives for murder. "The only thing we
haven't figured out is where Mark was at the end of the tour when
everyone else had collected by the shuttle bus. The tour leader
had to go find him."

"I can answer that," Reed said. "I took a closer look at the
surveillance tapes and caught a glimpse of him talking to one of
my employees after the tour was over. I didn't notice originally
because the clock on the recording was a few minutes fast, so the
first time through I'd stopped before I got to that spot, thinking
everyone had left by then."

"Did you talk to the employee?"

Reed nodded as he unwrapped a sandwich. "I was just
about to go find him on the factory floor when he came to see me.
He's new, and apparently he didn't realize I have an open-door
policy, so he'd wasted time thinking he needed an appointment to
see me. I have to admit, I was a little concerned that he hadn't
come to me right away since I don't know him very well. The
good news, though, is that he did eventually report that Mark had
tried to bribe him to steal some barrels with our logo on them.
The employee didn't know what Mark planned to do with them
and rejected the bribe before finding out."

I claimed a sandwich but was too stressed to eat, so I set
it aside for Lucas. Grad students never turned down a free meal.

"Are you sure the employee isn't just covering up his own actions, now that he knows Mark is dead and can't make good on any promises he made?"

There was a pause while Reed chewed and swallowed the large bite of sandwich he'd taken before I questioned him. "I'm sure. I looked at the footage again afterwards, and you can clearly see from the body language that Mark was pestering the employee, who was trying his best to end the conversation without being rude to someone who might be a customer. Mark, of course, plowed ahead and kept trying, but eventually the rejection was too obvious even for him to ignore and he left."

"And presumably the employee didn't attack Mark to get him to take no for an answer."

"Nope, no assault," Reed said. "Not by this employee, and not by anyone else between the arrival of the shuttle and Mark's exit from the factory." As if relieved to have established his employees' innocence, he began wolfing down the remainder of his sandwich.

"So you're definitely off the hook."

He shrugged and held up a finger until he could swallow his food. "In theory, yes, but gossips will talk unless the real culprit is arrested."

"That's what I've been thinking too," I said. "It's not good enough to just not be officially charged with murder. Unless someone is arrested and convicted, we'll all be viewed with suspicion—you, me, my sisters, and the shuttle driver."

"What are you going to do about it?" he asked. "Em said you had a plan."

"We've laid the groundwork for a trap. My sisters and I strongly suspect that the Hammett twins are the culprits, but we don't have any real evidence. We need them—or whoever killed Mark—to panic and make a run for it."

"And that's where I come in," he said, brushing the crumbs that were all that was left of his sandwich into the wrapper it had come in.

"You and Lucas, the shuttle driver," I said. "He should be here soon."

"Well, darn," he said, leaning back in his chair. "Here I was thinking this was all an excuse to spend some time alone with me."

"I'm afraid there won't be any alone time for us until the killer is caught," I said.

He grinned. "Ah, so you admit you were thinking about it."

"I'm not admitting anything," I said, feigning interest in a packet of chips. "I'll let the facts speak for themselves."

"Then as far as I'm concerned, the facts are saying you'd like to get to know me better. And not just to be sure I'm not a killer."

"That's why facts sometimes need a translator." I resolutely pushed the chips over next to Lucas's sandwich and looked up to meet Reed's gaze. "The facts are saying something different to me. They're saying things might have been different for us if Mark hadn't been killed, and we could have had some fun together this weekend, even if we're just ships passing in the night. As it is, though, there's no present or future for us. You're irrevocably tied to Cooperton and your family business, and I'll be heading back to DC on Monday after Noah's birthday party tomorrow afternoon."

After a pause, he said, "How come no one told me about a party?"

I laughed. "You really want to hang out with a dozen sticky, sugar-high toddlers?"

"Sure, if you'll be there too."

If only circumstances were different, I thought. We could have had a lovely weekend together. But I couldn't let myself get distracted at the moment. There was too much at stake for my sisters.

"Don't give me too much credit for bravery though," he went on. "I know something about the party that your sisters apparently didn't tell you. There won't be a dozen people at the party, let alone a dozen feral toddlers. Noah would find it overwhelming, so it'll just be family. And I'm practically family, so I should be there."

"I'll make sure it's okay with CJ and let you know," I agreed. "But there won't be a party if we don't hurry up and catch Mark's killer."

"Got it," he said. "So what's the plan to make sure Noah gets his party, and the B&B is saved from a death spiral?"

"Em has already laid the groundwork, convincing the guests that we have inside information on the investigation, and we're amenable to covering up the killer's guilt. If no one takes the bait, then first thing in the morning, we'll escalate, convincing them that the police have been talking to a witness who is reluctant to cooperate, but they think she'll crack before long."

"So what do you need me for? And the bus driver."

"To keep an eye on the guests and make sure they don't try to leave. They outnumber us, so we could get distracted, and the culprit could slip away. We need one-on-one coverage to watch for any suspicious activity. And to stop them if they show an inclination to leave before the deputy says they can."

"I assume you'll be at the front desk coordinating everything," he said. "Have you told your sisters that you'll also be acting as bait? If the killer feels cornered, they might be tempted to take a hostage. The rest of us will be out of sight, secretly watching over the guests, but you'll be right out there in public, an easy target."

"It's not that risky," I said. "It's not like I'll be in some deserted building, with help miles away. If it will make you feel better, I'll borrow the baby monitor that CJ uses when Noah's sleeping. I'll set it up at the front desk, and you can be on the other end."

"I still don't like it," Reed said. "But I have a feeling you and your sisters will go ahead with your plan even without me, so I'm in. And I'll take the Hammetts as my suspects to watch."

"Thank you."

He sighed. "Are you sure this will work?"

"If anyone can pull it off, my sisters and I can," I said. "We're invincible when we work together. Or at least that's what we thought when we were younger, and we need to believe it now."

"But you're out of practice at being a team," he said. "Might have been good to work together on something simpler than catching a killer."

He wasn't wrong. My sisters and I had stopped being a team over the years. And that was my fault. If we got through this weekend, I would make fixing that my top priority. But for now, I had to count on deeply ingrained family habits to kick in.

CHAPTER TWENTY-THREE

The food for everyone except the Hammetts was the first to arrive, so Em took the Millers' meals to their rooms—they deserved the special treatment, even if they hadn't asked for it—and I took the ones for the Dells and Readings. Reed stayed in the kitchen to make some phone calls.

Jonny accepted the Dells' delivery with a nod of thanks, and then I went down the hall to knock on the Readings' door. Shelly called out, "Just a minute."

I heard some rustling inside, and after a minute or two, the door opened just enough for Shelly to peer out at me. On seeing the bags in my hands, she pulled the door the rest of the way open and invited me in. "You really didn't need to deliver. We would have come down to pick it up."

"I don't mind." I stepped inside, noting that the daughter wasn't in the room, and carried the bags over to the desk. "You've been inconvenienced enough this weekend."

"But just think what great stories we'll have to tell our friends when we get home. Especially if the killer is caught before we leave." Her tone was as cheerful as her words, but her eyes were red and puffy. She must have been crying when I knocked, and the rustling had been her trying to compose herself.

"Are you okay?" I asked. "I should have realized before now that you must be upset by everything that's happened this weekend. You may not have been married to Mark any longer, but I'm sure you loved him at one point. His death must have been a shock."

"It was unexpected, but otherwise not all that upsetting," she said, pulling a tissue out of her pocket before dropping into the upholstered chair near the take-out bags. "For a while, I fantasized about Mark driving off a cliff and dying in a ball of fire or something equally gruesome, but I got over it. At some point, it just stopped mattering to me whether he was dead or alive. I accepted that his dying wouldn't bring back my B&B, and I refused to let him make me miserable one minute longer. It was right around the one-year anniversary of the divorce when he stopped by to wave his new will in my face. He left everything to some distant relatives that I know for a fact he didn't even like. Just so I'd know there was no chance of my ever inheriting from him and using the money to buy another B&B."

"That must have hurt."

"It did at the time, but I got the last laugh." She dabbed at her eyes, which hadn't fully gotten the message that she was over her grief. "Turns out, I like retirement. Now I can play bridge whenever I want, no need to be available for guests."

"Then why are you so sad tonight?"

"I'm not sure. I think it's just a delayed reaction to all the grief he put me through before. And maybe a bit of relief that he'll never be able to hurt me again. I've been putting on a good front for Candy because she doesn't need any more reasons to hate Mark." Shelly tossed her tissue in the waste basket, her eyes no longer watery. "In fact, it's a good thing she and I were never out of each other's sight on Friday, or I might have had to consider whether she killed Mark. That's something no mother should ever have to think."

"Did Candy really hate him that much?"

"Oh, yes," Shelly said without hesitation. "I feel some guilt over that. I should have listened when Candy said she didn't want him as a stepfather. I thought she was just resisting change—she's always been something of a stickler for routine—but she was right that he was an awful person."

"What did she think when Mark showed up at the restaurant on Friday?"

"She tried to convince me to leave right then and cancel the weekend. But foolish me, I thought we'd be able to avoid him. Okay, and I was a bit greedy. I'd wanted to visit here for years, long before you and your sisters bought the place, but I never had a chance. And to be honest, our budget is a little tight for luxuries like vacations, so it was hard to turn down a free weekend here." She sighed. "Still, I should have listened to Candy. Not that the Three Sisters B&B isn't wonderful. I love the way the three of you work together so well."

I was relieved that our squabbles hadn't been obvious to the guests. "Thank you. My sisters and I do make a good team."

Shelly nodded. "You're going to make a success of the B&B, I just know it. But it would still have been better if I'd withdrawn from the inspection team. I tried to ignore Mark, but he kept insisting he had to talk to me alone, starting the minute he saw me at the restaurant. I think he was as surprised to see me as I was to see him."

"Did you ever find out what he wanted to talk about?"

She nodded. "We were just finishing up lunch at the barbeque place, and Candy was deep in a conversation with the Millers at the restaurant. No one else was paying me or Mark any attention, so I went over and told him that if he really needed to tell me something, it was now or never. He followed me out to the corridor and demanded that I give him a toolbox he'd left behind with me. I wanted to tell him I'd thrown it out, just to spite him, but it was actually taking up space in my garage, an annoying reminder of him. I told him I'd leave it on the front porch, so he could pick it up. Then he got mad that I wouldn't deliver it to him. If we'd been truly alone, he would have had a temper tantrum, but we could hear that the rest of the group was starting to get ready to leave, and they'd be joining us in a few seconds, so he held onto his temper."

"I'd have probably agreed with Candy at that point and gone home."

"I should have," Shelly said. "But I was too angry to think rationally. Instead, I got stubborn and decided that I wasn't going to let Mark chase me away from a vacation I'd been looking forward to. I calmed down on the ride over here and pulled into the horse farm to tell Candy we were turning around and going home. But she'd changed her mind about the weekend. She hadn't been as oblivious to my conversation with Mark as I thought she had, and she thought he'd leave us alone now that I'd shown that I wouldn't put up with his antics any longer. We agreed that if he said one more word to annoy either of us, we'd leave, but we weren't giving up a nice weekend just because he might be a problem."

That all sounded reasonable, but Shelly did have means, motive, and opportunity to have killed Mark while out in the corridor alone. They may have been out of the others' sight for only a couple of minutes, but it didn't take long to lash out in anger, causing Mark to fall and hit his head.

I must have hesitated for too long because Shelly reached out to pat my forearm. "It's okay," she said. "I know what you're thinking. You're wondering if you can believe me when I've admitted to being alone with Mark, and I even admitted how furious I was with him. Luckily, there was someone in the corridor where Mark and I were talking. He can vouch for the lack of any physical altercation."

"There was a witness?"

"Oh, yes," she said. "In fact, I'm glad you asked me about it just now because I didn't think to tell the nice deputy when he took my statement originally. We didn't know then that Mark could have been injured at the restaurant. I distinctly recall seeing the owner of the barbeque place at the far end of the corridor, rearranging a display. I remember feeling relieved that if Mark got too annoying, there was someone nearby who would notice. The owner was too far away to hear our conversation, but I'm sure he'd have intervened if there had been a physical confrontation. He's a member of the tourism co-op and active in a number of local charities, so you probably know him."

I didn't, of course, but CJ or Em probably did, and they could ask the witness for confirmation of Shelly's story. I was already inclined to believe her, just not enough to confess our plan to identify the killer. I settled for asking, "So who do you think killed Mark?"

"It had to have been those horrible Hammett twins," Shelly said. "They're evil."

"Why do you think that?" I asked. "I know they're rude, but that's not the same as being evil. And you were happy to play bridge with them."

"Not any longer," she said. "All they care about is winning, even if they have to cheat. Which they did repeatedly during today's game. And we still beat them, which really made them angry. They knocked the table over again, this time causing it to fall on top of me."

"Oh, no. Are you all right?"

"I'm fine. I may act like a silly old lady, but I'm pretty tough, and the table was light. Didn't even leave a tiny bruise. Just saying, it shows the Hammetts are willing to get physical over little things. I could have been hurt and ended up like Mark, a dead woman walking. And the Hammetts didn't stick around long enough to find out that I wasn't hurt. They stomped out, leaving Candy and me to pick everything up."

"I'm glad it wasn't worse."

"Me too," she said. "But it was worth the risk we took when we goaded the Hammetts into a rematch today. I'd been hoping that when Candy and I trounced them again, they'd slip and say something incriminating about bribing Mark. But all they did was turn over the table when they lost. It does confirm that they're willing to get violent when they're angry, and they don't care if anyone gets hurt, but they didn't say anything incriminating that we could pass on to that nice deputy. I guess I'm not a real-life Miss Marple, after all."

"You'd make a fine fictional detective," I assured her. "But please don't take any more risks with your safety."

"I've learned my lesson," Shelly said. "In that split second between Beck grabbing the card table and it landing on my lap, I really did think I was going to die. So from now on, I'm leaving it to the professionals. I'm sure they'll come around soon enough to the same conclusion as we did—that it's got to be the Hammetts. There's no way the Millers could have done it. The way they've coped with Tanya's injury is nothing short of heroic. They wouldn't let something as insignificant as Mark's schemes get to them."

"What about the Dells?"

Shelly laughed. "No way. I'm surprised you don't know their reputation. Jack is practically a saint, and Jonny is on the same path as soon as he matures a little more. You must have heard about Jack's wife, Jonny's mother, and her terminal cancer. The two men were devoted to her, taking care of her at home to the very end while still putting in crazy hours at the restaurant. They made sure one of them was always at home with her. They even kept her cleaning business going as long as there was still hope that she'd recover. She was a member of the tourism co-op, you know. Pretty much everyone around here had a contract with her to clean their offices. I figured that's why the Dells got chosen to be judges this weekend. They aren't directly members of the co-op themselves, and it was a way of giving her family a little vacation."

"Do you know why you were chosen for the inspection?"

Shelly shrugged. "I assume it was because we have B&B

experience, and we were a member of the co-op in the past."

Before I could follow up, Beck Hammett's grating voice came barreling up the stairs from the front desk. "Where is everyone hiding? Do you really want another dead guest on your hands? We're going to starve to death if dinner doesn't get here soon."

* * *

Way too soon for dead-guest jokes, I thought. Not that the Hammetts would understand that.

Fortunately, as I reached the lobby, I could see the delivery vehicle with the Hammetts' dinner pulling up out front, and CJ was gesturing instructions to the driver for where to park. I hurried over to the front desk to listen to Beck's complaints—his brother stood beside him but didn't say anything.

I tried several times to tell them that the food had arrived and CJ would bring it inside any minute now, but Beck kept talking over me. I finally gave up and let him rant, although my calm patience seemed to make him even more angry. Reed's earlier words about my placing myself at risk came back to me, but I wasn't terribly worried. CJ would be coming through the front door soon, and in the meantime, I was safe enough behind the barrier of the front desk, which was bolted to the floor, making it impossible for them to topple it onto me.

When CJ did finally appear with the Hammetts' dinner, Beck broke off his rant, snatched their bags from her hand, and raced up the stairs with Benn at his heels.

Lucas came through the front door just as the Hammetts were disappearing. CJ whispered to me that she'd explained the basics of our plan to Lucas, and he'd agreed to help. We all adjourned to the kitchen to work out a more detailed schedule. I wasn't particularly worried that anyone would try to run overnight since Em hadn't told them the final lie. The one I thought would push the killer into thinking they were about to be arrested. At breakfast, she would tell them we'd learned who the purported secret witness was—Mark's new girlfriend—and that she was still refusing to cooperate since she didn't trust the police to, in her words, make the culprit pay. The police were convinced that she knew who had killed Mark, and why, and planned to use that information to take her own revenge if they couldn't convince her to reveal what she knew.

CJ and Lucas went back to the owners' quarters to get Noah settled for the night. I stayed in the lobby, just in case I was wrong, and someone did try to leave after they finished eating. Reed volunteered to patrol the grounds overnight. Em settled into the kitchen to catch up on B&B paperwork while keeping an eye on the veranda, where any guests trying to sneak out the emergency exits would end up.

The hours passed uneventfully, with the guests staying in their rooms. Shortly before midnight, I left the front desk to make a fresh pot of coffee for Em and Reed, both of whom planned to stay up all night. Em thanked me absently for the mug I placed next to her hand, engrossed as she was in the B&B's accounts. I took another one out to the front porch, where Reed, just back from a periodic walk around the grounds, had settled in a wicker chair. From there, he had a good view of the parking lot to his left and the driveway in front of him.

Reed took the offered coffee. "Aren't you having any?"

"No. I'm going to check for lights in the windows to make sure all the guests are asleep, and if they are, I'll try for a few hours' sleep before it's time to make breakfast."

"You don't need to check the guests' windows. All the lights are out and have been for at least an hour."

So there was really no reason for me to stay on the porch with Reed, but the sleepiness that had driven me to abandon the front desk had completely dissipated. I dropped into the wicker chair next to Reed's. "I wish I had more time here before I'm due back at work."

"Can't you take a few more days off?" he asked. "I could arrange a private tour of a popular local destination if you'd like."

I laughed. "I'd love a private tour of Hills' Barrels, but I just can't this week. I've got a full schedule booked, and my paralegal has been texting to warn me that critical things are piling up already."

"The offer stands whenever you're ready." He sipped his coffee while I admired the intense quiet and darkness of the spring night. It was never this serene at home.

"I'll take you up on the offer someday," I said. "The factory sounds fascinating. Whenever you talk about it, I can tell that you love your work."

"I do."

Reed went on to describe the basics of barrel making and the challenges of running a traditional business in a modern world. It clearly wasn't just a job for him, or a duty that had been imposed on him by family demands. He would make barrels to the day he died, and he would be tethered to Hills' Barrels almost as long until he could turn it over to someone with the necessary skills to keep the family business going for the next generation.

Reed cut himself off suddenly. "I do tend to go on and on about the factory. I should let you go get some sleep now before you pass out from boredom."

"I'm not bored," I said. "Just thinking that, like you, I love my work, but unlike you, I have some flexibility for taking time off. I really don't have any excuse for not having visited my sisters more in recent years. I'm determined not to make that mistake again." And if I just happened to run into Reed while in Cooperton, well, that would be a nice bonus.

"Maybe you'll fall in love with Kentucky and move back here permanently."

I could fall in love with more than Kentucky, my heart told me. But then my head reminded me of how impossible that would be.

"It's complicated," I said at last. "Getting licensed to practice law here would be easy enough, but I'm not particularly good at marketing myself, and I'm not sure there's even enough demand for my specialty in a small town.."

"Sounds like your career is more important to you than your family."

"That's ridiculous," I said, despite a tiny voice in my head—definitely my heart speaking again, not my brain—whispering that he was right. "I love my sisters, and I fully admit that I should have visited more often, but they are perfectly capable of standing on their own without me."

"What about Noah?" Reed asked, and I wondered if CJ had told him about the autism diagnosis. He added, "It's not easy growing up with a single parent, especially one who runs her own business. Extended family can make a big difference in a child's life."

"She's got Emma."

"Who also has other commitments. It's a little like how

you realized you needed Lucas and me to investigate Mark's murder. With two sisters to lean on, CJ and Noah will have more support than they can use, so you and Em could each have time for your own lives."

He made it sound so easy, but all I could think of was how overwhelming a project it would be to move here and start over. Especially with having to do it in a way that Em and CJ would appreciate, instead of seeing it as me being judgmental about their adulting skills.

"I'll think about it," I said and got to my feet. "But for now, you're definitely right that I should get some sleep."

"I'd better go patrol the yard again, so I don't fall asleep too." Reed stood. "But first promise me you're not just humoring me, and you'll really think about your options for spending more time with your family."

"I will." He hadn't really needed to elicit a promise from me. I'd already planned to spend the long drive back to DC figuring out how and when I'd be visiting Cooperton again.

CHAPTER TWENTY-FOUR

I was able to get about five hours' sleep before my alarm rang. It meant I wasn't too exhausted to think, or cook, or to fret about how little time we had left to identify Mark's killer. Just until a little after noon, when the sheriff received what could well be inconclusive lab results and would have to tell the suspects that they could go home.

I blearily grabbed one of the cobbler-style aprons from the pantry and set about making the biscuits and gravy that were a Sunday-only menu item. It was a miracle I didn't burn everything since I was distracted by the thought that maybe my plan for catching Mark's killer wouldn't work. It had been a long time since my sisters and I had worked as a team, and I didn't exactly have any experience with tricking criminals into a confession.

It was around seven-thirty, half an hour before the beginning of the breakfast hours, when I heard stealthy movement out on the veranda. It couldn't be my sisters or our two helpers. Lucas had been gone when I woke up, presumably to take over patrolling the yard so Reed could get some sleep in his truck. CJ had gotten up the same time I did, to feed Noah and get settled in the lobby, so Em could take a brief nap before she took center stage at the breakfast table, convincing the guests that Mark's girlfriend knew who had killed him and was going to either blackmail the culprit or get them arrested for murder.

I hurried out the back door without removing my apron and found David Miller tiptoeing across the veranda, pushing his wife in her wheelchair toward the ramp that led to the parking area. She had all of their luggage either on her lap or hanging off the back of the chair, so they weren't just going out to admire the scenery.

When David saw me, he froze guiltily, and Tanya looked over her shoulder at him to ask, "What's wrong?"

He nodded toward me, and she turned her head in my direction. "Oh."

After a moment, she smiled, and said, "Just getting some fresh air."

My eyebrows rose. "Airing your luggage too, I see."

"No one likes stale luggage," she said lightly with an apologetic smile. "But you're right. We were leaving. We decided it was time to call our attorney, and he confirmed what I thought, that we didn't have to stay here any longer or talk to the deputy if we didn't want to. And as much as I love your B&B and being close to the family farm, I miss the conveniences of home."

"I understand," I said. "But why don't you come in and have some breakfast first? It's a little early, but I don't mind, and there's no need for you to travel on an empty stomach. If you still want to leave when you're done, I won't even try to stop you."

Once they were settled at the table with a shared plate of biscuits and gravy, plus individual ham and cheese omelets, I poured myself some coffee and joined them at the table. I couldn't wait for Em to give the Millers the false information we'd devised, not if they might leave before Em showed up. I was going to have to do it, and the understudy was never as good as the star.

"I'm sure you'll be glad to know that the police are making progress with their witness." I paused to sip my coffee, as if expecting that they would indeed be relieved.

Tanya glanced at her husband and then answered for them both. "That is good news."

"Turns out, the witness is Mark's girlfriend," I said in what I hoped sounded like a gossipy tone, not an anxious, fake one.

The couple exchanged an obviously surprised look before Tanya said, "He had a girlfriend?"

"For the last few months," I said. "Since shortly before the attempts on his life began. The deputy thinks she knows something useful, but she keeps insisting she can get justice for Mark on her own, and she doesn't trust the police. They think she might be planning a bit of blackmail or extortion. Probably learned it from Mark. They think she'll try for some vigilante justice, so they're pushing pretty hard for her to reveal what she knows. Last I heard, she was wavering, but that was around midnight, so things might have changed since then. They may have already gotten the information they needed, and are making plans for an arrest, before they get their report at noon. I just hope the witness tells the truth. It would be terrible if she blamed the wrong person. But I'm sure you don't have anything to worry about. You didn't have any reason to want him dead."

"God will protect the innocent," David said with a covert glance at his wife.

"But He expects the innocent to do their part as well," Tanya reminded him before turning her attention back to me. "I might as well confess that we weren't exactly truthful with you when we said Mark had never done anything to harm the farm. In fact, he started a whisper campaign against Rackhouse Saddlebreds before he retired. He suggested we mistreated our horses and then bribed a vet to cover it up. Some buyers caught wind of it and threatened to cancel some major purchases. The vet denied it, of course, but Mark just claimed the vet was lying. If people had believed Mark, he could have ruined a perfect, two-hundred-year-old reputation for the farm. Survival in the horse business depends entirely on reputation. One little black mark, and you're done."

"Rackhouse seems to have survived," I said. "And so have you two."

"True, but it was difficult for a while," Tanya said. "Mark backed down eventually and claimed it was all just a misunderstanding. It was stressful though. For the farm's manager and for me. My husband and I depend on the income from my inherited interest in the farm, now that I've had to cut back to a part-time position as a judge, and David retired to take care of me."

"A threat to your security is a pretty strong motive for murder," I agreed. "And if you leave here without the sheriff's okay, it's going to look suspicious. They'll probably take a closer look at you, perhaps digging up your past with Mark."

"They can dig all they want," Tanya said. "We wanted Mark to pay for his crimes, not to die. Rackhouse handled him without violence before, and we were prepared in case he tried again. We'd gathered enough evidence to sue him over the previous defamation if he ever tried to lie about the farm again. We can use it to sue the girlfriend if she tries anything using Mark's tactics."

"Lawsuits can be unpredictable though," I said. "I'm a lawyer, you know."

"I thought you ran the B&B."

"It's mostly my sisters," I said. "I just help out as needed. Like this weekend, since CJ, who usually does the cooking, has an arm in a cast."

David nodded. "Family always has to come first. Behind God, of course, but first in worldly matters."

Tanya patted his hand. "I have the best family. Both by marriage and by blood. I was still in the hospital after my accident when the manager of Rackhouse started in on some modifications to the grounds so I could attend meetings and be part of the daily operations once I was ready."

"You wouldn't want to reflect badly on them then, by ignoring the deputy's request that you stay here until he's got his lab test results."

"Is that legal advice?" she asked.

"No, just common sense," I said. "Mark wasn't able to besmirch your reputation while he was alive. Don't let him do it from the grave. Wait until the deputy gives us the all-clear before you leave, so he doesn't start wondering why you ran."

Tanya asked her husband, "What do you think?"

"Whatever you want, dear," he said. "It's your family, your farm. You decide, and I'll be here to back you up. Both literally and figuratively."

She nodded. "All right. We'll stay. But we're putting our luggage in the van now, and we're leaving as soon as the deputy returns, no matter what he says."

"I understand."

If they tried to sneak off again after this conversation, they would definitely go to the top of my suspect list instead of at the bottom.

*　*　*

Shortly after the Millers left to take their luggage out to the van, while I was dealing with their dirty dishes, Em came into the kitchen and leaned against the end of the table.

I dried my hands. "Want some coffee?"

"*Definitely*." She melted into the nearest chair and leaned back, rubbing her eyes. "I can't pull an all-nighter any more, at least not without copious amounts of caffeine. I'm getting old."

"Yeah, tell me about it." I filled a mug and handed it to her.

"About what?"

She sounded confused, so I opted to let her drink her coffee without expecting her to talk. She finished half the contents of the mug before sighing in contentment. "Did you notice how happy CJ was last night with Lucas? He makes her laugh, even when things are bleak."

"I'm afraid I didn't notice."

"Probably because you wouldn't have known how unusual it was. I think this is the first time she's even noticed a man since her husband died. I mean, as a man, not as a guest or contractor. Lucas is definitely the first one who's made her laugh. A real laugh, not the polite hospitality laugh."

"Did she invite him to Noah's party later?"

"I think so." Em finished the rest of her coffee and got up to refill the mug. "Now I remember what I wanted to tell you before I got distracted by caffeine. Shortly after you went to bed last night, Reed told me that the Hammetts' lights had gone on again. I sneaked upstairs to listen at the door, in case it sounded like they were preparing to leave. Instead, they'd decided to get drunk."

I wasn't sure what to make of that. It could either be anxiety over the prospect of being arrested, or a celebration of having gotten away with murder. Or perhaps they got drunk every Saturday night.

"Could you make out any of what they were saying?"

Em shook her head and returned to the table. "It all sounded garbled. Mostly a lot of laughter. They probably couldn't even understand each other,"

"But they sounded happy, not nervous or depressed?"

Em took several thoughtful sips of her refreshed coffee, no longer desperate to chug it down. "Definitely not depressed. Can't say about nervous because drunken laughter always sounds like it's trying too hard. So it could have been real or it could have been covering up anxiety. All I knew for sure was that it was too loud, and I needed to ask them to keep the noise down before it woke up the other guests."

"How did they react?"

"Better than I'd expected," Em said. "A little grumbling about not being allowed to have any fun on the weekend, but I think they were ready to collapse already, so they didn't really argue. I decided to jump the gun a little bit and give them the story about the witness a little early since it looked like they wouldn't be in any condition to make it down to breakfast, and they weren't in any shape to run away. Or if they tried, Reed would be able to catch them single-handed since they could barely stand up on their own."

"That's fine. I trust your judgment. And I'm impressed that you confronted them. I'm not sure I would have had the courage to listen outside a suspected killer's door, let alone knock on it."

Em snorted. "You broke into their room to search it."

"Not when they were occupying it."

Em didn't get a chance to argue because the Dells entered the kitchen just then, and we had our assigned roles to play. I cooked the requested omelets while Em engaged them with her story about the witness who was, even then, on the verge of either wreaking her own revenge on Mark's killer or turning the culprit over to the cops. As far as I could tell, the Dells listened with the same calm lack of interest they'd shown for anything that didn't have to do with food, until I placed their plates in front of them, and then they didn't even pretend to care about anything else.

If they were worried about an imminent arrest or vigilante justice, they certainly didn't act like it. The two men lingered at the table, complimenting me on my biscuits, and making sure I'd packed up the jars of bacon bourbon jam they'd paid for the day before. They had a second cup of coffee while tossing ideas back and forth about how they could use the jam on sandwiches at their restaurant.

As they left the kitchen, Shelly entered to get a cup of coffee for herself and ask if it would be too much trouble for me to prepare plates she could take back to her room to eat there after Candy woke up.

I wondered briefly if Shelly might be trying to distract me while Candy sneaked out the emergency exit with their luggage, but then my sleep-deprived brain recalled that I'd largely ruled out the Readings as suspects. CJ had texted me the night before that she'd been able to confirm with the witness at the barbeque place that Mark had not been injured while arguing with Shelly there. She and her daughter could safely be placed at the very bottom of the list of suspects with the Millers. Still, I didn't stop Em when she went into her spiel about the fictional witness and the imminent arrest of Mark's killer.

I listened to their conversation while I compiled the cold breakfast plate that Shelly had requested. She seemed more relieved than concerned about the imminent prospect of the killer being identified and arrested. She just said, "It's about time the sheriff's office did their job," and then changed the topic, chattering about how much she loved the Three Sisters B&B and how she hoped to come back again sometime.

Eventually, she set her coffee down with a thump. "Oh, I remember what I wanted to tell you two. I kept thinking about what Jess said—wondering who had chosen the inspection team, so I emailed a friend on the board. She didn't get back to me until late last night, too late to bother you with her response. Especially since she didn't know the name of the person who chose the judges, just that we were invited as a group, not one at a time. She remembered how thrilled the board was that someone had put together a qualified team, so they didn't have to spend any time on it."

"Thanks for looking into it." Knowing that the team had been put together by someone other than board, presumably one of the team members, was interesting, but not as enlightening as if I knew who had done it. "I'll make sure the deputy knows. He may be able to find out more, although it's a bit of a long shot to think that whoever put together the team is also Mark's killer."

"If it helps, there's one more thing my friend was able to tell me. Whoever put together the team did it in February. She got the list right around Valentine's day. She remembers wondering if the B&B offered a special package deal for the holiday, something the co-op could promote in their advertising."

"That's interesting." Mid-February was right after the second attempt on Mark's life, giving a bit more credence to the theory that the person who set up the inspection team was, in fact, responsible for his death. It fit with the possibility that the failure of two spur-of-the-moment attacks had inspired the killer to be more deliberate the next time with a more complicated plan that involved surrounding Mark with people who hated him.

It was still just a theory, though, not one I felt entirely

confident about. Not even enough to share it with the deputy, especially since it would seem to rule out the Hammetts as the prime suspects. I could definitely see them carrying out spur-of-the-moment acts of rage. A slower, more complicated plan required patience, not something the twins seemed to have in any quantity whatsoever. Plus, I doubted they had enough contacts in Cooperton to know who, besides themselves, hated Mark but had the right skills to inspect the B&B.

What if I was wrong about everything? Not just the theory that someone had set Mark up to be surrounded by his enemies, but that that person was one of the guests who had then killed him?

Because if I was wrong about the guests being the only suspects, my plan wouldn't work. And so far, no one had seemed to even notice the bait that Em had waved under their noses.

CHAPTER TWENTY-FIVE

———

It was still a few minutes before ten o'clock when I finished tidying up after the guests who had had their breakfast and returned to their rooms. The Hammetts hadn't eaten yet. I didn't know if they were just running late, expecting to be served no matter when they showed up, like they'd done the day before, or if they were too hungover to get out of bed.

I prepared a tray with left-over muffins and a stack of napkins in case my sisters or our helpers were hungry. Em hadn't been ready for anything other than coffee earlier, and CJ had only picked at her food while encouraging Noah to eat quickly. Lucas was still outside, where he'd taken over for Reed sometime before I got up to start breakfast.

I tossed my phone into an apron pocket—my number was the one getting forwarded calls and texts from the front desk at the moment, so I needed to keep it close at hand—and carried the tray out to the lobby. CJ and Em were both behind the front desk, sharing a laptop and discussing B&B finances as a means of distracting themselves while they waited anxiously for the killer to make a move.

While I was placing the tray on a side table, Lucas came through the front door to announce that Reed was awake again, refreshed by a nap in his truck, and was prowling the front yard and parking lot.

"There's fresh coffee in the kitchen."

Em raised her mug to show that she was all set, but CJ and Lucas raced toward the kitchen, jockeying playfully for the lead. Thinking of what Em had said about the two of them, I paid attention this time. The young man definitely looked infatuated with CJ, but I couldn't tell if she reciprocated his feelings or had even noticed his interest as anything other than friendship.

I left Em to her laptop and went back to the kitchen to get

Reed some coffee and breakfast. Then we all went out to the front porch, where we could watch for any suspicious activity by the guests. We'd already decided that, if more than one pair of guests were acting suspiciously at the same time, Reed would focus on the Hammetts, Lucas on the Dells, CJ on the Readings, and Em on the Millers. I was supposed to stay back and coordinate the team.

It was such a tidy little plan, I thought as I placed the tray, now containing Reed's coffee in addition to the earlier collection of muffins, on the wicker side table next to the chair he'd claimed for himself. A place for everyone and everyone in their place.

At the thought, CJ and Lucas came out with their coffee and dropped into adjoining chairs. "Em will join us in a minute. She's encouraging Noah to read out here with us. He's your responsibility, Jess, if the rest of us are chasing down perps."

"Got it," I said, leaning against the railing and facing everyone else. A moment later, I heard the faint sound of an engine muffled, as intended, by the hedges surrounding three sides of the parking lot.

"Did you all hear that?" I asked. "An engine starting?"

Everyone else jumped to their feet and stared at the parking lot, but there was no one visible over the neatly trimmed three-foot-high hedges that prevented a clear view of the vehicles. Was the noise something other than a car engine? Possibly a tractor over at the horse farm?

And then I noticed a section of the hedge was shaking, as if a large animal was trying to squeeze between the shrubs. Or a human being who'd slipped out the back of the B&B while we were all out front. Definitely not the Millers, not with Tanya in a wheelchair. Unless that had been a lie too, intended to test the B&B's ability to deal with disabled guests.

"There," I pointed at the rustling of the shrubs. The plan was working, and the Hammetts had taken our bait. "Mark's killer is trying to sneak into the parking lot and leave."

CJ immediately vaulted over the railing and off the porch.

"Be careful with your cast," I shouted.

She ignored me, as I'd known she would. She paused only long enough to look back at Lucas and say impatiently, "Come on. I'll take the first one I reach. You get whoever's still standing."

He hesitated. "What am I supposed to do with him?"

CJ was already running toward the parking lot when she answered, "Whatever it takes. Block him or trip him or tackle him."

Lucas caught up with her. "I don't know how. I've never done anything like that."

"Really?" CJ grinned at him. "Time to learn. It's fun." And she picked up her pace.

By then, Reed was just a few feet behind them, having explained that he was going to try to shut down the getaway vehicle before vaulting over the railing.

Em emerged from the lobby with Noah, glanced at the running figures, and apparently correctly guessed what was happening. She urged our nephew over to a wicker chair set apart from the others. "Noah's your responsibility now since you're tethered to command central here. I'm going to block the driveway, in case CJ and Lucas can't catch them. I moved my car and CJ's out there before I went to bed. They just need to be moved into place."

I nodded, and she jogged off while I dialed 911. When the dispatcher answered, I said we needed some help with a guest who'd assaulted someone. Not quite the truth, but it would have been too confusing to explain that an assault on a guest was imminent, and that person would need to be arrested for murder.

The dispatcher asked if anyone was in immediate danger, and I had to think for a moment. CJ was never gentle when she was on an adventure, so it was likely that both she and the escaping guest she tackled would both end up with some bruises, and her cast might need to be replaced. In fact, she'd probably take the worst of the damage to herself and wouldn't inflict any serious harm on anyone else. Especially since Reed wasn't far behind her, and he could intervene if necessary. He wasn't as fast as CJ and Lucas, but he was bigger and more imposing. His looming presence would encourage the Hammetts to accept the inevitable, assuming they tried to escape after CJ and Lucas brought them down.

"No, there's no huge rush," I said. "Just whenever you have someone available to take statements and make an arrest. We'll sit on the culprits until then." Possibly literally, if CJ got her way.

As I was hanging up, the Readings came through the front door. "What's going on?" Candy asked.

I shrugged. "Pick-up rugby game. CJ's favorite."

Candy laughed while Shelly sputtered, "Where's the rest of the teams?"

"Are you volunteering?"

Candy patted her mother's back. "I think she's having you on, Mother."

Just then, as CJ and Lucas were closing in on where I assumed the quarry were crouched down, too low for me to see over the hedges, the tops of two identical heads rose into sight. I could see that they were moving in separate directions, presumably splitting up in the hope that one could make it to their car and then rescue the other.

They dropped back down and disappeared from sight moments before CJ and Lucas reached the abandoned hiding spot. I couldn't hear what CJ and Lucas said, but they seemed to have spotted their quarry and had split up themselves as planned. The Hammetts had probably counted on CJ being there as a cheerleader, rather than to actually tackle anyone. They were about to find out just how badly they'd miscalculated.

The hunt continued for several more minutes, long enough for me to realize there had been something off about the heads I'd glimpsed. The Hammetts had dark hair, cut in a standard if slightly long business style. But the heads I'd seen had been—

Before I could finish the thought, CJ's victory shout rang through the parking lot. I knew, without being able to see through the hedge, that she had forgotten about her cast and had tackled the escaping guest. The painful, sliding sound of her quarry landing hard on the gravel parking lot was audible all the way to the porch. A moment later, a matching victory cry rang out from Lucas, followed by another body landing and sliding across the gravel.

And that was when the Hammetts came out through the lobby and demanded, albeit in a whisper, to know what was going on, and why no one had responded to their texts inquiring about updates from the sheriff's office.

I finally put it all together. It hadn't been the Hammetts' heads I'd seen over the hedge. It had been the much lighter-colored, buzz-cut hair of the Dells.

* * *

Reed helped Jack and Jonny Dell to their feet and then urged everyone toward the front porch to await the police. Lucas looked like he was actually hoping one of their captives would run so he could catch him again, and I knew with absolute certainty that that was what CJ was thinking.

CJ held her cast-covered arm against her chest, but she didn't seem to be in too much pain. Maybe she'd just damaged the cast rather than the arm itself.

Lucas was limping. His face glowed with excitement though, so he probably wasn't even aware of the injury. He turned to CJ. "You were right. That really was fun. We should do this again sometime."

"Are you asking me out on a date?" CJ asked.

There was a slight hesitation before his face broke out in a grin. "Yeah, I am. So what do you say?"

"Have you ever gone bungee jumping? There's a great place not far from here."

His grin turned a little forced, but his voice remained enthusiastic. "Sounds perfect."

I texted Em to let her know we'd caught the culprits, and she should unblock the driveway to make way for the police. I hoped they wouldn't arrive too quickly though. I was already convinced that we knew who had killed Mark, but the sheriff's office might be skeptical without a confession. And I was the only one of us who had experience questioning witnesses, even if it had been in a very different context than a criminal investigation.

CJ stopped her prisoner about ten feet from the porch, presumably deeming it a safe distance from her son, and indicated that Jack should drop down on the grass next to the path that encircled the B&B to wait for the police. Lucas followed suit, herding Jonny to a spot just out of reach of his father. Neither resisted or tried to run, to CJ's and Lucas's disappointment.

Once settled on the grass, Jack, seeming truly bewildered, asked, "What on earth do you all think you're doing?"

"Making sure Mark's killer doesn't leave before the deputy arrives to make an arrest."

"You mean us?" Jack said. "That's ridiculous."

I'd forgotten the Readings were on the porch, leaning against the front railing, until Shelly said, "The killer can't possibly be one of the Dells."

I ignored her to ask Jack, "If suspecting you is ridiculous, then why did you run? At breakfast you said you were content to read in your room until check-out. And you didn't even collect the jam I put behind the front desk, so you could pick it up when you checked out. You'd already paid for it, so why leave it behind?"

"We don't have to tell you why we decided to leave. I just forgot about the jam when I got a call from the restaurant, saying they needed us, so we packed up and headed out. After all, the cops didn't really have the authority to force us to stay. We went along with it because we didn't have any real need to go home originally, but now we do. Besides, our leaving isn't enough to prove we had anything to do with Mark's death."

"No," I said, "but it's enough to get the police to take a much closer look at you and your son. I'm sure they'll find the necessary evidence, once they know who to focus on."

The Millers appeared on the path that led from the back of the house, having missed the chase and my accusation that the Dells had killed Mark. Nevertheless, David gave the men on the ground a wide berth, abandoning the path that they sat next to, for the more difficult terrain of the grass. He parked the wheelchair where he and his wife could be part of the conversation, keeping Reed between them and the two men on the ground.

"Why would the police be interested in the Dells?" Tanya asked. "We all know it was the Hammett twins who killed Mark."

Beck's denial from where he slouched in one of the porch's wicker chairs was a mere whisper instead of his usual shout.

"Mr. Hammett is right. They're not killers, even if they are jerks and won't be welcome at the B&B in the future." I was fairly sure my sisters would back me up on that. "The brothers didn't try to run after they heard about the existence of a witness to the murder, but the Dells did."

"They did?" Tanya asked.

"Yes," I said. "We already knew they had the means and opportunity to kill Mark. Everyone here did. I'm not so sure about the Dells' motive, but that may not matter so much. Once the police know who to focus on, it shouldn't take long for them to find the necessary evidence, maybe even come up with a witness who can fill in any missing pieces."

"Wait," Shelly said from the porch railing. "Your sister told us the police have already found a witness."

"She lied," I said. "Don't blame her. It's my fault. I made her do it. But I'm sure the police will find one as soon as the arrest is announced. That's something I recall vividly from growing up in a small town. There's always a witness, even when you think you're completely alone."

CJ added, "And everyone knows you, so they can always identify who they saw by name, not just a vague description. You can't get away with anything around here."

Jack let out a long sigh. "My son had nothing to do with any of this. Let him go, and I'll tell you whatever you want to know."

"Dad," Jonny said, preparing to scoot closer to his father, but Reed stopped him.

"No," Jack said without looking at his son. "Don't pay any attention to him. It was all me. Jonny is innocent."

I doubted that. At a minimum, I thought Jonny was an accomplice after the fact. But if it would get a confession out of Jack, I was willing to pretend I believed him.

I looked at Reed. "You can let Jonny go."

"I'm not going anywhere," Jonny said. "Not without Dad."

"Your choice," I said and crouched in front of Jack so I wasn't looming over him any longer and could seem sympathetic. I still kept my distance, so he wouldn't be tempted to try to take me hostage. "All right. It was just you. How did it happen?"

"It was an accident," Jack said. "We were arguing at the barbeque place, and he pushed me, and I pushed him back. It was hardly any force at all, but he dropped like a stone and didn't move. I thought he was dead, and I panicked and ran, pretending I didn't know he wasn't on his way to the B&B. It didn't feel fair that I'd get the blame when it was his own fault for being a sick old drunk. Otherwise, a tiny little bump on his head wouldn't have been enough to kill him."

He had something of a point, in that, from what I'd read, alcoholism and some medicines for strokes could make a person more likely to develop an epidural hematoma, but that didn't absolve Jack of liability for Mark's death. There was a saying in the law that defendants took their victims as they found them. It meant that a victim's pre-existing weaknesses were not a defense against responsibility for the harm done, even if a stronger, healthier victim would have been uninjured.

"Is that the truth?" I asked coldly. I felt some sympathy for Jack wanting to protect his son against a criminal conviction, but not with the claim that Mark's death had been anything other than pre-meditated. "Because it all looks premeditated to me. It wasn't the first attempt on Mr. Pleasant's life. You tried to run him off the road a month ago. Or was that your son?" I held up a hand. "Before you try to tell me you know nothing about that incident, remember that the police can compare the paint on your truck to the scrapings from Mark's car, now that they have a more limited pool of suspects."

Jack gave his son a long look, love and regret and apology in his eyes. Then he turned back to me resolutely. "All right. It wasn't an accident. Not this weekend, and not before. The first time I ran Mark off the road, it was just a spur of the moment urge to make him suffer a little. Not to kill him, just pay him back a bit for all the pain he caused me and my family. It was only after the second time, when it started to feel like Mark was laughing at us—at me, I mean—that I knew he had to die. When I heard about the Three Sisters B&B applying to join the tourism co-op, it seemed like the perfect opportunity to kill Mark in a setting where I could make it look like an accident. If anyone realized it was actually murder, then reasonable doubt would be on my side since everyone around him had a solid motive to kill him."

"But why?" Shelly called from the porch railing. "What had Mark ever done to you?"

"Not to me," Jack said dully. "To my wife. He killed her."

"No." Shelly's denial seemed involuntary. "She died of cancer. Mark was a terrible person, but he never killed anyone. I'd have turned him over to the cops myself if he'd hurt your wife."

"He didn't kill her literally," Jack said. "Just spread rumors about her business, turning her customers against her when she wouldn't pay his bribes. She'd have been able to fight the cancer if she hadn't been so worn out from fighting him and his lies. The threats started before her diagnosis and continued even after she was so obviously sick. She finally just lost the will to live. It was all Mark's fault, and he had to die. For her, and for the next person he would have set his sights on destroying."

I got to my feet, my glance falling on Jonny, who had collapsed into himself, his chest heaving and silent tears running down his face.

I could understand, if not forgive, the damage that Jack had been willing to inflict on the Three Sisters B&B to avenge his wife, but I just couldn't comprehend how he had been willing to risk destroying his son's future if they were caught. Whether or not Jonny had been directly involved in the murder, his life was never going to be the same. He might well end up in prison, convicted of murder alongside his father, and even if he didn't, Jonny was going to have to live with the reputation of being a killer's son and a suspected co-conspirator. His dreams of owning his own restaurant or even making a name for himself as a chef in someone else's kitchen were likely over.

Had Jack realized yet what he'd done to his son?

I looked down at Jack to say, "You had everyone fooled, including me, into thinking you were a good, kind person. But you're just like Mark was, so intent on getting whatever you felt you deserved, without any concern for anyone else, that you never even noticed that you were destroying your own family in the process."

CHAPTER TWENTY-SIX

The dispatcher had taken me at my word when I'd said we were in no huge rush for a cruiser to arrive, so it was a full hour later that the first one came up the driveway. It was operated by Deputy Shurette, who'd only intended to share the inconclusive results of the forensics report, but who'd called for back-up after I explained about Jack's confession. The deputy was as skeptical as I was about the son's supposed non-involvement in the crime, so both men were eventually read their rights and bundled off to the station for further questioning.

Noah's birthday party was pushed back from two to four, so CJ could make a quick trip to the emergency clinic to have her cast replaced, with Lucas acting as her chauffeur.

In the intervening time, I decorated the veranda with the party supplies, and Em checked out the remaining B&B guests. The Hammetts slunk off without saying much, still apparently feeling the effects of the excesses from the night before. The Readings and Millers both lingered a bit, assuring us that they would be turning in a positive report on the B&B that encouraged the board to approve the application despite the lack of surprise in the surprise inspection. Tanya Miller was confident they would accept their recommendation, and if not, she planned to give the board a lecture about how they'd brought some of this weekend's events on themselves by not being more open about the real reason for Mark's retirement. I had a feeling that the board would come around quickly, both due to the force of Tanya's personality and the realization of just how much work they'd have to do if they required a new inspection.

After all the B&B guests were gone, Em joined me on the veranda with Noah. There wasn't much left to do to prepare since Reed had been right, and no one other than family had been invited. Plus Reed, who'd invited himself and been approved by

CJ, and Lucas, who had apparently been invited by Noah himself.

By four o'clock, the veranda looked like an illustration from one of Noah's favorite books, featuring a tea party with cats. There were two tables, one for Noah and the cats, and the other for everyone else. Pappy had been herded out of the owners' quarters by Em—the cat still didn't trust me—and Beam had emerged from the propped-open French doors from the kitchen, with Taylor in his wake. The bowls of sardines on the chairs on either side of Noah probably had something to do with that, but he seemed convinced that they were coming for tea with their favorite human, just like in his book. He might even have been right since the cats stayed at the table even after their bowls were empty.

CJ returned from the emergency clinic, wobbling slightly, despite Lucas's hovering support. He mouthed, "pain meds" and guided her to a seat at the table for adults.

I remained standing, ready to help wherever needed but content to simply observe this little milestone in the life of my nephew. CJ had lost the slightly sullen attitude she'd had almost nonstop since the moment I'd arrived on Friday. She stayed safely in her seat but laughed and shouted encouragement to her son as Em brought out the cake and placed it in front of Noah to blow out the three candles. He spent a few seconds studying the cake before taking a deep breath and leaning forward, his cheeks puffed out like a chipmunk. After a gleeful glance at his mother, he suddenly reached out and quickly pinched each flame to suffocate it with his fingers before we could react.

Where on earth had he learned the candle trick? Probably from one of his books, I thought, but who put that sort of thing in a kids' book?

Reed came up beside me and elbowed me lightly before handing me a glass of sweet tea. "Looks like Noah's inherited more of his parents' daredevil spirit than anyone realized."

"I think fire is just about the only dangerous thing CJ didn't experiment with as a kid." I had a sudden thought. "At least not while I was living with her. For all I know, she could have taken up flaming batons after I left for college."

"Not that I've heard," Reed said. "And her husband wasn't interested in fire either, according to my brother. Let's hope Noah's interest in it is just a passing phase."

"CJ and Em will make sure of it."

Reed looked like he was going to say something but thought better of it. "I'm going to get some cake. Want some?"

"Sure."

The candles having been extinguished, the cake—I'd recognized the local bakery's logo on the box from one of the mugs in the kitchen—had been carried over to the adults' table by Lucas for cutting. Em placed a similar-looking one made out of premium cat food on Noah's table for his feline guests. She let him help her cut and serve slices to his little friends.

Meanwhile, Lucas skillfully blocked CJ from picking up the cake knife and had taken care of cutting slices himself. She wasn't in any condition to handle even a dull blade, but I was somewhat surprised that she let him take over.

The incident made it clear that she and Em didn't need my help, now that the Dells had been taken into custody. But that wasn't the point, was it? I'd always known that they could manage without me in normal circumstances, even if Noah did let his daredevil side show more often, just like they'd survived just fine without me after I left for college.

I didn't regret leaving home for my education or even for settling in DC afterward to practice law. It had been the right decision at the time. But I'd made some bad choices since then, mostly with respect to so thoroughly isolating myself from my only remaining family and hurting them in the process.

I wasn't as bad as Jack, who'd made much worse decisions with much worse consequences, but like him, I'd been so intent on my own goals that I'd been blinded to what was happening to my sisters and nephew. Unlike Jack, I still had the time and freedom to change my path, preventing any further damage.

It was time for a change, and instead of dreading how complicated it would be, I was starting to look forward to it.

Reed interrupted my thoughts, handing me a plate of cake. The sugary kind, not the fishy feline version. "You look too serious for a party."

"I've been thinking that I don't want to end up like Jack, unable to recognize when I'm following a path that will hurt the people I care about."

"You're nothing like Jack," he said.

"Maybe not, but from everything people have said about

him, he wasn't the murderous Jack of this weekend until recently. It takes time to lose touch like that. One wrong decision leads to another wrong decision and another and another. Before you know it, someone's dead and you're in jail."

"Does catching a killer always make you this melancholy?"

I laughed. "No, but it's gotten me thinking about the ways that I've hurt my sisters. There were always reasons—excuses, really—why I didn't visit more, why I couldn't be more involved in their lives even long-distance. Small things each time but still bad decisions, and they added up to our becoming distant from each other."

"That's not the same as plotting to kill someone."

"I know," I said. "But it made me think about how I could do better and make up for the past absence. I still need to discuss it with my sisters, but I'd like to move back here to help with the B&B. You were the one who reminded me that I could do that and still enjoy some time for myself. They don't need a lot of help, so I'd have the time to get to know my home state better, through an adult's eyes. I'd forgotten how beautiful this area is, and how much I'd loved it as a kid."

"I happen to know the owner of a really great tourist attraction around here," Reed said. "Once you're settled here, I bet I could get you a private tour."

"I'm counting on it."

Coming home didn't have to be *entirely* about my sisters, after all.

ABOUT THE AUTHOR

Gin Jones became a *USA Today* bestselling author after too many years of being a lawyer who specialized in ghostwriting for other lawyers. She much prefers writing fiction, since she isn't bound by boring facts and she can indulge her sense of humor without any risk of getting thrown into jail for contempt of court. In her spare time, Gin makes quilts, grows garlic, and advocates for rare disease patients.

To learn more about Gin, visit her online at: www.ginjones.com

ABOUT THE AUTHOR

Made in United States
North Haven, CT
30 August 2024

56767560R00136